That Taste Again

SEVEN DIREX

ISBN-10: 0-9816340-0-1
ISBN-13: 978-0-9816340-0-5

Cover Photo: Dawnetta Rakow
Cover Design: Hannes Charen
Myrmeleon Books   Broooklyn, NY
Contact: myrmeleonbooks@gmail.com

"Pleasure alone makes existence worthwhile. A pleasure-seeker has a difficult time parting from life. The person who is needy or suffers welcomes death like a friend. But the person who wants pleasure has to take life cheerfully as people did in ancient Greece. He mustn't shy away from indulging at other people's expense, he must never feel pity. He must harness others to his carriage, to his plow like animals. He must enslave people who feel, who wish to have pleasure like him; he must exploit them without regret for his service, for his delights. He must never ask whether they feel good about it or whether they perish. He must always bear in mind: If they had me in their control, they would do the same to me, and I would have to pay for their enjoyments with my sweat, my blood, my soul. Such was the world of the Ancients. Enjoyment and cruelty, freedom and slavery have always gone hand in hand. People who want to live like Olympian gods must have slaves whom they throw into their fish-ponds and gladiators who fight during their masters' sumptuous banquets—and the pleasure-seekers never care if some blood splatters on them."

      - cruel Wanda von Dunajew

When I turned 21, my mother began to be more officious with the credit card bill. She bought a big, neon-yellow highlighter and marked anything that was suspicious or too pricey. When I would come home for the holiday weekends, I would have to explain all the suspect charges. My mother has thick brown hair, a rainfall of curls, and is very elegant. She is not an authoritarian, so when she tries her best to be one, it is difficult to take her seriously. With my mother all stern and shoving evidence in my face, I would usually say, "Yeah, that's something I should pay for, but it really should not have cost so much money. It's a mistake. I'll make a few calls, and then I'll get back to you and tell you how much I owe you." This type of casuistry confused my mother enough to get her off my back, until the next statement came. However, one month she decided to make phone calls. She called me up after having done so. She was at home in a suburb of Chicago, I was in the stacks of Uris Library at Cornell University. She told me that she had just had three very interesting conversations with some ladies I had been calling since I was fifteen. "Which ladies?" "I talked to Rose, and to Susan, and to Ashley." "Oh, those ladies. What did they tell you? Lies, I'm sure." "I'm not upset about what it is you're doing, it must run in the family. But I don't think this is the reason we have given you a credit card. It is for emergencies only." "These are emergencies." My mother laughed. I continued, "You know I don't spend it on anything else. Books and Internet Research. I really don't think I take advantage of the card that much." "I can't believe you've been calling these companies for this long." "It was boring back home, I needed an outlet." "Well, it is out of the question that we are going to continue paying for this. If you really need to do these things, use your own money." "Okay, okay…" "And I am going to add up all the charges for the past few months and you're going to owe me that money, buster." "Yeah, okay, I'll talk to you later mother."

That night I called Susan to find out what had happened, if I was in big trouble. She laughed, told me that my mother was a very nice lady, and that she had not disclosed anything about the nature of her services. We did a call, and I used my debit card from Lasalle Bank.

When I called Rose about a month later, she reacted coldly and told me she would never talk to me again. She was very disappointed that I had lied to her, and was very embarrassed. I felt bad that I was going to lose all the good orgasms she gave me, but I was also aware of the expendability of people like Rose, and I figured she must have been thankful for having taken so much money from a minor without getting in trouble.

****

I went to Las Vegas for my 21st birthday. It was a present from my father. I took Dennis Mesorow who attended Cornell University with me. My father flew us out on a private jet. The limousine waiting for us at the airport took us straight to the Bellagio Hotel.

The entrance to the Bellagio had all these glass butterflies on the ceiling, there must have been a thousand of them, and the embroidered carpet had so many colors. The space was enormous, and there was fresh oxygen being pumped into the room to keep everyone wide-awake. My father gave us each three hundred dollars to gamble with, and he advised us to aim for breaking even. That way we could, at the very least, gamble for a long time. My father is a short, handsome man with big eyes and a Russian severity in his face. He is for the most part bald. He loves the game of Craps. I think this is because he is a physical person and you can throw those die pretty hard if you have good aim. It was quite a feeling to be standing in front of the rich green baize of the table, watching as the die skipped hazardously through all the stacks of chips. Everyone applauded when my number came up, all my neighbors got pushed hundreds of dollars, and one even tossed me a chip—to say thank you.

Dennis studied English Lit., like myself. He was born in Canada on a hippy farm in Horus. His family knew Timothy Leary, Ram Das, and Maharishi Mahesh Yogi personally. Dennis acted like he was above all these things, he behaved like a curmudgeonly old man. One night, in a snowstorm, he confided a lot of nasty stuff to me about a panic attack he endured when younger. He even broke down and cried. We grew closer after that. Dennis was a very handsome man. He had an old-fashioned, Austrian Prince nobility to his features—and many women envied his femininity. He always had one or two girls chasing after him, but for the most part, he seemed to hate women too much to want anything to do with them.

After we were done gambling and my father had gone off to bed, I suggested we go to CrazyHorse II, which I had heard was the best stripclub in all of Las Vegas. It took a lot of convincing, "Unlike you Jonathan, I don't have to pay for my women. I get them for free."

He came in the end, hoping I would make a fool of myself for his entertainment. We took the limo there, heading off the main strip to darker corners of the city. Inside Crazy-Horse II the women wore Satin and Silicon, and lots of makeup. Their skin was unusually soft—and they walked with their cunts or their tits leading the way. My eyes were glued on all of them. Dennis and I found two velvet sofas to sit in and were immediately served a drink.

"So you're telling me that you can cum, just by having one of the girls sit on your lap?"

9

"It's not about willing myself."

"How long do you need?"

"A few seconds."

I was staring in this one's eyes. She had on six-inch heels and daisy-dukes. She smelt of a poisonous flower when she came up to me. She whispered in my ear to see if I wanted a dance, she had delicious lips. She started dancing, I felt it growing, I wanted to control it so that I could enjoy it more, but she had conquered me from every direction—the cum squirted into the side of my jeans, above my right thigh. At that very moment, she started grinding her ass on my lap. She jumped up immediately, turned, and slapped me in my face. Then she spit at me. "You're friend just busted a nut all over me." "He can't control himself." "I'm gonna get the manager if you don't give me a huge tip." Dennis looked at me. He spoke in my place, "Come on baby, just part of the business right. You can't punish a man for his unwieldy desire?" "You gonna give me a tip or not?" I gave her a twenty, which was much less than she expected, and we sat back down. When we finally left CrazyHorse II, we exited into the blinding light of morning.

****

It was not until I moved to New York City that I found the site I OWN YOUR COCK. It was much different from anything I had ever seen before. The home page included an eloquently written manifesto:

If you are one of the many men who spend day and night searching the Internet for a phone sex operator who fulfills your wildest fantasies then brace yourself for what we at I OWN YOUR COCK have in store for you. We are not your regular company. *All our girls are handpicked by me, Alessandra, a 35 year old lifestyle dom. Since the young, precocious age of 13, I have been devilishly aware of the power I have over men. Having both a sexy body and a devious mind made it easy to get men to obey my commands. It was all the older boys at the high school who I first learned to toy with. Can you imagine sweet little me, with my budding breasts, and my long legs, telling boys eight years my senior that I was really interested in seeing their cocks? "I've never seen one before," I would say, "My mother told me a girl must be very knowledgeable about cocks, that way she can get exactly what she wants. Would you be willing to teach me?" When I would go up to their bedrooms, they would sit on their beds and take out their cocks. "Show me how to stroke it," I would demand. They would beg me to come over and put my tight ass on their thigh, or to put my mouth on their cocks. "How could you?" I would ask, coyly. "I am only 13, you shouldn't take advantage of me like that." I told them exactly how to touch themselves, every little detail, and because I was so young, and because they did not want to get in trouble, they did just what I said. When I got bored of playing around with them, I left. It made my nipples so hard to experience the desperation in their eyes, once they realized I was not kidding. If they did cum by accident, I promised them that I would never invite myself to their house again. I keep my promises.*

All the girls at I OWN YOUR COCK will keep their promises too. I made sure their experiences growing up were similar to mine, that each woman desired to dominate and torture men, and that each woman was a self-professed Goddess with her own unique way of turning a man into a little piggy.

You are all little piggies! You know that you are, and I am talking straight to you, and that is why you will never stray far from my site and my collection of goddesses. Whether you are a business man who is in charge of a giant

11

corporation or a young pervert with his daddy's credit card, we will quickly get inside your head and control that head of yours which decides real matters. Beware! And I mean this. We are all very addicting and we intend to be, and we do not care if this costs too much money or ruins you financially— Financial Domination is one of the many fetishes we are interested in. We will take that cock away from you. Every time you stroke, you will be worshipping one of us beautiful goddesses. And you will not be able to cum, even if you want to, until we have given you permission because WE OWN YOUR COCK! Please enjoy browsing through our website, and looking at our pictures. We look forward to hearing from you soon!

****

Around the time that I found I OWN YOUR COCK, I met Dolly. Dolly was a Freshman at NYU studying at the Tisch film school. She was intellectually precocious and hot on the trail of stardom. Her background was Russian. She was one of the few with red hair, freckles, and pink skin tone. We met on Halloween in costume. I was dressed up like Max from <u>Where the Wild Things Are</u>. I had on a sweatshirt with bunny ears poking out of the hood. I spent most of the night flipping them on and off. On my shirt were written the words, "Be Still!" Dolly was wearing a purple wig, and had a colorful dress which accentuated her delicious little body. She came up to me. I can be very shy. She told me that I was cute. We got to talking, and soon enough we were kissing outside of Tompkins Square Park. She took me to her dorm room, and we spent the night rubbing our bodies against each other. In the morning I saw her thick red curls, they were everywhere, and her whole face was buried in freckles. Her lips were so angelic and so pink. Her breasts were big enough for me to put my whole mouth around, and her nipples gave her so much sensation that I could never stop touching them.

She was surprised when I called her a day later. She thought it was very nice of me to ask how she was doing. When she came to see me, she again expressed her disbelief. She was not accustomed to men being chivalrous. She got all dressed up for me. She had on earrings, and had fixed her hair so the curls held close to her darling face. We were going to go out, but instead we spent the whole night in bed again. We fell for each other real quickly. I wrote her a lot of poems and sang her a lot of songs. We took a trip with my family to Mexico in December. It was on the beach down there, after we had drowsily discharged ourselves from a water taxi, that we both confessed to loving each other.

Dolly learned very quick how to use my cock. Her hands were very soft and very small, and her mouth did not open very wide. She sucked on it the way a small pet will lick on your hand, and she got lost in this dream while she did it. She always made me yelp, and then I would want to make her cum. I would touch her small, shaven pussy, and search for her clitoris, but nothing would ever happen. She told me it did not matter, that she lived vicariously through my cock. This was not good enough for me, I wanted to please her. She admitted that she had never orgasmed in her life. I kept telling her that she should go to a sex shop and buy herself a vibrator. She would get very possessive and say how she did not care that much about cumming. I would come over to visit all horny and she would be too apathetic to do anything. She would fall asleep around 10:00 PM. I would stay up the whole night, my hard on transformed into anxiety.

We ended things because of our sexual differences. I was broken up about it. She haunted me all summer long. I worked as a Reading Teacher in a Supplementary Reading Program. Everyday I had to drive out to a different corner of the TriState area and teach three two-hour classes to all levels of readers. One class would have toddlers, another would have graduate students. I had to follow a timeline and carry big boxes of books into synagogues, churches, and school-houses in strange corners of strange towns. Sometimes it would be at a University surrounded by Junipers and Dog-woods, other times I would end up in some crappy ass church with soiled windows. When I was carrying my books, or when I turned my back on the class to write something on the white board, this chill of regret would flash through my body. At nights I dreamt about her. I would wake up angry and tor-mented. I had this one dream where she became a lesbian; I had another where she told me that I was too serious for her and that she preferred boys who accepted that she was a tease. She wore these tight jeans, and her breasts were pronounced, and she would put her mouth right next to mine, and I could get a hint of what was to come, and then she would flitter away.

****

Initially ten women were mistresses of I OWN YOUR COCK. The home page constantly refreshed which of them were taking calls. Some nights eight of them would be avail-able. A whole phalanx. Each woman would have a picture, and her face was always very seductive. Though small, the icons were big enough to give me a whiff of what was waiting for me on the other line. Some liked to pose with the eyes of an ingénue, others liked to look straight at the camera.

I OWN YOUR COCK had a forum where the women posted sound bytes and essays. The men responded with praise, and some wrote scripts which they begged the ladies to record. I never wrote on any of these forums, but I kept a regular eye on them. A lot of the men would write poems or songs about how much they worshipped their favorite mistress. A few of the men would write detailed posts about the type of sessions he was having with his Goddess. One man had been put into a CB3000 and had sent the key to his mistress, Ariana. In his post he included a picture of his cock in this chastity device. He had to spend every night listening to his mistress painting her toenails, and when he got hard, his dick got stuffed up against the hard polymer. His wife was part of the whole thing. They were experimenting to save their marriage. They lived in Idaho, and they owned a textile factory. After work they spent all their money listening to Ariana painting her toenails, and he would get really hard, and his wife would get on the phone, and the two ladies would laugh about how much he was suffering. When the man was mailed back the key, he was allowed to masturbate, but he was still not allowed to cum. His wife would blow him right up until the edge. Then she put the CB3000 back on... A week went by like this before he had the best orgasm of his life, and he kept thanking his mistress, and his wife was really thankful too.

Other men sent all sorts of pictures to their mistresses. They dressed up in pink party dresses, wearing high heals and makeup. They were mostly fat, hairy, middle-aged men. One of these men sent pictures of his cock with a q-tip stuck in the pee-hole. Another one sent a picture of his cock drawn all over with lipstick. Most of the men at I OWN YOUR COCK were what you call sissies, and a lot of them enjoyed humiliation. The women would record minute long QuickTime files (they would be scratchy, and you could hear the mistress bump her lip into the microphone): "You are not a man. You are not worthy of my beauty. You have a pinprick, you piece of turd. You like to wear lipstick and lick panties after I have cummed in them. And not from you, you little maggot, but from my very hot boyfriend. I need a magnifying glass to see

15

your pathetic cock. And when I tell you to cum, you do it immediately, because you are pathetic and weak, and I am strong. But I didn't say that you could cum, you need to call me." Other times the women would be more creative and tell stories. The stories would take place in prison halls, or at a psychological ward, or in an interrogation. One woman, Lindsay, liked to write fantasies about seducing criminals. She would turn a murderer or a robber into a whining piece of turd.

Some nights I would find myself stubbornly unwilling to make a call. I was fed up with myself. To avoid this thought I would browse the web, rereading the mistresses' blogs, looking through their pictures, and listening to their recordings. Often enough I would be led to other sites and different places. One night I stumbled upon a site offering erotic hypnosis. There was a picture of a fat, ugly dom with red nails, blonde hair, and a crystal ball in her hand. She had giant tits, a crystal pendant pressed inside her cleavage, and a terrifying glimmer in her green, hypnotic eyes. Her name was Cruella Deville.

Cruella offered hypnotic mp3s, all about 30 minutes long. On the home page all the mp3s were listed in alphabetical order: *Anonymous Mind. Brainwashed into Oblivion. Cum on my Command. Death to your Identity. Elimination of your Identity. Female Orgasm. Groveling at my Feet. Happiness in my Cleavage. Ignore your conscious thoughts. Jezebel's Revenge. Kingdom of Cruella Part 1. Kingdom of Cruella Part 2. Kingdom of Cruella Part 3: Eternity. Licking my Toes. Mind Massage. Never Think. O- for zero: your soul. Puppy's Parade. Queen Cruella in Boots and a Strapon. Raping my sweet pet. SLEEP! Tele-minds: de-distancing you from me. Under my Spell. Vagina for my pet. Woman. X* (WARNING: this is only if you want to permanently erase all memory of your life before you met me). *Your Evil Genius. Zzzzzzzz.* Next to each listing was a link to a sample. I clicked on the sample for *Cum on my Command.*

The recording had a lot of echo effects in it. Cruella had a serious voice. The way she said Cum got my cock rock hard. I went back to the main page and found that there was a free induction.

Cruella advised that I pause the tape to get a pair of headphones and that I then find a comfortable position where I would not be disturbed. I did this immediately. I had a desktop computer on a little table. My bed was on the floor not more than a couple yards away. The cord was not that long, and I had to lie near the edge of the bed to avoid pulling the plug out from the socket. Cruella's voice carried into my ears: "Sleep... Five, Four, Three, Two, One, Sleep... Take a deep breath. As you hold it in think of everything you did today, everything you did yesterday, now breathe out all these thoughts and listen to me. My voice is the only thing that exists. Every word you hear, every syllable, makes you very sleepy. Picture in your mind one of those old-fashioned alarm clocks with bells on each side. The numbers have been changed. There is only one arm. Where there once was a Twelve is a Ten, and where the One should be is a Zero. The hand is pointing to the Zero. It begins to move clockwise, slowly, towards the One. As it moves you get sleepier and sleepier. When the hand reaches Ten, the bells on each side will be activated. Instead of a loud ring, they will vibrate silently. That vibration will be more and more sleepiness in every part of your body. When the arm gets to Ten, you will be the sleepiest you have ever been in your life. You will have no thoughts, all you will have is my voice. You will be easily suggestible. You will obey everything I say. The arm moves towards Two, the arm moves towards Three... all you hear is my voice. You have no thoughts. Four...Five...You are overcome with the richness of my voice. It gives you so much pleasure, you feel so very weak in comparison to my powerful voice. Six. Your chest is filling up with sleepiness. Seven. Your head is filling up with sleepiness. Eight. Your legs and your arms are filling up with sleepiness. Nine. Your cock is getting harder and harder. Ten… The bells are vibrating sleepiness all throughout your body. Feel it rush from the bottom to the top of you. Obey my voice. You are in the deepest sleep you have ever felt in your life. You have no thoughts. You are my slave. Repeat after me. 'I am Cruella's slave.' That's right. You WILL do whatever I say. Repeat it again. 'I am Cruella's slave.' Repeat it." I repeated these things.

"I am now going to put trigger words into your head. Some of these triggers I will imbed into your unconscious so that they take effect in your everyday life. These recordings are not the only time you are under my power. You will always be under my power, permanently. And this idea makes you very hard. Do you feel your cock getting hard? Throbbing for me. The more your cock throbs the more you cannot think. The more you cannot think the harder your cock throbs. Your first trigger is Throb. Every time I say Throb your cock will twitch. Throb. If it is soft, it will immediately get hard. Throb. You like this word very much. Your cock throbs, and your thoughts disappear. You obey me. Throb. The next trigger word is very fun. The word is Touch. Touch is such a fun word. It makes you want to touch your throbbing cock. And you cannot help yourself, you grab for it greedily, crazy. You pump it, you touch it every way you can think of. But it is me guiding your hand, everything you do is what I have told you to do. You can never cum until I tell you to. Remember that slave. No matter how badly you want to explode, you can never cum until I say Cum NOW. That is your final trigger word. Cum NOW. It makes you so horny to think of me saying that. Maybe I will even say it at the end of this induction. Let's play for a little. Say after me… I am Cruella's slave. That's my good pet. Throb for Cruella, forget all your thoughts and Throb for Cruella. Mmmmmmmmmmm…. Now Touch. Touch it all over. Make it feel so good. Everything you do is what I would do. You have never felt so big, so hard, so horny in your life, and still you cannot cum. Try to cum, just try? See what power I have over you and your throbbing cock. Your whole body is tingling. The bells on the alarm clock are humming through your body. When this induction is over, you are going to be addicted to me. You are going to want more and more. I want you to purchase one of my mp3s. I want you to purchase one immediately and listen to it over and over again. You will not be able to touch yourself until you do so. Every time you try to touch yourself before you have bought one of my mp3s, a sharp pain will shoot through your mind, and your hand will tighten up. You are my stupid, brainless robot. I am going to count down from 5 to 1. When I reach 1, I am going to say those words that you really really want to hear, and you will have the best orgasm of your life, and everything that we have talked about in this induction will be permanently imbedded in your unconscious. You will immediately buy one of my mp3s, and you will become more and more addicted to me. You will be wide-awake when I get to One, and you will have forgotten everything. Remember to forget. Remember to forget. Remember to forget. Five… You're cock is throbbing, you are so hard, you cannot hold it in much longer. Four… you will worship me forever. Three… you are getting so greedy, you cannot control your hand. You have no thoughts, Two… all you have is my voice, One… CUM NOW! CUM NOW, slave! Let it all out, let everything sink in…that's a good boy…"

The induction stopped. The orgasm that I had was immense. My legs were shivering. My cock had pumped so hard before squirting. My cum had shot all the way up to my neck.

I immediately went back to her site to find an mp3 to buy. I read all the blurbs and listened to all the samples again. There were pictures next to each mp3. Next to *X* was a picture of an empty cage. Next to *Woman* was a picture of a skinny woman's midsection. Next to *Raped by Cruella* was a picture of Cruella herself wearing a strap-on. I decided to buy *Cum on my Command* (next to it was a picture of an empty bowl). I waited until later in the night to listen to it. I went out of my bedroom into the hallway to do something else with myself. I could think of nothing to do. I wanted to go away in that world. There was banging above me and yelling from the streets.

I went back to my computer and looked through Cruella's site over and over again. Though she was so very ugly, I let myself get pulled into her eyes. I imagined that I was a little itty bitty person trapped inside the crystal between her cleavage and that I was cumming all over the walls of this cage. I turned off the lights, got comfortable, and listened to *Cum on my Command*. It was not very different than the induction. Cruella used the same techniques over and over again. However, *Cum on my Command* was produced a lot better. It had echo effects which were very well mastered, and there were even guitar notes being played in the background. Cruella was giving me reasons why I should sacrifice. She was motivating me. When I finished *Cum on my Command*, I wondered if I would ever be able to forget about Cruella, if she would haunt me forever. How would I read, or meet a real girl? She did not seem to care about these problems.

****

Around October of the next year Dolly sent me a text message. By then I was teaching high school at a Yeshiva in Midwood. The message said that she had been thinking about me all summer in a very genuine and pure way and that she missed me. I called her five minutes later. I caved when I heard her voice. She wanted to see me. I told her I would come by later the next day. My heart raced the whole subway ride across the Williamsburg Bridge. Sun flares were caught in the water and squeezing through the spaces between all the buildings. It reminded me of the taste of Dolly's skin, the innocent look in her eyes.

My heart beat so goddamn fast, and then I was lost in ChinaTown, before I found her dorm hall on Lawrence Street. I waited by the security guard for her to come down and check me in. And there was little Dolly; she had bought cat-eyed glasses since I last saw her... She snuggled up against me right away. A few of the other college students looked on. The guard took my identification. We were in the elevator staring at each other. She had on a green dress, it was high above her knees. The dorm room she lived in was enormous. The ceilings were ten feet high, and the entrance wrapped around to a living room and a kitchen. Nobody was home, and I found out right away that she had nothing on underneath. It was reassuring to stick my hand down between her legs and find it warm and moist. I ran her wetness up along the insides of her pussy lips, lubricating the whole thing. I was kissing her frantically, my pants were down, I was back on her breasts, we were on the couch, and on the floor. We were by a large crate of folk records, and underneath posters, then we were in her room, there were butterflies on the wall, and a picture of Dolly and her blonde girlfriend posing like nymphets.

Dolly lay there all cute and inviting, and I was clawing and cooing, and her body was getting wet and hard, and her mouth was opening, and this slight parting of her mouth, every time I caught a glimpse of it, redoubled my desire, and I went ahead frantically, touching her with supreme precision. She commented on how much love there was, how much affection.

We slowed down for a minute to compare our summers. I told her about my awful teaching experience; she told me about having worked at a gourmet restaurant, having kissed up to a lot of rich people, and having spent her days off riding her bicycle along the Atlantic coastline. She told me that she had finally done what we had always talked about, she had gone out and bought herself a vibrator. She had spent the whole summer getting herself off underneath her covers. She even said to me, "You were right, I should have listened. But I hadn't known what it was going to be like." My eyes glimmered. I was back on her body. It took me a long time to find her clitoris, which was small and buried beneath lips and asymmetrical ripples of skin, and her instructions about chasing past the mountain and entering into the river were not very helpful. I followed the patterns of her breathing. I wanted to overwhelm this pristine little girl. There was something so violent about her innocence. Finally I secured my index finger into a small crevice within a little knot of skin. I did not move my finger. I merely shifted it up and down ever so slightly, loosening and tightening its pressure. She was arching backwards. I had hit the spot. Her mouth parted even wider, and it was all pink and freckly. Her tongue was coming out. Her nipples were hard. Her breasts were above every other part of her body.

The area was drying out from my finger, and I took a chance, moving my finger down to her wet opening, dashing back to where I had complete control over her. She said, "You are right there." I could feel all her sensation in my hard cock. I lay down close to her sweating chest and her panting mouth. My cheek nestled against hers as I closed my eyes. My finger was pointing electrical pulses to her every extremity. It felt so powerful to be there like that, to watch her writhe, to build it up and up, I slowed my pressure when she was near to screaming, she looked at me despondently, she knew the power had all of a sudden shifted between us...

Her body was so excited to embrace me when she came. Her hip had gone numb, and she was very happy that I

22

had been the first man to make her orgasm. She was sweaty and she was pink, and wet, and totally in love with me.

Then she did not call me. She had to work a job to pay off loans. She was also interning at an experimental film production company to get her foot in the door. Between her homework and her extracurricular activities, she had no energy for anyone. Bad clichés worked their way into my psyche. I started calling this girl at I OWN YOUR COCK named Sylvia who was very good at reacting to the oscillations in my breath. She would get me touching myself and then pant with me. Coo. Occasionally she would ask me to describe how I was feeling, to tell her, "Sylvia owns my cock, she knows how to please me. I cannot be pleased unless Sylvia tells me what to do." I did not like to talk much, but being forced to express worship was different than talking. Sylvia would start to laugh at me when my excitement had me whining, which I did to keep from blowing my load.

****

Dennis had moved to New York, and he and I began to hang out because we both read and played music, and it was important to get a second opinion on all these things. Dennis was very determined to project himself as someone in the know. I respected him for his pugnacity, he would get drunk and scream at people about how dimwitted they were. It was great to live vicariously through him. He played the Prince of Denmark, and he did so in leather jackets with gelled black hair. He was always on the verge of making a miraculously profound statement, and it always required that he deface that which was around him, be it the eccentric failed poet at the bar every night, the pop jingle playing at the supermarket, the flimsy chairs supporting us restaurateurs, or the hoax of an installation piece drawing everyone into Chelsea for an after-noon of pretense. Everything was ready to be diminished, and his good friend Jonathan was in no way immune. But it felt good to be bruised by him. He hated me for almost everything I chose. From my careless word choices to my choice in women. He also hated on me for my lack of interest in Ren-aissance art, and he also hated me because I was not con-stantly referring to the Holocaust and World War II as something every serious conversation had to consider. "Do you even know who Hitler was?" He would exclaim with ec-static fury. "A real bad guy?" This kind of joke would bring out Dennis's ferocious scowl. He had big lips which curled down towards his chin, and there was always a cigarette there, like an exclamation mark. "One day when you grow up from all your Internet games, you'll feel the real stakes Jonathan, and I'll have forgiven you. Though, trust me, it has not been easy." I would grow red in my face, and it would be thrilling.

He was the one who pursued me. I had a hard time getting away from my home. I liked to be close to the com-puter because of the possibilities which it offered, and my books were important to me too, so the idea of going outside was never that appealing. Dennis would call me up after he got off work. He had a job at an Advertising Company in Midtown which he hated immensely. He would make fun of me until I agreed to have a drink with him.

Everything was Romantic when I made it out on the streets. I got the feeling that the leak in my pants had an aura about it that might show in my eyes. I was never too shy to share them. I felt like I was groping everyone as I wavered along the sidewalk. My street was festive, and since it was ethnic the cleaning services did not bother coming around that often. Garbage, chicken wing, confetti spray, toilet paper, chalk lines, spray paint, and a bevy of crumbs were soaked into the corners of the curb and the cracks between each slab of sidewalk. The hip-hop music was loud, and all the high school boys with baggy pants were playing with their cell-phones or their video game consoles. The women wore tight jeans and gold earrings, and if they had not yet turned thirty they were real sexy. Once over thirty all the women got pregnant and became obese, then they shrunk to midgets in their fifties. The older men were very delicate, and they must have been talking about the island or about going fishing the next day in the Hamptons. Some drug deals took place: a few homeless men and women came by skinny and strung out looking to buy from Sammy, a short, hyper man who was the default mayor of the block. He gave me a high five whenever I passed by. Once I turned the corner everything blackened out, and it was the brownstones which were most pervasive, and if it was clear out, the moonlight.

Dennis had this power over me. He made me feel weak and I waited for his validation. He seemed to under-stand the deeper questions, and he was writing articles for *Teleopoiesis*, which gave him a certain credential. Most im-pressive about Dennis was his ability to seduce women, and he lorded this over me. My entire situation on the Internet, and with Dolly, it was all because I was a loser who could not get any women. Something about this revelation attracted me.

He lived in ChinaTown, on a skinny street that smelled like cat and dog cadavers. One shop sold some cheap, spicy pork wontons, which was a good thing, as I was usually starving when I headed out to see Dennis because lying in my room never required much energy, and I had learned to over-come my urge to nap by jerking off. These were very weak and sweaty and sad jerk off sensations where I would be so dazed that all I could do was race myself to an orgasm, and then I would be even more tired, and there would be cum all over me, and I could care less about preventing it from getting over my sheets and my clothes. Some nights my shirt had dis-creet cum stains on it, but I liked the smell, and it kept me in this introverted mode. Dennis would make fun of me for how

I smelt, so I would try to smell worse and worse, just to piss him off.

He was really into his heroes. They included Walt Whitman, Lawrence Durrell, Bob Dylan, Leonard Cohen, William Shakespeare, Herman Melville, and Henry Miller. Dennis considered himself a Luddite. He looked fondly on the days when stone churches had been erected, and frescoes draped the ceilings. The time was out of joint, so he said, when he was born: he was too talented, too keen, to be amidst us. It was the twilight he used to say, before we were swept completely under the grips of the forces of kitsch and capitalist tyranny.

We would talk about women almost all the time. We both hated them. I hated them because they had broken my heart all throughout my life, and they were very precious with themselves, like little felines licking their fur. They were just so precious. He hated them because he was partially impotent. We would sit out on his porch in the back of his building. The porch had thick, dark wood pikes outlining its narrow shape. The pale white exterior of the building across from us was plagued with gray splotches. It made the place feel ghostly, as if the whole area had already passed away. We would sit out there smoking cigarettes, talking, and playing guitar. Dennis talked really loud, he had a gruff voice, which he parodied when he was griping about females. To him the female was subhuman, she was incapable of higher thought, and that was about all he said really, and he would say so very forcefully, as if he had written a new law. When he talked about specific women in his life, he would complain about lumps they had on their skin or about the way they tried to align themselves with feminism when in fact they wanted to be domestic cows as soon as possible... His flare for the dramatic was humorous. And he had striking eyes, maybe lilac, which had a calico, oriental enormity, and he always tried to make them look doughy and sad.

Dennis prided himself on being a connoisseur of pornography. He was obsessed with Rocco Sifreddi, a strong Italian with a big cock and a patient, vibrating voice. Rocco's voice was very low, and it would feel like a tremor of sensation when he was ordering the girls to get down on their knees or to spread their ass cheeks for him. Rocco was famous for fucking girls in the asshole, and this was Dennis's favorite thing to watch. Rocco would fuck them as hard as possible. He would slap their faces and squeeze their cheeks. He would turn their mouths towards him and squeeze the lips open and then spit in their mouths. Sometimes the spit would miss, and it would land on the girl's eyes, and she would try not to blink, and she would try to keep her pretty pink lips open so that she looked sexy for the camera. Rocco abused his women, he pounded and pounded them, and when they were sucking his cock, he made them choke and gag, and then all this spit would come out of their mouth when he removed it, and the women would gasp for air. He was one of the most famous porno stars. He made the women look sad and pathetic. They were crying almost all the time because they were being forced to deep throat something too big, for too long. Dennis said that he could only get off when the woman was enjoying herself, and this came in the form of the high-pitched screams she let out when being fucked up her ass. Dennis bragged about his own sexual romps. He loved to take a girl's face and turn it to the side and bang his cock against her cheek. The cheek had to be blemish free, soft, and from the Mediterranean for him to really enjoy this activity.

Dennis had five women who were obsessed with him, and they would come over and visit whenever he called. They were all what Dennis called bluestocking girls, and these were the most pathetic type of women who existed, those who read Rilke or Rimbaud with undo affection, those who worshipped the ground of Joan Didion or Mary Wollenscroft, these women did not know anything about the literature they loved, except for the prestige which loving it gave them. The moment these pretty ladies would arrive in their makeup and tight fitting blouses, Dennis would find something about them to make fun of. If they were wearing sandals, it might be the size of their big toe or the crudding up of nail polish. If they were wearing jeans with an insignia or studs on the back pocket, he would mention this as something horribly tacky. If they had not put on makeup, he would say, "You look awful." He committed the ultimate taboo and commented on their weight, whether too thin or too large. The girl would always be defending herself while she walked into the living room, before she had even sat down, before she had even said hello to me.

I was the friendly pervert who seductive Dennis had around for entertainment. My conversation with the women was scarce and ironic. It was also important that I kept my mouth shut about Isabella, who was Dennis's actual girlfriend, and who knew nothing of the exploits that took place at his home every weekend. Dennis would offer us beer and then without fail he would grab his guitar. He whispered to himself, looking up from time to time with his doughy eyes. We both would sit there watching him. When he finally started, his face transformed into something very melancholic and woeful. His heart retched while he sang, and though he hit all of his notes, and though his melodies were catchy, the smug assuredness of his personality came out in his lyrics and in his bland, Eddie Veder-esque crooning. He had one song that began, "Face too pretty for a mind so fine/Eyes like diamonds from a distant time." Another song, "Truth is I have never met someone like me/Curse me for being so bold and so free." And he even had a song whose chorus repeated over and over again, "I cannot go on."

These songs were all Bob Dylan folk style, with a bit of Elliot Smith in them. He kept the rhythm in a very clunky, persistent way which absented each song of joy. Still, the fact that his lyrics were so far flung in their attempt to be honest, that he sang so loud, and that he looked so woefully pathetic kept us captive. He made us feel embarrassed for not under-standing his profundity. When he was done and he put his guitar down, the girls, who were threatened by his emotional-ity, would sit on his lap. He would have me turn on a new CD he was into, and he would drum along to the beat on the thighs of these little girls. It was usually around that time that he would make me sing. Singing to strangers was something I desired to avoid, and Dennis made me sing because I was like something zoological to him. I turned red, I tried hard not to apologize before starting. I began to thrash away. My songs were all schizophrenic. I had one where I said, "If you got a problem with your civilization/Bring it on down to the mer-chant poet" (which was a reference to the Solon described in my high school textbook), and I had another one where I cat-erwauled, "I sent my dove a brain out to sea/It came back whimpering I couldn't find a leaf." The words and the chords spat out arhythmically and atonally. And I hated the way Dennis and the girl would urge me on. Dennis always asked me for another song after I finished, and I always asked for a cigarette, though I did not like to smoke. I wanted to do any-thing, smoke, drink, anything so I could not feel so embar-rassed to be myself. When I left, I had my Internet perversions to look forward to, and it was so nice to be able to lie back and listen to my headphones.

****

The feminization mp3s led me down a twisted, sleepy tunnel, until finally breasts formed, my nipples became overly sensitized, and my cock was replaced with a cunt, which my Queen, my Master, Cruella, toyed with any way she liked. She slapped my fresh ass. Other times she wore a strap-on and fucked my pussy. Then there were the parties she had, where I had to suck lots of cocks, take them in my every orifice. These feminization tracks took more concentration than I was used to. In the cum hypnosis tracks the fantasy was not so different from the situation. There were my hands, her voice, and my cock. Now, I had to find a way to present myself to myself as something I was not and make believe that I was receiving the sensations of this make believe creature I had become. To imagine the sensitivity of my nipples being heightened was not very difficult. They were an erogenous zone I had experimented with before, and with Cruella's sultry voice it was not hard to imagine that they were indeed bigger, fluffier, and always sending shockwaves down to 'my cunt.' As for my cock, I transformed the foreskin into my clit. I never grabbed it, I would rub it, put lotion all over it, feel it as something moist, which had tremors in every particle, every corner, between every vein, and this gave me very delicious, warm feelings—to be present to my cock and my body as if they were constantly reaching out of me. There were more tears in my chest, a serpentine eloquence came over my bodily gestures, and I started to pant like a little girl, just like Cruella told me to. "Pant like a little girl, let all that sensation come over you. It builds so slowly when you rub your clit for me." My lips felt moist and pouty, and my cheeks lowered. I sat there crying, like a puddle. I became all leaky. My orgasm built up slowly, made me scream before it arrived, and then I blacked out as I came all over my stomach and returned to my manhood. It felt so good to be a little girl with pouty lips. I always wanted more when it was done. I wanted to think about Cruella every second. I had access to some of her other slaves, through Yahoo Group, and they made the most amazing confessions:

Bootslave: I am Cruella's slave. Cruella owns my mind, my body and my soul. I wake up every day and say a prayer to

Cruella, just as she has told me to do. My breasts have grown so big by now that Cruella has me wearing a bra to work everyday. She tells me that this bra will make my pussy wet, and it does, my pussy is wet the whole day. Cruella has been kind enough to talk to me on the phone, which only her lucky and servile pets get to do. This is notice for all of you out there who are looking for more and want to be completely owned by the beautiful, commanding Cruella. If you are nice to her, and email her, and buy all her mp3s, she comes closer to you. She is thinking about letting me go and see her. All I can think about is being in her presence. To have those eyes in front of me in reality, this would make my pussy shoot streams of juice on the wall. I am touching my pussy right now just thinking about it. Humping my hand. Pumping and thrusting. She makes me feel so good. I cannot take it sometimes. I want to burst. She is the most commanding, the ultimate goddess. She deserves all of your attention. Give it to her! I can never get her out of my mind. She has set up so many triggers that my unconscious is always sending me the message she wants: I must obey Cruella. I must obey Cruella. I MUST OBEY CRUELLA. My tits are so hard, I am so milky for her. Cruella wants me to have her baby for her. I would do this, I would get fat for her. I never thought a dream like this could come true. To have a beautiful woman in my life who makes me horny all the time, and all I have to do to earn this is to forget my desires and please her in every way. Cruella, because she is so special, has to lead a very expensive lifestyle, this is why aside from all the money I spend on mp3s and phone calls, I also send her $300 at the end of every week. She has asked me to collect more money from all of you. Don't you want to feel like me? Don't you?

****

Dennis could never let up an opportunity to brag. He would burst out, almost upon greeting me, all that had transpired the past few nights with his cute girly girls. They wanted him to be physical. They wanted him to choke them really hard. He could never do it the way they wanted. They wanted him to kiss them passionately. This was pathetic and Romantic, and he refused to do this. They wanted him to stay hard inside their pussies and make them cum, but he hated the way they spoke about Hemingway as if he was a good writer, and he hated the way they had gained some weight in their thighs, and he hated the music that he heard coming through the ceiling, so he could never give them what they wanted. They wanted to jump into the flame of sexual tension, as he put it, but he knew that these flames were tenuous and if over-indulged they would just snuff out. Sex for him was a major burden. His cock was never hard, and it was like he was always trying to play catch up. He would run after stiffness, run after affection. He would try to focus, and it was too hard for him to do. In his own words, it was his Sartrean existentialism that caused his impotence. He was too aware of the sensation of sound coming from the curtain, too aware of the masks girls wear, too aware of the ignorance of everyone walking down the streets, everyone in their apartments watching Television, everyone in an office making money, everyone everyone everyone was naïve, and it pained him, and his cock felt the brunt of this awareness, for the enjoyment of the cock was a false pride he could not muster. He orally diagrammed his sexual experience. It wavered. It reached a point where what had felt like an ensuing climax subsided and dropped all the way back to the beginning. He would grow despondent, remain in this trap, the girl would be underneath him with her freckled breasts, and all he could concentrate on was his limpening dick, and then he would double up his efforts, he would imagine a different girl, one who turned him on, and that would

32

help him lift off from the bottom, and he would get closer, and the girl's red lips would part, and then, her tooth, a tad too sharply pointed, would make him think that this girl was not worthy of his affection, that he was indulging in something kitschy, so he would return again to the bottom. This was when he pulled out his final stop, his most drastic fantasy, he imagined that the girl was cheating on him, that she was in fact fucking another guy, and usually, he admitted to me later, this guy he imagined her to be fucking was me, and this is when he would lose control and cum inside of the girl.

Dennis, who was half Jewish, liked to talk about the superiority of the Jewish ethos. "The strongest rebellion one can have against authority is Messianic. Thinking that you are the Messiah is the greatest feeling a human can have. Only the Jews are still allowed this luxury, Jonathan. In Christianity everything has already come, everyone is resigned to submission. You see what I am getting at, Jews are allowed to come, in fact, if they do come, they save the world." This is why the Holocaust was so telling of the world. Jealousy of the victor, he called it. Hitler, to him, was the prototype of an impotent male. He would read me passages from <u>Mein Kampf</u>. The book had lots and lots of exclamation marks. These were substitutes for the orgasm he claimed. If you cannot get it up, if you cannot please a woman, you have to compensate through signage. He would continue on Hitler, gleefully, "Here is a man, he has failed as an artist, as an architect, he has failed at everything, god only knows how he failed with women. I can guarantee there are some embarrassing nights with his cock falling limp, I can guarantee you this, Jonathan. And he is so desperate, that he fabricates his cock. He makes it out of propaganda, out of thick blocks of stone, out of the steal knife, out of erect marches and bolstering screams, he makes it out of fields pouring with the blood of the potent, how potent are they now he screams, and he marches, marches like a cock is up his ass, and that is how it feels, to the impotent, like they have been fucked by the world's order. It is the man with a defunct organ, not a woman, who experiences the most excessive penis envy, and this is Hitler."

"Are you saying the Jews have the best cocks?"

"If you're their representative, darling beaver."

****

Dolly contacted me a year later, and we went up to visit her mother in New Chatham, CT. We went straight into the woods. Dolly walked slowly, and I walked behind her. We were covered on all sides by a play of light and shadow best evoked by the Russian pen. And Dolly was Russian, so everywhere were the ingredients for those descriptively seasoned novels. Dolly found these ripe wineberries and ate them without hesitating. She picked up a flower which had white, diaphanous scepters encircling the stamen, and she pushed her mouth into it and nibbled on its edges. She found another plant, and she found a cluster of seeds underneath its petals, and she ate them too, then she fed them to me—they tasted like garlic. She was wearing a sun hat and sunglasses. Every so often I came up next to her and held her tightly in my arms. I kissed from the bottom of her neck, to her cheek, to her lips, and I would suck her lower one gently into my mouth, nibbling on it and the edge of her tongue. I pushed my cock against her thighs—when I finally tried to devour her mouth...

We made it into a clearing, and the fields were all shades of yellow and green. A walkway led us to a bench which overlooked an undulation of prairie chords. She bit into a peach she had been carrying with her, letting the juices fall onto her chin. She told me how wet I made her. I took this as a cue to put my hand inside, but she stopped it, and told me to wait until later.

Back through the shade of the trees we watched the sun lower, it left impressionisms on the water and the lingering sailboats. Corn stalks carried on forever right beneath our eyes. The surface of everything said fuck Dolly. Behind a bend we found a small area with a wooden swing. Dolly sat on it and arched her chest upwards. Her hair, against the elm leaves, was so striking in the low sunlight, the color of a strange anesthesia. Everything was brought in from the mountains. She let me swing, I glared at her like a devil. I pulled the ropes taut, leaned back, I smiled as she took a photograph of me. She came towards me, twirling a dandelion in her hand, whispering to it. We started to kiss real strong. One of us kept snapping photographs. She took a picture of me soaking in her presence, a curl on my lips. I took one of her, her wild hair all about her wild face. When she bent down to grab my cock, I captured how small her face was in comparison, how little her hands. The medallion she wore from her Grandmother in Russia, with an etching of Mother Mary, hung near my cock. When we came together we took a picture. The sun was highlighting our hair, and the world did not seem balanced. We scrambled to get dressed as we heard noises coming up the road. I took one more picture, her hand blocking visual passage to her pussy. Her fleshy legs fore-grounded the trees.

We sat on a pier, with a little child chasing a seagull, and the sun set in her hair, 'cause I was curled in her lap, whispering sweetly as I smiled up towards her. And I knew that there was the most delicate shimmering going on out there, I could smell the salt, and the excitement, and I could hear the repetition of the breaking waves.

We went to her visit her mother, Dasha. She lived on the Ocean, in a beach house. She greeted us warmly and gave us food she had set aside. Some rosemary olives and some figs. She opened a bottle of red wine she had been saving. Dolly's mother used to be very beautiful. She was born in St.

Petersburg and she married there. After only a year in America, when Dolly was six years old, Dasha divorced her husband. She had ballooned a little since then, but her arrogance from her prettier days gave her a certain charm. We sat in the dark of that small home as the smell of garlic and olive oil started sizzling near the stove. While we were waiting for the food, we went outside to grab our bags, and on the gravel of the driveway, it finally became clear how far we were from the city. Back in Dolly's bedroom we got to kiss for a few minutes. It had a bed and nothing more. When we went back out to the kitchen, I had precum all over my pants. I was given more wine and Dasha asked me about my teaching. I talked about the Yeshiva a little, about how the kids were difficult. Dasha's mother started to talk about how lonely she was. We finished up quietly.

Dolly was in her pajamas and she was distant from me. Being back in her home was difficult, and she felt for her mother. She turned over, the kohl beneath her eyes was smearing. She asked me to leave her alone because she did not want me to see her in that way, nobody ever had. I tried to talk to her very abstractly about disarming sadness, but she was adamant about it being something out of her control, something which took hold of her, making her feel so distant from the possibility of existence. I said this was something which she indulged in, in this feeling, in her own debilitation. Her sadness was all over the room, it was inside me. It had no reason for being there. We could have been fucking sadness out of ourselves. The scene out the window, with the tall trees and the vibrating of the wind chimes—Dolly's sadness brought it into focus; it was more than in focus, it was exaggerated, and as I looked at the shadows on the ceiling I imagined that that was where Dolly was, for she was not in her body anymore—if she had been, I would have been in it too. I went outside. The blue tarp covering a sailboat was flapping next door. The sea was cold and it was crashing loudly. I found a cigarette butt in my jacket pocket and lit it with the flame from the barbeque along the side of Dolly's home. The wind came straight into my mouth. It came fast, and my jacket rippled. I walked to the edge of the lawn, which was raised up six feet from the sand of the beach. I was going to jump, and then I finally did, and my knees and my thighs felt the shock—I lost my breath for a second. Clouds were in front of the stars out East, but to the North and the South and the West they were everywhere. The wind brushed up against me too firmly and I got anxious and cold. I had dreamt of staying out all night and I lasted only five minutes. I went back inside and fumbled around the bathroom quietly. Dasha's door was slightly ajar. Bruno the big goofy bulldog Dasha owned was lying on top of her, snoring loudly. I went back to Dolly. She had fallen asleep. I tried to imagine I was something magnificent. I tried to think about the morning.

I woke up and there was cum all over my boxers, and I felt the sheets and they had been stained too. The sun was coming in from all sides, Dolly was opening her eyelids shyly. I started to rub all the cum into anything dry. I rubbed it into the sheet, I rubbed it along my arms, I rubbed it into my boxers, and I rubbed some on Dolly's pajama leg in the guise of showing her affection. She made a noise of discomfort and rolled away from me.

I had gone into Dasha's room to say something to comfort her, Dolly was already asleep. She asked me why I was not with Dolly. "Dolly is tired." Dasha understood. She let me lie in bed with her, and she began to stroke me. She took off her sweatshirt, and I played with her big breasts. She stuffed one in my mouth and told me to suffocate. When I had lost my consciousness, she led me into Dolly's room, her hand tickling my cock. She shook Dolly, Dolly was moaning in her sleep, her breast had fallen out of her pajama shirt. Dasha noticed how badly I desired Dolly. She shook Dolly awake. Dolly moaned louder. When she realized who was standing

above her, Dolly said, "Mom," just like a child. Dasha re-
sponded, "You have not been very nice to our guest, and he
has been so nice to us, I have had to take it upon myself to
give him the hospitality he deserves, but he wants you more
than me." "Mom... I'm tired." Dasha took her hand and
placed it gently on Dolly's cheek. Then she slapped her face.
Dolly's tears formed, she came up to me and kissed my stom-
ach and she licked my nipples. Her mom lubricated her hand
by placing it in Dolly's mouth and started rubbing my cock at
the head. I was buckling over from all the sensations. Dolly
started to crawl around me, like she was a little spider. She
sucked on my neck, on my back, then she was curled up be-
tween my ass cheeks, flicking my asshole with her tongue.
Dasha was telling her where she should go, how hard she
should press up against me... She told Dolly to get off of me,
"Lie on the bed and be naked." They both stopped rubbing
me. We were in this little room. I had all the sensation-
residues of Dolly's tongue glowing on my skin. Dasha let go
of my cock. She saw the way I stared at Dolly, she laughed.
Dolly giggled too, she stretched out and then fell asleep.
That's when Dasha grabbed me from the side, leaned up
against my ear, and told me to cum all over her daughter
while she lie there asleep... I did as I was told. I drew a line
from Dolly's right knee to the cavity beneath her right eye.

Dolly went to shower. She moved as if the sunlight,
as if the waking shore; she moved as if the stovetop frying, as
if the crooked door; she moved as if the leaf, and the leaflet on
her dresser; she moved as if she knew that movement was the
answer. I lay in bed. The water was running. Dasha came in
and asked me if I wanted to come out and have some breakfast; she made a joke about Dolly having been a poor host.
The sun was lined up with the window, it lay across the sea,
the white walls of the home were on fire.

****

Dennis had asked me in the dead of winter to pick him up at Newark Airport. He was returning from a week long vacation with his estranged father on a small island called Mariposa off the coast of Mazatlan, Mexico. The island had no electricity, one telephone, and was reached via faerie. Dennis came up to the curb with his luggage, he was wearing a straw cowboy hat and he had a nice tan. He got into the car and gave me a big hug. I could smell his cologne and his skin. The scruff on his cheeks scratched mine a little, and I still felt the imprint as he animatedly praised the nights and days he had just spent in paradise. New Jersey was dark, the factory smokestacks were shadowy, and the highway winded us down into the Lincoln Tunnel where we breezed past a blur of fluorescent lights. Dennis had seen a scorpion, his eyes were livid. He slept in a hammock dangling from the ceiling of a wood cabin. The sunlight in the morning came in with the wind coming off the hot Ocean, which, said Dennis, was as still as a sheet of glass. He walked all day... to the little town where meats and vegetables were sold, into the pathways trellised by tropical trees, and his skin and the sand were covered in a network of shadows. "Arabesque," he said proudly, "You have to see the pictures." He told me about James who had lived out there for twenty years. "A real man's man, these handsome dark eyes, he would set up everything for us. You know my father Jonathan, the prototype of the absentee academic, he can't do anything. James would set up the lights and patch holes in the roof. He would come back in the afternoon with these neon fish he had caught with his trusty knife." Dennis thrust his arm out to give me the full effect. "My father and I really got along, it was unusual." "Did you guys come to any earth-shattering conclusions?" "Only that when the next life form comes down, they will call all of us idol worshipers…" "That's pretty good." "Oh, there was something. James told us about this tribe in South America, the Tupi, the Guyaki, Guarani, one of those." "Tupi?" "Just listen Jonathan." He was getting giddier than I had ever remembered him, and I enjoyed playing along. "Is it about Hitler?" "Yes! It's about the opposite. The potent chieftain." "Important to sneak your favorite word in there." Dennis ignored me, "The chief is chosen to be the chief because he is the one who speaks most eloquently, he is the most generous, and he is the only one who gets to fuck more than one woman. The tribe does not listen to him. They get rid of him if he stops being generous, and the women all devour him with their lust, so he is always tired. He takes on the role of chief solely to defuse its political authority, and in his generosity the tribe can live harmoniously. There is no hierarchy, no classes. The man with the biggest cock expends all his spunk for the betterment of the community, instead of using it solipsistically. I do not understand it exactly, but I know this is profound. When I go to Oxford this is going to be my dissertation, comparing this chief to Hitler." I was laughing, "I think this trip was very good for you. You make a much more charming fool." Dennis straightened up, "I do feel happy, I am going to project happy confidence from now on." We put the radio on, and turned onto Delancey…

We parked underneath the BQE and walked a few blocks to my home. The Dominicans were all on the porch. Dennis stopped to show them some special Mexican Rum he had brought back with him, and they were all excited, and he let them take a few swigs. In return they let us smoke the joint they were passing around. When we closed the busted black gate behind us, we were whirling with all this excitement, and Dennis put his arm around me. He started effusing about how we were the ones, the only ones. Then it dawned on me, and I could not get it out of my head… He was very handsome, and I didn't know how to talk to him without him reading right through me, because we were so gentle when we talked and we looked each other directly in the eyes. We went into my living room, where we had played a lot of guitar. My bookshelves were in there too. We turned on a desk light and pointed it towards the wall. The room took on the character of some place elsewhere. Usually the shouts outside were deafening, that night it was all silent. Dennis handed me the rum, then he lit up a cigarette. The rum was real syrupy, and it was clouding my mind. I was so fucking nervous. Dennis wanted to show me pictures. He took out his digital camera, and I sat down next to him on the couch. He lunged his leg into mine, and his elbow was on my ribs as we looked through hundreds of pictures. The Ocean did look like glass, in the brightest shots it had a ruddy hue. The shadows, in the trellised trees... the alpaca colors of the hammock, and there were a few of Dennis without his shirt, he had no hair on his chest, the smoothness was apparent in the pictures, he had really big lips, and it would have been nice, I thought, to touch them, if just with my fingers. I was jealous of Dennis. I wanted to live without electricity and wake up on an island, do nothing but feel the water on my ankles. Hiding away... the enormity of the dreams that could have come. The spirits at night... He had one picture of a fifty-year old woman spreading her legs flirtatiously on the floor of his father's cabin. I shifted to the floor and sat on all the dust. Dennis was drinking the rum, he was looking at me, I was fidgeting, my fingers were crawling around, pulling at the edge of my shirt, spidering through my hair and the fuzz of my chin. I said, "Dennis, I feel really weird saying this, but I also think I would feel retarded if I didn't. I feel a lot of sexual tension, right now specifically. I have felt it before. I do not know what to think about it. Maybe I'm crazy, is this something you feel too?" "It's interesting, isn't it, especially because we are both heterosexual?" "Yeah, I guess because we talk about our sex life so much, it is hard for your fantasies not to become mine. It seems almost

inevitable, like it would be unempathic not to want you."
Dennis let out one of his crude chuckles. He explained why
we should not do anything about it. How that would destroy
this beautiful sexual tension we had.

We ended up lying in bed next to each other fifteen
minutes later, head to toe. We were fully clothed, Dennis still
had his shoes on. His rigidly crossed arms were against my
stomach. He was explaining, very mechanically, what it was
he hoped we could partake in together. He hoped that we
could be a pair of prizefighters, swinging our cocks against
each other, bounding about with our strength and our 'virility.'
We would jerk each other off, cum on each other's skin. He
told me that he had fantasies about fucking me in the ass, that
he had them at night, that he jerked off to these fantasies. It
was not the same with me. The one time I felt it most forcefully was when he greeted me with a joking kiss on the cheek.
"I can only imagine it beginning by kissing you, rubbing up
against you, maybe starting by your chest and working towards your mouth." Dennis laughed, "You're so Romantic.
It's part of what bothers me so much about you... I guess it's
admirable." We were very quiet. I hated him for making me
do it, because I thought he was the dominant and I the submissive, but I was getting tired of waiting; I reached towards him
and flipped him over to my side. I put my arm around him, so
he was right up close. We were breathing on each other. He
smelt fresh, like some minty herb, it reminded me of the Muir
Forest outside of San Francisco... He turned so his head faced
the ceiling, and he repeated over and over: "You just annoy
me so much... Do you know how much you annoy me...?"
He shook his head and said it again, "You really annoy me."
"You annoy me too," I said. He turned his back to me and we
went to sleep. In the morning he was already dressing to go,
he thanked me for a sexy evening.

****

Princess Gianna came up on Google when I typed in erotic hypnosis. She was a cute blond from Portland, and her pictures seemed authentic. The severity of her face was softened by the patient way she stared out from her blue eyes. I lingered over her face, weighing the possibilities. One part of the site had suggestive pictures of her ass and her cleavage. Another part of the site had pictures of different rooms in her home. The kitchen had all these pans, the bedroom had a television and a cat, and the bathroom had a toilet. It was like a scene in a David Lynch movie, where you wait hesitantly for the pathology hiding behind the couch. The rest of the site had a lot of literature, but I was so anxious to call her that I did not take the time to read it.

It took three nights for me to get in touch with her. Her voice was perky, perky and grave. She wanted $300 for her first call, and she wanted it sent through Western Union. The demand for this much money cut my restraints right out of me, and I asked for the details. I had to call up Western Union and give an account number, an address, and a credit card number. In my rush to get back to Gianna's voice I made the decision to use my mother's credit card because I had not used it recently and because my own bank account was missing the $6000 the Rabbi owed me. I gave all the information and called back Gianna. Gianna checked her bank to see if the transfer had gone through. It hadn't. I grew a bit despondent. Part of me figured it was a good thing, that something was protecting me, something which knew much better than I how wasteful I was being.

My phone rang and it was my mother. It was one in the morning where I was, midnight back in Chicago. The nice people at Western Union had called up my mother to get the cash transfer approved. Since I was not the main account holder, they had to get her authorization. My mother and the phone receptionist at Western Union had no idea what service, what kind of person Gianna was, so everything was very vague to my mother, not to mention that she had just been woken. I told her that it was a mistake, that I had no idea they were going to call her. "I will rectify everything, go back to sleep, Mom." She did.

I called back Western Union and gave my own credit card number. I asked the phone operator to double check to see if the transfer had gone through. When it was confirmed, I called Gianna back. She checked her records and the money was there. We were both very happy. She asked for my name and then told me that from now on my name was puppy. She observed that I had been surprised by the charge of $300 and asked if I had not read all the literature on her website before calling. This was what the website instructed me to do. I told her that I had been so excited I had not looked over everything. "Do you know what it is I do?" "Yes, I think so." "And what is your experience so far?" "I have been downloading mp3s from different sites, I have never called anyone who is a hypnotist. I have done phone sex calls before, but never hypnotic ones." "Have you ever done any of this for real, with a girlfriend, or a dominatrix?" "I went to a dominatrix once, that's it." "So you know this first call is going to be an hour long, do you have enough time right now? I need at least an hour to implant all my triggers in you." "I have time." I scurried into my room and got underneath my covers. Everything was dark. The echoes from my building and the shouts from the street were very small.

She wanted me to go to her web page. On that page was a link to a giant colored spiral which moved in flash animation. She wanted me to look at the center point of the spiral while I listened to her. I forget what happened after I got it up. Hypnosis is about forgetting. I remember saying yes to her when she asked if I was the most hypnotized I had ever

44

been. I was so happy to say that. I remember falling, feeling my shoulders slump, and her voice shot out and spread through my body. I was vibrating, and I was listening to what she had to say. I went to bed that night having made promises, I think we gave each other our home numbers and we were working out a sum of money which I was going to pay her monthly. She also had demanded that I only touch my cock if I was looking at her pictures or talking to her, and I could only cum if I was given permission by her alone.

Fall was turning into winter, and I was waiting anxiously for contact with Gianna. Every time I called I got her answering machine. I felt myself falling, dragging through the lattice of holes on the phone from merely the few words she had to say about calling her back. I had to skinny up on food, the Rabbi was not running the school correctly, and the money I had from my parents I refused to spend on anything but phone sex. So I was skipping meals, and that was part of the sensuality which was coming over me, and then, finally, Gianna called me. "Hi puppy," she said. "Hi princess." "That's a good puppy." And I was panting like a little doggy, "Oh, you remember everything I told you, good puppy." And I was panting again, like a good puppy. She purred... rolling her tongue, a large quantity of Rrrrrrrrrrrrrrrrr rushed at me, and I leaned against the wall in the hallway. "How does that feel, puppy?" And I panted like a dog. She stopped teasing me like this and began to fuss about her kitchen. She made herself tea and told me about the different faces her cat was making. She had a regal, fat, white cat. We needed to talk about expenses. She charged $1200 a month. That did not include the first payment. If I paid $1200, I would be able to call her at any hour of the day, and she was going to call me too. She asked me about my life. She liked that I was a schoolteacher. She felt something special inside me. She spoke to me about how much she liked sushi and how she had to fix her car, and I waited and waited for her to hypnotize me again—but she didn't, and I felt broken when I got off the phone with her. I could not jerk off without her permission. All I could do was figure out how much I was going to pay her for the month. I had told her my situation with the Rabbi and with my parents; she wanted me to be honest because she wanted it to work out between us. She told me to do some thinking, make some calculations, and get back to her with how much I could afford.

****

"Isabella read all my emails. She's going nuts. She thinks I cheated on her over fifteen times since we've been together. She sounds like she's going to kill herself. I told her that when I'm with her, I give all that I can. How can she expect me to stay faithful when she's not around? Women are such fucking idiots."

"She checked your email when you were sleeping?"

"I used her computer and my password saved. She clicked in. She didn't read one or two emails Jonathan, she read everything I've written for the past three months. To Joanne, to Imogen, to Susanna."

"To Magda?"

"Everyone Jonathan, all of them."

"I told Isabella I did not believe in love. I told her not to get caught up with me, that I would never be faithful to her. I don't know what planet these fucking creatures live on, acting like we can be robotic sycophants to their shallowness our whole lives. Give them our sperm. What the fuck, are they crazy? I have my own life to live."

"What life, Dennis, what life you got to live?"

"I have my ideas, I have my art, I have my own way, and if someone is going to get in the way of that, they can stay the fuck away from me."

"I thought Isabella was the only girl who got you hard?"

"More or less."

"So why're you fucking around with other people anyways? For bragging rights?"

"You wouldn't understand Jonathan, seeing as you can't get a woman unless you pay her money to talk to you."

"I reached a new low recently."

"Yes...?"

"I'm paying some girl a monthly rate to be my phone-in mistress. She is going to be on call, or I am going to be on call. I don't understand it yet."

"I don't get it."

"I like to be exploited. It is very fun for me. Extort away, I say."

All of a sudden, an old woman turned around. We were waiting in line at San Loco Tacos on Ave A. across from Tompkins Square Park. We were drunk and starving. This old woman turned around, and her eyes lit up as she said, "I'm an extortionist." She said it very seductively, even though she was old and nasty. "Oh yeah?" I picked up on her tone, "That's wonderful, what do you extort?" "What would you like me to extort from you?" "There is only so much one can extort from someone. I prefer to have either my cum or my money taken from me, as I have little else." "Yummy," said the woman. Dennis was horrified. I liked her eyes though, they were blue, and her forwardness made her saggy chest look sexy. She sized both of us up, "He's no fun. I can see that." She pointed to Dennis. "Yeah, he thinks he deserves certain things." "Do you want to leave him? I live right around the corner." I looked at Dennis, "Oh, what the fuck, I'll come and hang out with you two pervs."

47

We walked up 9th street to her apartment. Clarice worked for Vice magazine. The magazine showed ugly, naked women with herpes. Clarice was in her late 40s. She played the Clash for us on her record player. She must have done lots of cocaine and heroin, but she was now living in a brick-walled apartment with eclectic furniture and super high ceilings. Clarice had just returned from Jamaica where she had almost been robbed. A Jamaican boy ran up from behind her while she was walking the beach one night and grabbed for her purse. It stayed hooked around Clarice's arm, and she refused to let go. She very theatrically showed us herself being dragged along the beach, cussing and scratching as she went. She held on for so long, the boy gave up and ran away. She took off after him swinging her purse at his face, yelling, "You're an amateur, you're an amateur. See," she elaborated, "I'd prefer a pro stealing from me, at least do a good fucking job. It's embarrassing when an amateur tries to rob you, for you and for him. I whacked that boy in his face. Fuckin' amateur," she laughed, falling on top of my lap. She lay there with her head down, her forehead was feeling for my cock. She sat up to face me, "I really want to suck both of your cocks, you guys're hot. I can suck really good cock." Dennis was sitting at the other end of the black leather sofa, he looked like he was going to puke. "Go for my friend first, I need to make a phone call."

"A phone call?" She seemed perplexed.

"Yeah, I have a mistress. She won't let me cum unless I ask for her permission."

I ran off to the bathroom and left Dennis there without looking back. I sat down on the toilet and dialed Gianna. She answered the phone gruffly, "Yes?" "Princess, this is your puppy John." "What is it?" She was not happy I called, I felt like apologizing. "I'm not gonna talk to you until you figure out how much you're gonna pay me." She sounded as if she was going to hang-up. "Hold on, hold on. I'll pay you… 600.

But I can't pay it all at once, I'll start with 300." "I need it all, that way you can be assured the attention you want puppy." "Okay, okay, 600, I'll get it to you tomorrow." "That's a good puppy." I was so happy she was going to stay on the phone and listen to me. "Why is it you called me puppy?" "I am in a sort of situation, and I thought you would prefer me to call you." "What situation?" "My friend and I are about to both get blown by this woman who picked us up." "You can't get a blowjob unless I'm there with you." "What?" "Just hand the phone to this woman and let me talk to her, let me listen while she blows you, okay puppy?" I panted for her. "That's a good puppy." I panted again. "RRrrrrrrrrrrrrrrrrrrrrr…" I felt myself dropping a little, "Go get us a blowjob puppy."

I walked out of the bathroom, my cock was rock hard. Clarice pulled her head up from Dennis's lap, she was kneeling before him. He had not moved from the couch. Dennis twisted his neck, and I saw this terrible pain and shame in his eyes. "You're friend can't get it up. It's his fault. I know I give fucking good blowjobs."

Dennis turned red, he was not saying anything.

"I'll give it a go, but my mistress wants to talk to you, if that's okay? I know this is weird."

"It ain't that weird, let me talk to her. What's her name? You're a fun kid you know."

"Her name's Gianna." I handed over the phone.

Clarice said hello and then was giggling and nodding her head. She pushed the glass table off the carpet so I could lie on it. She handed the phone back to me, "I'm gonna go puppy. You have my permission to cum. Call me tomorrow and tell me everything." "Thank you princess." The phone clicked. I was trying not to look at Dennis, I did not want to feel his judgment. I lay down, and Clarice pulled out my cock, excited to see how hard it was. Dennis walked away, I could hear his anxious steps on the wood. "You're much bigger than he is, " Clarice notified me, as she began to deep

49

throat my cock. She made a suction which worked it like a pump, and it kept getting tighter and tighter with each swallow. I closed my eyes. I did not want to look at her thin, balding head nor at the buildup of skin and wrinkles around her cheeks. I closed my eyes tighter. I started to wonder about Dennis, whether he was watching me or not. I thought that this woman must be diseased, and that she was slobbering herpes all over my cock. I tried to focus on my Princess and her desire for me to cum in this hag's mouth, but then I thought about how she wanted 600 dollars from me, and where the hell aside from in the mouth of an old hag was that getting me? I opened my eyes. Clarice was sucking me voraciously. I turned, Dennis was around the corner, between the kitchen and the bathroom. He was looking at me, his face was blank. His mouth, usually curled in disgust, was hanging stiff, unsure how to react. His left hand was in his pants. I turned back to Clarice. She looked up at me, a few bubbles of spit dribbled onto her chin. I asked, "Can you take your top off?" She did so very reluctantly. Her breasts were large and they were old, they were older than her face, because her face at least had this spark of desire in it. Her breasts were drooped and wrinkled, and when I tried to touch her nipples to get them erect nothing happened, and for a second I saw this horrific expression come over her. I stopped touching her, and she hid her breasts between my legs. I closed my eyes real tight. I did not want to let her down. I thought of nothing but the sensation, and it started to rise. I came hard in her mouth and she swallowed it all. She gave this awful look and I apologized, "Maybe that was a bad thing to have done?" She lay on the couch, put her head on my lap, and said that it was okay, that she wanted to, that she felt happy to have pleased me, because I was hot. I ran my hands through her hair, just once. I could not muster more affection. I only had this hypothetical empathy. She yelled that we should go, and though she may have wanted us to deny her request, we eagerly accepted.

****

Wiring the first 300 dollars to Gianna made my cock hard. I walked from Union Square to 6th Avenue with precum on my pants. The sky was blue, I dashed through the cold air. The buildings with all their fancy windows were as soft as the shoulders of all the bundled people I bumped up against. I called Gianna the moment I got home. She was in a hurry but promised we would talk later.

She called me—after leaving a bar where she had just beat some friends of hers in billiards—to tell me she would be home soon and that I should get into bed, naked, and lay there thinking about her until she called. It must have been a half an hour. I stayed put, because I did not want to miss out on the effect. She started to "RRrrrrrrrrrrrrrrrr" the moment I picked up the phone, and I dropped way down for her, and she had me call her princess, and she had me go deeper, and get sleepier and sleepier, further than ever, and she told me the rules, how I was going to lose my voice, how whenever she asked me how I was feeling, I would no longer know how to speak in English. I would recede to a primordial status, that of doggy. And all I could do was bark like a doggy. Once she made this take effect, she asked me if I was feeling good, and I barked like a dog, but she wanted it louder, and she wanted me to keep barking like a dog, and she turned my whole body into a dog, and another dog was there too and it was fucking me up my ass, pounding me into my bed sheets, which I humped over and over again, and the dog pounding my ass was me as well, so I was barking and humping myself, and when the dog fucking my ass came, so did I, and it must have been an hour or so, I do not know, but I was shivering, sweating all over, and Princess made me pant for her. She said, "That is what happens to good puppies." I was starting to prove myself to her, and she had some very serious plans for me. She made

51

me think of her breast lying against my nipple while I panted and licked her cheek, and then she said goodbye.

I could not sleep that night. I feared that my objective eye had been destroyed. And in a way that was what I wanted, humping my bed with all the vestiges of sex-energy that were still worming around inside me. I fell asleep for only a few minutes and entered a lucid world, like that of the Sirens. I woke up. The sun sort of crept in...

My window faces the other side of the building, so it is a gray haze which enters in the morning. Gianna lived on the West Coast. I was waiting for it to be 11:00 AM, then I could confess to Gianna about what happened. She was the only one who could help me understand. My heart beat more and more. I could not understand if my dream had come true. I wanted to jerk off with an extreme rage, and yet I could not do anything until Gianna gave me permission. The barking which she had instilled in me had given me new access. Every new sound I made was a new sensation. My heart could barely pump enough blood to compensate for this expansion. Gianna had performed a surgery on my body. The sparks of sensation became hallucinations in the morning, and I could not see straight anymore. I showered, and it was hard not to touch myself, I wanted to lay down and hump the tile, hump the wall, hump my soap. I took a walk down my street. I shied away from all the Dominicans. The sun was pouring and it was Gianna, and the buildings with their erections were Gianna, and the soft breath coming out of my mouth into the cold air was Gianna, and my feet against the sidewalk, the feel of cloth on my legs, the gloves holding my hands, it was all, in that it was sensation, and in that Gianna wanted me at the extreme for her, it was all Gianna, and I was hurting to call her, hoping, in some backwards way, that she would undo this, when in fact she could very well have wanted to intensify things even more.

I went to a coffee shop, everyone in the coffee shop had laptop computers and they were all staring at them and typing away. My coffee tasted good, and good reminded me of Gianna, and I wanted more good. I kept looking at my clock, wanting it to be the time when I could call her, everything that morning was about a strategic wasting of time. I wanted to be in bed shivering with pleasure again.

By eleven I ran home. Gianna was happy to hear about my symptoms of obsession. She said that I must have never felt so much before, and that I would get used to it. I must have lied to her. I must not have told her how paranoid I had gotten, or if I did tell her, I told it to her in a way where it was just a form of flattery. And maybe that is all I wanted to do anyways.

****

Dolly dressed up for me that evening. She wore a purple dress and tied her hair into braids which she twisted into a bun. She put a pink gloss on her lips and powdered her cheeks. We took a walk to a park with her mother. Dolly was way up the road ahead of us. The park was flat and surrounded by federal style buildings. Dolly's presence was not coming out from inside existence, it was glued on, bursting off the seam of reality. I was talking to Dasha and staring at Dolly, and Dolly was a tiny thing in the distance. Dolly was ignoring my stares. She also was doing everything so that I could continue staring at her. I wanted to taste her. I wanted to lie inside her. She flitted about with her cuteness, wiping it in my direction, and that got me chasing after her. The sun was lowering down very properly. Dasha and I caught up with Dolly, and she was not happy. I wondered what had happened without saying a thing.

We went over to Dasha's friends' house. Dasha's friends were rich and had two children, a four-year old boy named Christopher and a six-year old girl named Rebecca. They also had two enormous St. Bernards, one of who, Bruce, was in love with Dolly and pounced on her the minute we entered. The home had once been a church, the ceilings were vaulted all the way to an attic-like space where the husband and wife slept at night. The absent husband was an Architect and an Extreme Sportsman. Samantha, the mother, in sweats, was busy cutesying up the kitchen area, arranging the Chinese take-out on paper plates. The house, with its enormous brick walls and its long wood floors, had a quaint ruddiness to it, which back dropped piles of toys, running children, and dogs. The bathroom's wall was a giant aquarium that jutted out into that main room. Everything was oversized.

Rebecca and Christopher were in love with Dolly, she was this fairy who made believe with them, dressed up with them, and taught them all about being open-minded. And she would make sure they knew what creativity meant, it was cute to watch. Soon enough though, quietly, I snuck my way into their hearts and turned whatever game Dolly was encouraging them to play into some dramatic affair which always degenerated into the throwing of toys and I getting pummeled with fists and bodies

No sooner had we arrived at the home than Dolly was out of her purple dress and in a Poison Ivy outfit. The green sequins complemented all that was red about her. The kids knew me well by then. Samantha told me how they had been asking all about me. Rebecca, who had long straight brown hair and was bossy cute, kept tying my hands behind my back no matter where I went, and when I got free she took some punches at my ribs. I didn't tell her to stop, I thought it was fun. Samantha and Dasha yelled at Rebecca for being rude, and when she did not stop even then, they joked about how she was flirting with me. She blushed and bulldozed her head straight into her mother. Christopher had a thick face with what Dolly saw as a delicate heart bleeding out from his every drooling expression. He had a slight problem putting words together, but he was enthusiastic, and he followed Rebecca religiously.

Dolly came out in her Poison Ivy outfit and this got Rebecca riled up. She wanted to be in an outfit too, and she wanted to be in the Poison Ivy outfit, and she started to pull at it. But Dolly liked the plastic leaves in her hair, and she liked that Christopher came up to her with a great grin on his face and said, "You're pretty." The mothers laughed, and I looked at Dolly, who looked at me, and she grew shy.

Rebecca got all dressed up as Wonder Woman, she even had pink heels, and Christopher put on a Batman vest and a Dracula cape, and I put on a Viking helmet and a tutu. We all grabbed different weapons. I picked up this giant stuffed snake and wrapped it around me, and in a French accent told them all, "I will whip you with my snake." They laughed and screamed. Rebecca took two rubber balls and said, "You get killed if you get hit by one," and Christopher screamed for the same thing, so she gave him one of the balls. Dolly was about to decide what her powers were when Rebecca jumped over to her and said, "You have to try to kiss us, and if you do we freeze." How cute Dolly looked as I leered at her.

A ball socked me in the face, and I had to lie on the floor for a minute. I heard running all around the room, I tried for a second to be existential, to think about what it all meant, but I was getting kicked in the ribs by Christopher... Dolly was creeping over towards Rebecca, who was dancing on the couch in celebration of having hit me directly in my face. Instead of running away from Dolly, Rebecca let her kiss her on her forehead. I jumped up with my snake and began hissing and swinging it around. It was bigger than I and had this cartoonish grin on its face. All three of them ran away to the bedrooms, where a giant wall structure split into two sinuous hallways. The mother's and I were briefly alone before I entered, and I made sure, with my eyes, that I was not being too ridiculous. They thought it was all a riot, so I went in. I took a right, and I found Dolly lying on Christopher's bed, which had tons of pillows and books all over it. I let the snake go limp at my side and dove straight for Dolly. She kissed my forehead and turned me onto my side, and she kissed my ear, and her tongue was in my ear, which she treated very sweetly, and I got the chills, and my cock began to get big, but then she got up, screaming, "I took care of Jonathan." And she ran out of the room, and I counted to one minute without hurrying, taking seriously the impact of her kiss.

I was alone, my snake had fallen to the side of the bed. I picked it up and wrapped it so that its head was atop my head, and I went crawling and hopping through the sinuous hallway into Rebecca's room, which was pinker than Christopher's, and had a giant doll house. The three of them were armed and whispering on Rebecca's circular bed. Dolly screamed, "Now!" I would have been pummeled with balls and even a plastic power tool did I not somehow manage to whip the snake, blocking all three toy missiles in one perfect stroke. The two kids, seeing me rear the snake back, took off to the stairs leading into the bathroom, and I had to follow them into the shower stall, where the puffer fish and the white eel floated languorously.

I finally lashed them, and I sashayed the snake back around me knowing that Dolly was watching from the doorway, and I took off after her, back into Rebecca's room, cornered her on the bed, and lashed her with the snake. The kids were counting out loud, and they were only at twenty, so I started smothering Dolly with kisses and grabbing at her chest, and when she said that I should stop, I reminded her that she was frozen and could not move. She took me so seriously that I had to squeeze in her cheeks to get at her tongue, and the kids were at forty, so I reached my two fingers to her nipples and got them hard and that got me hard, very hard, and we were so happy to be like that, playing and playing, and the kids got to sixty, so I turned around, but they had already entered the room, and Rebecca was leaping towards me, viciously, in revenge, and I had no time to move. She was spread full out in the air, and she landed her cheek on my cock, and it hit her hard, and she started to cry, and I curled into a ball, because a seventy pound child had just put at least half of her accelerated weight directly on my cock. I was yelping, and she was sobbing, and the worst was that I knew I had let Dolly down completely.

Dasha and Samantha came running around the corner when Rebecca had not let up. They did not ask what happened. I did not try to comfort Rebecca, I feared that my touch might remind her. I looked at Dolly, I did not know if Dolly had seen, if Dolly put two and two together. She was not looking at me, I was heart broken. They took Rebecca out of the room, I kept fearing that she would turn and in a fit of spit and tears scream, "It was him, it was him. It was his cock." She never did. Dasha got an ice pack and held it to Rebecca's forehead. A terrible air of silence came over the house. Christopher would not let me read a story to him, he would not even let me stay in the room when Dolly started to read. I asked if Rebecca was okay, and Samantha answered me nice enough. That made me feel better. I just wanted to go away.

I went outside. They had a large patio, I went to the staircase leading up to the patio, it was covered in vines. I knelt down, so that the vines were all I saw. I picked one elliptical hole in the fence guarding the stairs and placed my eye up against it. I could see little thorns coming from part of the vine, and I imagined them scraping my eye so that blood started to tear down the meat of the plant. I kept imagining this over and over again, and it made me stop worrying about having bruised a girl's head with my cock. The stars were overhead, I thought about them. It is so hard sometimes to know what to think about, how to think about things, just when you think you have caught the winds of chance, you find it was all a false sign, and your strength cracks. I wanted to writhe in those vines, see myself all bloody, but then I realized this was like Jesus, and I felt like I had thought something very tacky.

That night Dolly asked me if it was my cock. I told her it was. The lights were out. The Ocean was snoring. The wind was silent, no chimes. I could feel the musky air of the darkness pressing against the window the entire night. I had lost Dolly for the third time.

****

"So it is going to have to end with Gianna. She called me on the phone the other day. A week ago. She was coughing and said that she had pneumonia, and she wanted me to comfort her. I hadn't heard from her since she made me bark like a dog." Dennis made a very condescending facial expression. I lowered my voice shyly, "Anyways, she calls me out of the blue and she's coughing, and we talk for an hour, and she says that she has no money for medicine and that she needs me really badly to get the other 300 dollars I owe her."

"300 dollars more?"

"Yeah, she wanted 600, and I only paid her 300."

"I thought you already paid 600."

"The first three was for the first call. Listen, it aint a bad deal. 600 a month for a full-time phone girlfriend, and she knows what she's doing."

"Do you hear yourself?"

"Yes, I think I do."

"Go on…"

I took a deep breath, "She reminded me of how I felt, and I cannot tell you how erotic I felt walking through Union Square, heading to the bank, I had jizm all over, my cock was hard. This woman gets my cock hard, when I think about her, just like that, spontaneously. I've never had that before…"

"You're actually considering doing it?"

"I'm walking to the edge, so to speak. Seeing how I feel there."

"If it's your parent's money, it's not a big deal. Richard has millions. He could pay for thousands of these women to talk to you every night and it would not chip away at his fortune."

"It's my money. I have to wire her cash. I can't use the credit card. And I don't fucking spend 600 dollars on my parent's credit card."

"Not at once at least."

"Right… Okay, wait, it gets worse. She called me a few days later and unloaded this horrific story on me. She was married once. She is 32 now. She has a daughter who is ten years old. The daughter lives with Gianna's ex-husband, who apparently abused Gianna when they lived together. Gianna says she is being brought to trial on criminal charges for having molested her daughter. She claims, however, that she never did such a thing and that the father is convincing the daughter to say these things because he hates her guts and he wants money. Also there is this weird thing, about how she was really submissive to her ex-husband, and a lot of her rage, or her desire to control men, comes from her realization that she did not always have to play the role of sex object, and she is liberated now that she is dominant. I asked her if she thought that maybe she had done things which were not appropriate. I could imagine that she would rub her child, and it would feel very sexual, and she was just trying to be affectionate. I don't know, maybe she is making this all up, to get

59

more money out of me. And the idea of being ripped off is not entirely demeaning to me. You know there is this fetish on-line called Financial Domination. These women advertise themselves as goddesses, female supremacists, major cunts, and you are supposed to pay for their goddess lifestyles, that is it, you don't cum, nothing, all you do is send them money, and I swear to god there is a fucking lot of them, so it must mean that it is in demand. These women will dress up real slutty, show their juicy lips with lipstick, or they will have a cigarette in their mouths and be raising their curse finger at the screen with the text "LOSER" written above the pic, and they will ask for 25 or 50 or 75 dollars. It is totally fucked up."

"Have you done one of these?"

"I tried it once. You know, I try everything once, or twice. I paid $25 to this one blonde chick who has all these puppies who send her money from New Zealand, England, Germany, the whole fucking world, I think she's from Canada, and I was hoping it would feel good, or she would email me or make a puppy out of me, I don't know what the fuck I'm hoping for, man this Gianna is driving me crazy, I'm gonna just stop calling her. She is gonna be pissed, I know it, I'm afraid a bit. I don't know."

"We are living in hell, Jonathan, this is hell." He shouted this to the smelly corner of ChinaTown where we sat on chairs.

"Yeah."

"We were born in the wrong generation."

"What generation should we have been born in? The mid 20th century Europe?"

"At least then…"

"At least then what, we had record players instead of CD players?"

"I'm a Luddite, okay."

"I don't know what that means."

"That's cause you're an idiot."

****

Melanie Dearheart had the most twisted mp3s. Cruella's were gross, Melanie's tracks, because she was sexier and because she did not cater to the sissy loser types, were more insidious, and she claimed to be a certified hypnotist. She also knew how to edit sound with expertise. She would have eight tracks of audio, all of the sound levels chosen well, and they would sometimes be in the left ear and sometimes in the right, and though she used echo, she never used it with blind assurance, like Cruella did. Melanie had one track where the low sound of a heart beating played for the entire thirty minutes. I found Melanie on a site called NiteFlirt, where there are what seem to be millions of girls offering phone sex, videos, live web cam shows, and recordings. Most are into control. Feminization, financial domination, hypnosis, and other freaky stuff. Some are real women at home, others are ex-porn stars, and then everything in between. The girls get rated, and the rating system is treated very seriously, so girls who suck, who hang up, or don't take the calls seriously are immediately discovered. Melanie had the highest rating. The average rating was around 100, hers was 20,000. Nobody came close. She had a radio show, and she was like Cruella, this big woman, except she was cleaner than Cruella, not as old, and had very pretty juicy lips, and these captivating eyes.

The first mp3 of hers I listened to was called *My Body*. She spoke very fast, elocuting impeccably. Her vocabulary was dense and well chosen. She spoke in a way where she was trying to confuse me. And then, all of a sudden, another voice came up in my other ear, and this voice was my response to her commands, so as she started to take me down, I heard myself respond, "No, I am not your slave." And she would be saying that she was turning me into her slave, very elaborately, it was all very confusing, and it was meant to eliminate my thoughts, and it was very convincing, especially with a few more voices in the background whispering about my cock getting hard. What she wanted was to place herself in my body so I could feel her breasts and her power. She would make my mouth twitch, and she would make me drool, and she would humiliate the size of my cock so that it was all of a sudden a little clitty. And then that voice, which was mine, which had been saying, "You are not inside my body, you do not control me," it changed, it affirmed, it said, "I am so horny, I am worshipping Melanie Dearheart. I am in love with Melanie Dearheart." And I felt this too, I felt this strong compulsion to hug and kiss this image of Melanie which were these breasts that were giving me so much pleasure as I touched my own nipples, and I wanted to love Melanie forever, and she wanted me to love her too…

Bootslave: I have given up everything for Cruella: I only have my job so that I can give her money. She let me see her. She let me see her. I have been so good. I drove down to South Carolina, and I do not remember anything after she greeted me at the door. I think she used Chloroform, and she told me she fucked me for three straight days. I remember waking up in drool. I am so devoted to Cruella. I never knew somebody could know so well how to take away my control and fulfill all my fantasies. Cruella has become my religion, I bow down to her every morning.

****

Mornings sucked! No sunlight came into my room. I grabbed a book and ventured outside for coffee, the process took over an hour. One day in January I was reading The

Function of An Orgasm by Wilhelm Reich. Wilhelm had invented a machine called the Orgone Box which captured the orgasmic energy of the universe. I had just started the book. I had only bought it because of the quote on the back: "*I maintain that every person who has succeeded in preserving a certain amount of naturalness knows this: those who are psychically ill need but one thing—complete and repeated genital gratification.*" Wilhelm had a sexy, blonde, Eastern European wife, I saw the pictures. He was put in jail, here in America, and he died in prison. I was reading all about this when Dr. Samuel Horkheim came bursting into my life.

Samuel was a hefty man with a baldhead, a graying goatee, and ears which stuck out perpendicular to his face. He was dressed in a crumpled sports jacket, and it was as if he was always there because he talked so fast and knew so much, and he had over ten things, at least, to say about the book I was reading. He sat down across from me at the wobbly table and we drank our coffee together. He mentioned other authors, de Sade and Walter Benjamin, and George Bataille, all of whom I knew a bit about. He was a professor of Architectural Theory. He taught at Yale and The New School. He studied undergrad at Princeton, did his Masters at Cambridge, and his P.H.D. at Harvard. He was fluent in Italian, French, German and Yiddish. We talked for an hour and it went by real fast. He suggested over ten writers that I should read. I asked him if he knew Vilem Flusser, who had written a lot of vignette essays on the future of design. He hadn't. He appreciated my suggestion. He told me that I was knowledgeable for my age, that I had read a lot. I thought he was being nice. My hair was all scruffy from the baseball cap I kept shifting around my head, taking it on and off.   Samuel pointed outside to the Dominican Church at the corner when I asked him what exactly Architectural Theory entailed. I thought the building was very ugly. It had fake plaster pillars on it. He said that it was the Diva of the street. The only building which was really asserting itself. He showed me how it indented very cleverly at the corner, and he said that the plaster was merely representative of the historical period in which it was built. "But I can dismiss an entire historical period, right?" I pointed to the rich brownstones that carried on down the street, said I liked these better, merely because of their color. He said he liked them better too, that they were like home-grown Johnny Cash whereas the Church was like Tina Turner. I did not notice certain details about him that first time, it took all my energy just to follow his stories and ideas. I thought about him a lot when he left. He was flying to Boston to teach a class on the city of Rome which, he complained, was not his expertise. He ran out of the shop and I went back to <u>The Function of the Orgasm</u>.

****

The day before Dennis left for Oxford he slept at my house. We got drunk and then got into bed together. I told Dennis about having met this interesting Jewish intellectual who was quite flamboyant, but Dennis was caught up in his future so he paid no attention. Dennis had gotten into both the Art History program and the English program. He had de-cided to do Art History, he wanted to be well-rounded. He still had to choose between concentrating in the Renaissance or in Surrealism. He was blabbing on and on about how he hated Surrealism, about how Colombia taught a course on it called: *Surrealism, a Cultural Irritant.* He saw Surrealism as a false profundity, as something only hippy kids and sopho-moric enthusiasts of art were into, he imagined what prestige it would earn him if he knew all about the Renaissance. I was sleepy and turned toward the wall. I said, "I wouldn't do the

Renaissance, too much stone, not enough electricity." He laughed really hard, he said, "That's pretty funny." I was happy he complimented me. "What're you gonna be doing in December?" he asked. "Why?" "I have a month off between semesters, I thought we could meet up after this long separation, go off to Corfu or the Andaman Islands?" "I'll have to see when I have off for Chanukah. But it sounds doable." "Maybe then, far away from all this bullshit, we can consummate things between each other." "Yes, and then we can have children. You can study in the tower, and I will man the nursery." Dennis chuckled again, heartily. It was a rare moment of him letting go. He took the opportunity to start in again on fantasizing about me. We took our cocks out and started to jerk off. I took my shirt off. I felt very agile, and I crossed my legs, looking down at Dennis as he got hard. His cock was about my size. It was dark, it felt strange to look at. He was moaning a little. I could not get hard at all. He noticed, and I felt embarrassed. I went to the bathroom, told him I would get it hard there and then come back. I tried to think about something else. I thought about Cruella demanding me to cum, but my cock stayed stretchy. I was gone for over five minutes. "I can't do it." His cock was really hard, I grabbed his balls, brushed my fingers against his shaft, and he came right then, a little of it got on my fingers. I joked that I was disgusted; really, I felt neither here nor there. He left the next day for Oxford. I was so happy to be free of him.

My heart is beating very fast. It is late in the evening. I can't do anything right, right now. I can't explain how I feel. I want to explain that I feel really freaked out. I don't know when I am going to go to sleep. The idea of lying down on my mattress, closing my eyes, and, instead of sleep, having the onslaught of thought keep me awake for an hour or two, frightens me. My heart keeps beating faster, or it is just beating at the same speed. I should jerk off, look at some pornography, that will get me out of my head. And maybe it will tire me out a bit... I sat up, I reread what I wrote, my heart is still beating fast. I liked what I wrote. I think I feel the same, right now. I want to explain that I feel really freaked out. I don't know when I am going to go to sleep. The idea of lying down on my mattress, closing my eyes, and, instead of sleep, having the onslaught of thought keep me awake for an hour or two, frightens me. My heart keeps beating faster and faster, or it's just beating the same speed. I should jerk off, look at some pornography, that will get my out of my head. I wonder. I wonder about so many things. I am inattentive to them. Maybe they have to do with a very pretty landscape. I can't tell. Maybe I am wondering about the universe. I hate that I said that, it doesn't feel profound, and I feel so profoundly aware of my innocence in the face of all of this, that I could cry almost. None of that comes out right. It is better to return to my beating heart. It fucking is going to keep me awake for a long time. I am trying to laugh about it. I am going to stop writing soon, I feel like this is a lot. I fear what too much would mean, and then I fear what too little will mean. They both make my heart beat fast. But, it is beating despite these things. I could scream for me not to stop writing. It will be so scary when I do. I will have to be pathetic and jerk off, and the cum will be all gross, and I will have wasted my energy and my money, and for nothing, just to hide myself away from my anxiety. I could cry, I could write something beautiful, oh I wish I could. I can't muster this. I feel nauseas. I am going to jerk off, I'm sorry.

part 2

Late in August I turned a corner on Rivington and saw Dolly walking towards me. She was alone. Her hair was tied back, she had on a red t-shirt with her name inscribed in gold. Her jeans were tight, I smelled her as we hugged. "I knew I was going to run into you," she said. We walked all the way to Washington Square Park. The day was sweltering. Everyone was out. We lay down away from the dog run, away from the fountain, on a patch of grass. For over an hour there were only Dolly's lips, her freckles, the branches of the trees, the blue of the sky, and an occasional wisp or fold of cloud. We laughed about how silly we were. I kissed her with as much delicacy as I could. I wanted to prove something to her, to keep her with me forever.

She was living on 22nd and Park in the apartment of one of her classmates. As she explained it, she had seduced this sweet kid named Matthew into letting her stay the summer for free. She had difficulty repulsing his advances until he left unexpectedly at the beginning of the summer, so Dolly had the whole place to herself. She said, "All these Beautiful Rich Men I have in my life." I got her naked, her body was so fucking tight, her skin folded gently, her freckles were all these little sensors. She leaned against the wall, standing on the mattress. Outside the summer lightning ricocheted off the windows. The terrace had a view of a giant movie poster— windows and stone carvings reached out towards an unidentifiable horizon. I bent down on my knees and ran my hands up her thighs, I buried my face in her pussy. I was more patient than ever with my tongue when I put it inside her folds. She kept getting hotter and wetter. She bent down to grab my cock, I didn't let her. I laid her down. She said, "I don't know what you do to me." I started to fuck her, it was all so strange. I barked just like a dog. I do not know how else I could have prevented myself from cumming. She was saying, "Fuck me harder big boy." She was so little, so cute, I pulled out and came all over her belly. She rubbed around in it like a feline with her catnip. I lay between her legs and built up a slow orgasm for her. We fell asleep naked and sweaty.

I was desperate for her the next day. I consciously thought about paying her to stay in my life. We went to Park Slope. We lay by a tree beneath berries and starlings. She wore a flower dress and no panties. I lay my ear beside her green eyes and her pink lips and put my finger inside her. She came three times on the slope. Every so often I put my cheek on her shoulder to see the hundreds of people around us.

Dolly had wanted to see the Jamaican drum circle that took place in an obscure corner of the park. We could hear the drums in the distance and we followed the low reverberations through hills and shifts of greenery…

The circle was enormous. Over a hundred people were there. It was on the outskirts of the park. Booths selling figurines and incense were lined up right outside a parking lot.

We shared a joint I had in my pocket. The men all around us were dense, like wood. They had dreadlocks—dark hands. The number of rhythms being played were incomprehensible. Tambourines, and all sorts of bongos. Inside the circle a few were dancing. One African lady in a green and yellow dress was moving majestically. A white man was sitting completely still in a yogic pose. Dolly started dancing. I wanted to think she was sexy and that I could kiss her, but she knocked my hand away when I put it on her hips. The whole scene was very serious. A little girl held a stick and was casting spells on everyone around her. She saw me staring and immediately extended her arm to strike me with her spell. I ducked. When I got back up, I smiled at Dolly, hoping she had seen my little encounter, but she just kept on dancing. She could vibrate out from her hips. I tried to dance, to imagine these people, the skinny men with torn khakis and tank tops, I tried to imagine them as real people. I saw a cardinal land on a tree, this was like a secret only I knew. I was dancing too—the whole time.

Dolly looked uneasy. I said, "I don't know why we had to smoke—everything was so nice." She smiled in agreement. "Do you want to go?" She did, we walked away. My nerves calmed a little. We found a pond to sit in front of. Kids were running about on one side. And further off a family was whacking away at a piñata. Dolly took some pictures of me. "Look how beautiful you are..." She had taken one where I looked dreamier and prettier than I ever imagined myself to be. She lingered over the image awhile, then she talked about how when she was dancing it felt like every muscle in her body was taking part in the rhythm. She grew cold. She said she was nervous, she apologized, and thanked me for being so patient with her.

On the subway we did not say a single word and the fluorescent lights were immense. I wanted to grab her, I wanted to escape, to feel her grace, and since it was not there, I stared at the splotched paint on the subway floor. An anonymous human figure with six arms was chained into the patterns of paint. He was on a metal bed, his head was arched forward, his face was in agony. I stared at him for the rest of the ride home.

Dolly and I went back to her place, she snacked on blueberries and raspberries. Something subsided in both of us, and we were naked on the gourmet white sheets of Matthew's queen-size bed. The imposing skyscraper next door bore down on us in the low refractions of sunset. She put my cock in her mouth—every tremor was pleasurable. I made adorable noises. Baying. All different types of animals came and went within me. I hummed. I kept reaching what seemed like the climax, but I managed to turn it into a higher plateau. "I'm not going to cum, it's too good." And the break which was this sentence did not interrupt a thing, and I went back to screaming. The speed of light was coursing through me. She said, "It's your will versus mine." It took her less than a minute to get me to shriek after she spoke so boldly—and my cock twitched and pumped everything into her cute mouth, and I rolled about in the bed laughing at the top of my lungs— and I didn't stop for at least five minutes. Dolly curled up aside me and we fell asleep.

Then she left for Europe. She was to spend two weeks with her grandparents in St. Petersburg, and then it was on to Prague, where she was studying for the semester at a famous film program. I helped her pack. I sat up all night as she slept nervously, nervous about her first real adventure. I drove her to the airport. In the car she said, "I'm so lucky to have found a boy who is so nice to me, and does so much for me." I hoped she would not forget this. She encouraged me to get in touch with Dasha if I needed a break from the city, saying that her mother was my biggest supporter. In the airport we hid behind a concrete column. We made each other wet and hard. Dolly looked at me and said, "You wear your heart on your sleeve. I have to be so gentle with you." I smiled and kissed her... She kissed me so hard the last time, right before she turned to go through the security checkpoint. It felt like the first time she had moved in my direction.

It hit me the moment the JFK veered away from the sky tram. I was deep in Queens. Dolly was soaring up in the air above me. I doubted her capacity to look back... She was so flighty, and I knew she would fall in love with the shingled roofs and circuitous streets of Eastern Europe.

Aug. 25th

Around four in the morning I began to realize I was doomed to consciousness here and now in the middle of the night. I went to the kitchen to pour myself a glass of water. I turned on the light, which stung--five baby cockroaches crawled around the sink as my glass filled. The light went off and the water did not go down the right pipe. I tried to sleep on the couch in the living room but the fire alarm

72

continually beeped, and I was a little distraught about having been kept up by you. I wondered for the millionth time if I'll be able to keep my wits about me in your absence. I went back into my bedroom. I began to imagine you as the most brilliant being in the world, a submission I allowed myself, to overcome my disjointedness. And in the pace of mist soaring off the horizon your image came to hover above me. I have this one where the kohl beneath your eyes gives you a morose sensuality. Your hair is tied up in a big bouquet of flowers, and you lean coyly upon my chair. You do these stretches, and move your wet-lipped mouth with all-knowing satisfaction. My penis began to twitch. I was surprised, but quick to seize. I cautioned myself to concentrate on your concretized form. I can, in paranoiac moods, receive such a flurry of diced images that instead of arousal it is fear of insanity that climaxes inside me. But I held you so tight honey, and not just your image, it was your warmth I felt, it was you building up my orgasm, I let it go so slowly. I pictured your delicate fingers inside the folds of your nether lips. You stroked yourself at the same pace I was stroking, and as my erection grew so did you moisten. Then you were above me, your whole body, your face right there. You had a few whispers, a few 'loves' and 'dears.' In that ghostly realm your image sunk inside me, and your every particle dissipated to the ends of my skin. I was at the mercy of your seduction. You were still playing with yourself. Your pussy is marvelous, love, and with your fingers there so sweetly controlling it, I wish for its flavor. Your head worked down and down my penis. Your freckles, your prim and proud nose, the fire of your sweet skin. You finally appeared above me, and begged me to cum inside you, a command I was willing to obey. Then you were gone, and I decided that aside from wiping off my stomach in the bathroom, I should also write down the happenings of my evening. Please do not fear honey, the shower water is not running.

All my love,

John

    She did not respond. I couldn't eat for a week. Or when I did, I had terrible diarrhea. At nights all the most terrible fantasies came to me. She became violent in her treatment of me. She took me through corridors and made me watch as she experienced a pleasure greater than any I had ever given her. She laughed at me while I jerked off. She told me how desperately I needed her, how she could be anywhere, enjoying anything, and I would still be obsessing over her ghost. She was so vivid. I could not sleep. During school, when I turned away from the students to write something on the white board, that was enough privacy to sting me with longing.

I kept rereading the first email I had sent her to find a single word that might have been out of place, might have confused her—but it was all so adoring. And this made the fact that she was not responding even harder to bear…

…She wrote me then:

Sept. 4th

Baby, oh baby. my mind is rumbling like an approaching storm. I'm reading "The Idiot" at the moment and just hours ago read a passage concerning a letter from a dying man, in which he cursed those healthy people wasting away their living minutes. "I could not endure that poking, bustling, eternally preoccupied, gloomy, and anxious mass of human beings that scurried about me on the pavements. Why their eternal dolefulness, their eternal anxiety and bustle; their eternally gloomy spite? Whose fault is it that they are unhappy and don't know how to live, each with sixty years of life ahead of them?" In a (hopefully?) (maybe?) less melodramatic way I confess to feeling parallel thoughts right now. How many times did I turn away your kisses and your cock...under what pretenses? That I was tired/sore/not in the mood? Curse the former me! I would do anything for you right now. Sitting in the kitchen trying to keep up with conversation and all I can picture is you arriving at my door and how I would jump up and wrap my legs around you. I'm going through a shift in phases and I'm swallowing it as well as possible.

Anyways, I wrote you a poem baby, sweet and simple. Here it goes:

To Be Alone Out Here With You

days out here are warm and lazy
night time storms reshape my dreams
plants and flowers grow in mazes
and we've got everything we need

dinner, we go out and pick it
beer's a bike ride to the store
chickens lay eggs for our eating
puppies are what playing's for

grandma strips inside the sauna
hitting birch twigs on my skin
grandpa swigs his homemade whiskey
coaxing me to drink with him

full and drunk i lay upstairs
on patterned quilts beside the trees
musing, as i'm prone to doing
of you sitting here with me

eyebrows furrowed near these curtains
writing scratches in your book
and all it takes (of this i'm certain)
is to offer you one look

and you would follow to the garden
to the greenhouse, to the field
you would follow even further
till i told you there to kneel

you'd lift up my country dress
and rip the ribbons from my hair
our hands frantic, faces pressed
breathing in the country air

to be alone out here with you
i could find a thousand places
between the lines that people build

and the thick forest erases

to kiss inhale devour love you
and fall asleep in tired sweat
but it seems these merely musings
are as close as i will get

****

    I ran after Dr. Samuel Horkheim the next time I saw him—around 10:00 PM on a weekend night. He walked robustly a hundred paces in front of me. I could tell it was Samuel from his baldhead and his demonic ears. He wore a leather jacket and jeans. He overcame the ridiculousness of his appearance with an opulent air of joie de vivre. I sprinted up to him. I came out of breath. I said, "Sorry, we met at MidSummers Café, <u>The Function of the Orgasm</u>. I know you're a smart guy. I need a smart conversation." Samuel was happy to talk. He was on the way to a bar and asked me to come along.

    "I must have had quite an effect on you. It's not very often I get chased down you know."

    "I thought a lot about our conversation. I even started to read <u>Minima Moralia</u>—"

    "Yes, <u>Notes from a Damaged Life</u> by Adorno. That is his most personal book."

    "I like it, he's funny."

    "He's the angry Prince."

    "He says, 'Slippers are a monument to the hatred of bending down.'"

    "Yes, he can be very dramatic. He becomes a parody of himself. I am quite impressed that you started to read this. Many people have trouble with him. Next to Foucault he is my favorite 20th century theorist." Samuel said this last line with a big dose of irony.

"I don't know about Foucault. He fits everything into his paranoid structure."

"Yes, maybe it's a bit easy, but he's a beautiful writer. In French at least."

"You should talk to my friend Dennis, he is much better at these conversations than I am."

"I'm not sure why you say this, maybe you have an intellectual insecurity. I wish my grad students could converse like this."

"My friend takes it more seriously. He is studying art history at Oxford."

"I studied there briefly. He must be studying under Martin Kemp. He's one of the premier Leonardo scholars. A bit stuffy though, if you ask me."

We walked underneath a highway overpass and stopped briefly at a stoplight. Samuel smiled at me very flirtatiously, and I smiled back shyly, lowering my eyes.

"You know now that I think about it I think I know your friend Dennis. Does he write for *Teleopoiesis*?"

"Yeah."

"I met him at an art gallery opening. I don't like that boy at all. I'm surprised you're friends with him. We got in this tedious argument about patriotism. Dennis is one of these cocky, conservative, young intellectuals. He is not very subtle at all. And he is not so impressive." Samuel was shaking, like a worm had just crawled inside his skin. "I really don't like that boy. It's a shame too. He is very handsome. But then, my god, when he opened his mouth. He is a beautiful shell. Is he gay?"

"That's difficult to answer. He usually is just into women, but he and I had a sort of thing, or a sort of nothing."

"Oh, this is very interesting. So you like men? You could have fooled me. I can usually tell by the way a man looks at me."

"I think I'm straight, for the most part. Maybe I just haven't found the right man."

"Well well... You really know how to say things don't you."

"I probably should become gay. Women really tear me up inside."

"Of course you know what Plato's opinion about all this is?"

"That it's the ideal, being gay?"

"No, I mean these terms did not even exist back then."

"Okay... So the ideal was a man with another man."

"I don't think it was *the* ideal, but he did see it as *an* ideal. Even Nietzsche, who was never with anyone after he got Syphilis from a prostitute, recognized the relationship between two men as an ideal..."

By that time we had reached the entrance to a gay bar, and we quieted down as the bouncer looked us over. Samuel seemed to know the bouncer, and they exchanged a few words before we entered. We sat down on stools in a patio outside. We were surrounded by a lot of skinny men. We kept our jackets on because it was cold. A trellis woven with grape vines hung above our heads. I liked so many things about Samuel. He had a very pretty smile, and with his extra weight he seemed warm and cuddly. His way of speaking was intoxicating. He said I had a utopian streak because of a long story I told him about having taken a homeless man to have a drink with me. I told him all about Dolly and how she haunted me at night. He shrugged off my woes so flippantly that it made me feel like I was playing out some stupid drama. He had a way of referring everything back to gayness and books, and if I heard him correctly, my gaze was aimed in the wrong direction. I asked him if he was proselytizing, but he denied it. He

78

was unbelievably masterful, he could weasel out of anything, even were I to accuse him of weaseling out of everything. "Charm is knowing that you're charming. Yes, I know this is a tautology, but there is some truth in this way of phrasing it." Time sped up in his presence in such a way that I could no longer linger in my longing. I felt closer to the truth with him than I ever had before.

Back at his apartment we were surrounded by shelves of books. Samuel's expertise, though he was an encyclopedic phenomenon, was in Renaissance Architecture, and his favorite writer was the renowned Le Corbusier. Samuel had recently published a translation of a very difficult book called, When the Cathedrals Were White. He pulled it off the shelf, he showed me everywhere where his name was printed. He had just won a very prestigious award in his field, though because his field was minor, the prize only amounted to a couple thousand dollars. He put that book away and then pulled out Le Baphomet by Pierre Klossowski. "His brother Balthus painted my favorite painting in the whole world—" I began. "Ah yes," he always knew before I finished, "The one where the man is stoking fire…" "Yeah," I got excited, "And the young girl sits on a chair admiring herself in a hand mirror." "It is about class differences and gender roles." "I don't know, I always take it literally, that the man is working hard at the fire so that the woman can sit and drown up in the flames of her vanity." "Oh, this is much more complex than my interpretation. You have added an economy of exchange." I was happy to have penetrated him: I had no way to measure what my seduction felt like.

He told me all about Le Baphomet. How it was about the Knights of the Templar, and ghosts, devils, saints, and men interchangeably fucking each other up "the arse." It became so complex that the reader could not distinguish the living from the dead. He compared it to de Sade who claimed, in The Philosophy of the Bedroom, that the ultimate pleasure was when the master got filled up the ass with the cum of the slave. Samuel said everything with such enthusiasm. He was sitting at the edge of his bed. I was crouching on the floor below him, fingering all his books.

"Have you ever fantasized about men?"

"Yes, a few times."

"What about?"

"I don't know, kissing, taking it from behind."

"You know, I'm known for making fantasies come true."

"No, I didn't know."

"Tell me about this experience with Dennis. Was this you're only experience with a man?"

"Yeah, the only one. It was a complete failure. For me at least. Dennis didn't want to kiss or anything."

"I don't know why he wouldn't want to kiss you, maybe he was afraid of liking it."

"Maybe. I don't get Dennis, and I don't want to."

"If I were to see the two of you at a Sauna, I would be immediately attracted to Dennis. He is beautiful, but then I would realize that you were much more interesting. I think you have your own beauty. You hide it. I was not attracted to you at all the first day I met you. Now I see you are a combination of an angel and the devil, with very pretty lips." I blushed. "Do you find me attractive? I think maybe you haven't noticed that I have pretty eyes." He pointed to them, they were large, green, and apricot-shaped.

"I think you're attractive." He came down, knelt beside me, and put his open mouth on mine, we kissed four times with our tongues, but then I couldn't do it anymore, so I pulled away. He went right back to the bed. "How was that?" "It was fine. I think the hair on your goatee confused me a bit." "Yes, I imagine it must be strange. You are very brave. It didn't feel like you had never done something like that before." He tried to come close to me again, I held my arm out and pushed him away. He sat back down on the edge of the bed. "You get used to the rough hair. It is the dialectic between soft and hard. Do you feel different, you probably feel like you have crossed a giant threshold."

"No, I feel like my tongue just touched your tongue, not that it was bad."

Samuel lay down on the bed and crossed his arms. His belly protruded, and he took up most of the mattress. He yawned. We talked like that for a while. He asked me if I had seen all the pictures on his walls. They were arched between the bookshelves across from his bed. In descending order there were small black and white photos of Charles Baudelaire, James Dean, Walt Whitman, Friedrich Nietzsche, Theodor Adorno and Glen Gould. I didn't know who Glen Gould was so Samuel put on a record of Gould's Bach fugues. Samuel said that once he played piano for me I would never be able to resist him. I lay down next to him with my arms crossed. The first rays of morning lit up the fire escape out his window. We talked and talked. Everything was playful, and everything was honest, and there was no bullying, no intimidation. He was very patient with me.

He went for it one more time, he leaned towards me, he kept himself light despite his physique. He was like a teddy bear. He pulled up my shirt and put his mouth on my right nipple. He sucked it until it was hard, his other hand found my cock beneath my pants and began to play there. I closed my eyes. All the sensations were recognizable, and I stayed focused on that. My cock started to get hard, I was feeling something I couldn't describe, nebulous words came to mind: airy, translucent, liminal. When I lost my focus, I had him stop, it was too difficult. We crossed our arms so that we each held hands above the other's chest. It was a very strong pose, brotherly, it felt equanimitous. "I feel like we're in a movie," Samuel said.

I went to the bathroom, it was really cramped and there was green on the wall. The sink was pealing. I smiled at myself. I felt weathered. My eyes shone in a way I had never seen before, same with the patient expression on my face. My hair was long and disheveled. I felt so pretty, just like a little girl. I kissed Samuel on the cheek, he said he wanted to see me soon, but he was going away for a few weeks to Italy. The sun was screaming as I walked back home in a daze.

****

Ever since Dennis had gone off to Oxford, we had been sending emails to each other at a rate of three a week. As I was always opening up my account hoping to see a message from Dolly to see Dennis's name come up in bold face was a minor consolation. For whatever reason we stumbled directly into a heated, competitive battle about war, war criminals, and virtuality. Dennis called us, "Neophyte Kitties." At one point he wrote:

Sept. 5th
Yes, the forest over books any day. I sense you are "feeling your oats." It took restraint in my last email not to get testy, but higher ground tends to pay off. You apparently thought I was competing with you, when I had imagined throughout that we were on the same team. Now don't ruin the whole matter by getting defensive again...my guard is down, and I would hope yours is too; else it would seem this "new" mode of communication has had negative effects on our discourse. Certainly I don't think you would lash out at me that way in person. If I come off "strongly" in print, please don't take it personally--you hit rather George Foreman like yourself (and probably with less self mocking irony). And my you inherit the rhetoric of these reactionary thinkers rather naturally...(again, b/c I label does not mean I'm trying to

avoid implication). You should have been a philosophy student, what with that mathematical brain of yours.

Send me a love poem,

D

Sept. 6th
I will bestow you with more affection once I recover from yesterday--I talked far too much, and my throat ripped up. I never wanted to cause you to take the higher ground. In retrospect your self mocking irony may be the very thing which frustrates me. Anyhow, I have a tendency to tug on heartstrings through prose which my conversational voice is too weak to excite. Please don't fear that our communication will be decaying. The distance which these machines impose on us invents a space where we can stab each other through and through without there being actual consequences. A statement I sometimes am willing to test. It is not my ultimate goal though…. And if you must team up with Dolly and demand I manufacture some words of love, so be it. I can never resist an order. You'll get it when my head clears, love.

J

This love was strange to see in print. We had often hugged and said, "I love you man," but this had always seemed political—since Dennis never made me feel comfortable enough to let my guard down. I was already considering my life without him. No more secret cult of genius. No more misogyny. No more self-congratulation in the midst of vicious camaraderie. But here he was sending me emails with an affectionate subtext. He began to speak of our vacation in December to a bower in some imaginary land. I was relieved when he spoke like this because when he spoke rationally he felt very distant… He had been attending balls in the Gothic Churches, walking through empty, large stone hallways and dark plazas at night, and through the meadows on Sunday afternoons. He hated England and the people there, he wanted to return, have the two of us go away to an island together. He was nostalgic for New York City, kept saying what a motherfucking kick ass time it had been back in ChinaTown with our books and our guitars. The Oxonians were dull, despite their intelligence. The professors were dinosaurs who refused poststructural French thought, and the library system was antiquated. It was closed on Sundays and too scattered to have all your books in one place. Dennis complained, wailed, and since there was no mention of a woman who was getting on his nerves, I assumed he had not yet met one.

****

Dolly sent me a single email with the subject line "Send Love Letters To…" The text included her address and a brief apology for being in a hurry. I was thrilled to have her want something from me. I made a project out of it. I found these skinny cards with an assortment of Henry Darger montages on the cover. Dolly loved Henry Darger. She took me to see a movie about him: *In the Realms of the Unreal.* Darger was a janitor from Chicago who spent his life in solitude. When he died a whole world of paintings, stories, and songs were found in his bedroom. Tenants remembered him talking all night long and stamping about his room, but they never presumed he was talking to himself. The montages were of these seven prepubescent girls with little penises. They were angelic and always in danger of being attacked by corporals. Sometimes they would be shown dancing in skirts or with their penises hanging out, other times they would be hanging from trees, tortured, dead, and bleeding. Darger had a Manichean ethos. Dolly liked the fairy nature of the little girls and the weirdness of the profanities. I bought four cards and on each card I wrote about my unrelenting desire for her. Holding back would have been cowardly:

Sept. 17th
All my sensations are spliced
I hear the fire alarm
I remember the granite sunsets on the Gorge
You wiggle your butt, press your face to my forehead…
What is it I feel or see?
Your correspondence with me has chickens
and grandma fat on the palate
Or are your whisky lips
Parted as you fiddle your sex?
Riffling through your calendars of song

The Blackness of these Moments:
Neither the notes I know you hear
Nor the face which I hold dear
Are in me now
I am much further away from imagination and sound
I AM longing
Every crumpled attempt to enter a fabricated hope
Disintegrates
I see the fine threads of shadows in the darkness
And I long for you
Like a galactic force
I am not human
No, I am the size of the universe

I am the size of the universe
And I am begging for your body.

I asked her in a Postscript if there was any way I could go up and visit Dasha—as she had suggested. Dolly did not answer my letters so I chose to call her. We had not spoken in over a month and she sounded irritated. She said she was in the middle of cooking for her friends. I asked if she got the love letters. She said they were perfect, she said she did not know why she had not written to thank me, why she took from me without returning and then continued to encourage me to give. I asked her if there was something concrete which was distancing her from me. She said she was disconnected from her life back home, that she was becoming something phony in her film program, that she was just as cold to her mother. I told her that I could only handle so much. She agreed with me. The last thing she said to me was that I should definitely go see Dasha, she would be thrilled to have my company.

****

I waited outside the New Chatham train station in the crisp Autumn air for no longer than a minute before Dasha pulled up, leaned over the passenger seat, and motioned me into her Sedan. She seemed overjoyed to have me in town and gave me a big kiss. I was feeling very anxious about being there and just about Dolly in general. I fidgeted with the glove compartment and the CD's as we drove away. I felt very handsome and grown up being with Dasha. She continually commended me for being a teacher. I joked, "Not just a teacher, the kids call me Rabbi." Dasha mentioned how lucky Dolly was to have met me. "I don't know Dasha, she never calls me." "She never calls me. You have to know she loves you. I remember one day we were driving in the car and she said, 'I miss Jonathan.' That is how I know she loves you. She is not very mature for her age. You have been very patient with her." "I don't know, I sent her all these love letters and she never responded... I know I shouldn't demand a response, but knowledge that the letters were received, this would be enough to settle my stomach." "This is Dolly. She loves life so much. The other day she met this woman who spoke Russian and they went to the top of a hill to look out at the city, and she remembers every detail. She loves life too much, it is hard for her to remember us."

We were driving through the fall leaves. The Ocean came into view. We turned fast around a corner where kids played on a sliver of beach. The seagulls were getting blown far into the streets. We drove slowly through the narrow lanes that led to her home and parked on the grass. I was relieved to smell the autumn air and stretch my body. I longed for Dolly, it was immense how much shelf life my longing for her had. It kept coming up at the end of every breath, at the end of every joy, whether it be from the overcast sky or the smell of fish and salt off the Atlantic, whether it was the little wood home and all its decorations or the sandwich which Dasha made me, whether it was the awkward pauses in conversation Dasha and I shared or my excitement for the nighttime and the hard blowing wind—or the way the oak and maple trunks shadowed the darkness, each of these followed with the gasping psyche which was Dolly's absence.

Inside on the bookshelf was a collection of photographs stacked in cardboard boxes. I could not help myself. Every picture of Dolly stung me. In a couple she was walking proudly in the woods, wearing a fleece, stretching underneath a fence, and there was a strange boy about my age walking behind her. I saw him in another picture: Rebecca sat on Dolly's lap, and Dolly was wearing that purple dress which she once had worn for me. I found three pictures of her lying in bed in her pajamas. Without makeup, her only ruse was the innocence she expressed. The fullness of her cheeks and the green of her eyes were never more pronounced, and she held her lips so delicately. The bulldog, Bruno, was humping her in these pictures. I put them directly in my pocket.

That night the cowbells were ringing. I opened up
Ecce Homo. I was lying on the white futon running alongside
the living room, the big window there captured the blackness
of the Ocean. Samuel suggested I read Ecce Homo, which he
called, "Icky Homo." I was surprised by how much I enjoyed
reading it that night. I only read the first couple sections so
nothing much stuck out, save the hardness of character which
Nietzsche expressed, his unwillingness to fall prey to anything
that would burden his conscience. He also had a section on
the vengeance of women, how the infertile woman was the
most dangerous creature imaginable. I was convinced that
Dolly was infertile, and this was a soothing notion. I read
longer than I had intended to read, and Nietzsche even said as
much, that readers find themselves reading him late into the
night. I put him down and listened to the noises outside my
body. I took the pictures I had stolen earlier out of my pocket
and placed them inside Ecce Homo.

Dasha was taking pictures of me in the morning.
Bruno the bulldog had jumped on top of me, and I was buried
beneath him, trying to sleep despite his heavy breathing.
Dasha thought I was asleep. Really, I was posing for her pictures, knowing they would end up in Dolly's email box. I
tried to look as cute as Dolly had looked in those pictures now
book marking Ecce Homo. I wanted to show her that I was
the gypsy she only wished she could be, and that she had not
won anything over me. Dasha finished taking the pictures,
and I waited a few more minutes before rising. The sunlight
and its reflection off the white walls of the home made it impossible to keep my eyes closed for very long. I thought about
Nietzsche, and I was happy that I thought about him instead of
Dolly.

Dasha made these pancakes which had ricotta cheese
in them, she had Vermont syrup too, it was all very delicious.
She left me to go to work, and I had a whole home and a

sunny day to myself. I had a bag full of books, but I kept reading and rereading passages from Nietzsche:

"May I here venture the surmise that I know women? That is part of my Dionysian dowry. Who knows? Perhaps I am the first psychologist of the eternally feminine. They all love me—an old story—not counting abortive females, the "emancipated" who lack the stuff for children.—Fortunately, I am not willing to be torn to pieces: the perfect woman tears to pieces when she loves—I know these charming maenads—Ah, what a dangerous, creeping subterranean little beast of prey she is! And yet so agreeable!—A little woman who pursues her revenge would run over fate itself. Woman is indescribably more evil than man; also cleverer; good nature is in a woman a form of degeneration." I could not help picturing Dolly's cheerful smile and her waifish little body while reading this passage. And when I jumped down the six-foot stone ledge to walk a foot from the tide line, I thought of malicious Dolly far off across this Ocean, sinking her vengeful, infertile hips in the way of every man she passed, trying to destroy each one for being incapable of redeeming her with a child. The sky was gray and I was bundled up, and the wind was strong. I had brought cigarettes but decided instead to inhale the brisk, cool wind every time I desired to smoke. I climbed on the rocks near the edge of the tide, kneeling down to listen to the plash of the waves. I stomped all over the shells, jumping up and down—the whites of the water skipped about.

I must have stayed outside for three hours. When I came back in, I immediately noticed a folded piece of paper by the photographs I had looked at the day before. I went over and opened it up. It was a printout of a photograph of Dolly wearing kohl and holding her right hand behind her right ear in a canned sexual gesture. She was wearing a flower-shaped skullcap atop her thick curls, which were tied behind her ears, and her face was angled downwards, temptingly, eyeing her cleavage, which filled up the base of the photograph. It was terrifyingly seductive to me. I took out the other pictures from <u>Ecce Homo</u> and closed myself in the bathroom. I turned on the shower water and balanced the pictures on the side of the radiator so that I could look at all of them in succession while I jerked myself off: Dolly in her pajamas, and Dolly looking like a two-bit whore. I was so horny and angry, and my cock was so erect, and then I could not finish right away because I wanted so badly to capture this lust and shove it in Dolly's face, so I went to my bag and got out my camera. I set it up on the ledge of the sink, turned the timer on, and took two pictures of me sitting on the toilet jerking off to Dolly's pictures.

Later, Dasha came home and asked if I had found the picture of Dolly she had printed out for me. I told her I had and that I couldn't look at it because it tormented me. "But she looks so cute, I thought you would love it. She just sent me that from Germany." "I folded it up and put it away."

We went over to see the kids, Christopher and Rebecca. I was amazed at how happy they were to see me. We played many different games. The two mothers watched me as I played around. I went over to their computer to see if Dolly had written me anything. She hadn't, I sent a letter to Dennis instead:

Oct. 19th
Dennis,
Sorry for the lack of communication. In true sociopathic fashion I have traveled to Dolly's home in Connecticut and inserted myself with ease into her mother's goings and comings—this includes playtime with her mother's friend's children. I do not have much time right now because the children are begging me to play batman. I shall be home tomorrow, then I can detail the conclusions about myself made on this odd journey. One has been a communion with Nietzsche— who I hope to make my closest friend in the upcoming months.

I have discovered a tyrant in me. Beware,
john

I went home the next day, the transition from being above ground to slowly grinding down into Manhattan was like watching my breath steal away from me while I stood apart from myself in a glass chamber. It was trees and the blue sky and then it was columns of cement and steel, I had been lowered into a crypt.

****

Oct. 21st

Funny you should say so, I was going to advise you—but was afraid of appearing pedantic—beware yourself of Nietzsche et al...from your words (whether they be fitting or not) I would say you are among the susceptible... Sat in the Christ Church meadows and read some "Genealogy" myself this afternoon—I can't figure out who he is talking about at each moment, and it all seems part of the grand deception. Like I said, beware.... That said, nothing wrong with feeling stupider. And also, remember, that it is those who have brooded (a good German word) longest over their stupidity who will appear the most clever. Again...Don't be fooled! Love to you J....Kill the Tyrant...seek the Human Alternative,

D

Oct. 22nd

It is true D. I am susceptible to N. He intoxicates me. So, yeah, go wipe your nose or something, bitch, cause N. is where it is fucking at—and your nose is bleeding.
Please, please, know I send my love, my allegiance to the dubious "human alternative."

In ten years, you and me my love, we better be on the beach—for I made a covenant with the Sea up in CT., and those pacts don't fade for Millenniums. Sometimes I wish I had had the nerve you know, to break your silly heart down—but I was not yet a hyperborean.

O that this chalice never cease to pour! I also
discovered this: women, you know those lithe creatures with the
demure looks, they are in charge! Nowadays, they think we are on to
them, so they are crying murder. Please think I'm cute and
innocent—because I can be powerful too; just look how true it is as
I plant my slender leg into these black leather boots. Yuck, D. Yuck.
 I am tortured from all directions by Aphrodite and her witchery,
disguised, packaged just as I want it to look. Good Lord, D. I
admire your ability to torment them, but I know it only causes you
more pain than they; for they are unconquerable. Please D, Advise.
I hear the red-headed Lilith cackling down my door.
john

Oct. 23rd
I get concerned, John, b/c "intoxication" is a form of myopia, and in
your particular case there is a great deal of what N. would term "ressen-
timent" mixed in w/ your intellectual ambitions...Beware... And I only
say this w/ the most tender of intentions (and moreover b/c I refuse to
underestimate you)...DISINTEREST is the essential foundation for all
aesthetic reflection, and when this ceases to find its correlative in the
social sphere we can sometimes arrive at Tyranny. Call me the "weak-
hearted" humanist if you will...give seed to your dynamo visions...I will
be shepherding the children of gentler nourish to Pala--if there is a sea
we are to meet on, I prefer Huxley's Polynesia to Arnold's Dover...
-D

****

"The web keeps getting tighter and tighter. You feel me
around you. If you try to refuse me, the strand only thickens.
The harder your cock gets the more you are my slave. The
hornier you get, the more your thoughts become vacant, your
mind is filled with the sound of my voice, it pours into you
again and again, it ties itself around you, you can feel it in
your legs, in your chest, in your brain, you have never felt so

blissful, you will never leave this web. Try to leave this web. I dare you too. You don't want to, do you…? Ha, ha, ha… You are too weak to get away. A red light is flashing, stare at this red light. You are bound to me forever. Ha, ha, ha, ha, ha, ha, ha…."

****

I tried my best to open up to Samuel the next time we saw each other. I wore tight jeans and one of my cleaner dress shirts. In the mirror before I left I was fascinated by the parting of my lips. I got lost in his speech. He took me places when he talked, through history, up above in the dialectic of thought, and down again to ecstatic absurdities. He said, "I bet you never guessed you could meet some one as silly as me." He meowed when I looked at him, then he said, "Cow as a puppy!" He had this way of baby talking even when he was philosophizing, accentuating everything with a demonstrative awareness of its pretense, and then saying it just the same. Those who read Deleuze were *Deleuzional* or part of the *Grande Deleuzion*. And Syllogisms were *suck-my-jisms*. He had a theory about a world without women. "No, it is not a misogynistic theory because no women exist in this world." It entailed the erecting of a giant incubation vat in the center of town where men could jerk off into tubes. The tubes led to a giant pool which fed into fertilization chambers. The babies came out on blankets in a finely furnished atelier around the corner from the machine. The only chromosome sent to the eggs to be fertilized would be Y, so only more boys would be produced. When they came of age, they too could jerk off in the center of town. One of the privileges of old age was to teach the newborns how to properly work their penises. "If women really want to come to our town, they can wear long flowing dresses and swim around in the cum, that is the closest they can get." "What would happen if one of these women got impregnated while they were swimming in the vat? And then she had a female baby? Would there be a revolution?" "Of course not, these men would not be interested in the female." "Wouldn't it become the transgression?" "No, because it is utopia." As we walked down the street, Samuel meowed and swung his head around at every sexy boy he saw. When girls walked by, girls who captured my attention, he would act astonished that any reasonable soul could fall for such "vampirism and kitsch."

We went back to his place. He had moved. He lived by Harlem in an apartment filled with antique dressers, dusty bookshelves, and a miscellany of odd door handles and Greek figurines. We sat on the edge of his bed. His bookshelves surrounded us. He had the most complete library, the whole Western Canon. We were on the twentieth floor. It was dark outside, but I could sense how far I was from Brooklyn, with all the books and with the classical music Samuel played on the radio. I started talking enthusiastically about Nietzsche. I always hoped that I could make insights which would impress Samuel, but he would add fifteen to mine before I finished my sentence. As an historian he hated overarching generalizations. Everything was singular, everything had its own facticity.

I emphatically declared, "I don't care what you say, everything Nietzsche says is right, even when he's wrong." And that was when Samuel kissed me, and I did not stop him. My lips curved open, Samuel's facial hair pushed into the crevice between my upper lip and my nose. Partly drunk I drifted far away in the sensation of his tongue, feeling his big body caving in all around me, he held my thigh firmly. He pulled my hand over to his lap and placed it on his hard cock. I pushed my hand against it, I heard something within him jump excitedly at this action, and I squeezed gently outside his pants, doubling his excitement. My cock was not hard, but I was pleased with how I felt. Samuel kept getting more and more excited. I was becoming feathery, light, distant, he was charging at me, and I wanted to please him.

I felt sad when he found out I was not hard, so I dropped to my knees and pulled his pants off, he helped me get them off, and I saw his cock, it was thicker than mine, and he was much hairier, his butt was fatty, and there was hair all over and I could smell shit too, but he was so sweet, and I put my face in that smell and licked his balls, and then moved up to his shaft. His penis had a small flap of skin protruding from the shaft, and this scared me, and I thought I was going to get AIDS, and I asked him what it was, and he reassured me, apologizing for not having told me sooner. He said it was from his circumcision, that he had recently been tested, that he was clean, so I continued, and I put his cock hurriedly in my mouth because the conversation had been a bit of a buzz kill, and I wanted to return to that smell, and I liked the way my hand felt so graceful against his thigh as I teased him. I put the cock all the way in my mouth, I made sure not to put my teeth on it. I have a big mouth and I opened my big mouth wide, and I let the cock head reach back into the pocket of my right cheek, and I swirled my tongue up and down the shaft, and he was getting very very excited, and I was scared that the cum was going to be all in my mouth, but he took it out and started to jerk off. He spat on his hand, then he jerked off vigorously, and I licked his balls, and put my other finger down by his asshole and circled it around there, and when I put it inside he started to say, "That is very good Jonathan, you know exactly what I like Jonathan. Oh, that is very good, very good." I pushed my finger deeper, and all the skin was around me, and that smell, and I pulled one hand up to his nipple, to tickle it, and he came right then, with some heavy grunts, and he was so happy with me, and he told me that I was some sort of erotic god, that I was better than 99% of the gay men he had

95

been with, and he had been with over 500 I later learned, and it was nice to be in his big arms and chest then, and to talk about Dante or Mahler or whoever...

He snored all night. He had a terrible snore. I curled up inside the sheets trying to escape, but this did not allay the sound. I took one of his books with me into the bathroom and ran the shower water. At some point I ended up back in bed staring at the morning light and the high windows across the street... He woke up horny, he grabbed me into his arms. My back was turned away from him, I could feel his cock against my ass. He told me stories about his Russian Grandmother, he did her voice perfectly, "'Yes I've been through Russian Revolution so nothing surprises me but let me ask you Samuel: Do you get it put in or do you put it in?' I'm versatile Grandma, I do both. 'Yes, yes I was not born yesterday. This means you get it put in.'" I was laughing, and I was suffocating too, but I kept laughing, and he started kissing me, and I kissed him back, I was still so happy with him, and I gave him another blowjob, this time I licked his asshole a couple times before finishing him off.

We were on Broadway Avenue in the morning. The sun was pouring down the street. We had scarves on, and we were laughing. A group of young girls passed by us singing, they were so ridiculous. "What is this they do?" "Sirens." We had breakfast at a café, then we went to a bookstore, Samuel suggested over twenty books, I remembered them all. He joked, "You know my students pay outrageous fees for this kind of information." "Well, that's why I pay you in other ways." He purred and we kissed goodbye.

****

The first thought that occurred to me when I saw Dolly's name lit up in my email box was about the pictures I had taken of myself jerking off to her photographs. I had never sent her these pictures, and I wondered how they would have impacted her. Since she had not reacted lovingly to my patience, maybe she would have preferred a glimpse at my impatience. Nonetheless...

Nov 21st
How many times have we Met?

and yet each time i cut myself out of your days or disembark or fade away i always find
myself feeling i never
showed you the best side, i find myself teeming with regrets. although i remind myself
constantly that it is
necessary for me to be away, i find you living as a phantom in my brain, and i'm not quite
sure how your living
quarters are up there, i'm not sure how to be a good host for your ghost. seeing you is diving
into a lake,
seeing you is running through cardboard, seeing you is shadows made by candles seeing you
is blue green and
grey. i dont really know what to say, except you're still sitting in my attic-mind, fidgeting
your knees and
scrawling onto my skull and all i can feel is that i need to apologize. for hiding, for not
communicating, for
giving you scraps and retreating. i don't know where i am at right now, it's been a lot of dark
days and i'm still
alienated by everything and everyone. i'm so happy for your constant progress into greater

and greater spaces,
and i orbit around the desire to see you and share thoughts, only to
find myself spinning
away from those
urges with a plummeting feeling in my core. i'm like a snowglobe, frozen in my daily life,
until the thought of
you or a letter shakes my whole self, and pieces of my doubtful brain
float around the
murky space. Maybe this is just a long way of saying that i can't meet
you in Venice. I know we would be beautiful together, but i cannot
handle that right now. i want you to be happy, i wanted to say hi.

Nov. 21st
Hey D. What's the deal with December? Dolly has deserted me. It is
too long and too predictable to explain. Recently she wrote me an
email saying how I am a lake, and blue and green and that I am like a
tornado which whips against the fragile shack that is her mind. We
were going to go to Venice with each other in December, but now I
am all yours, so.... ?
john

P.S. Do you know Dr. Samuel Horkheim? he says he knows you.

Five days before I left for Venice, Oxford and Morocco, Dennis sent me the picture of a girl in his Art History
program. She had thick waves of blonde hair. Her face was
hard to make out because of the flask she held to her mouth,
but her blue eyes were enormous:

Dec. 6th
The subject read: Our would be Travel Companion

And beneath her picture: Victoria Everheart--she likes whiskey (as you
can see) and Jesus, which is perhaps less apparent.

****

It took me a day and a half to arrive at my pension room around the corner of St. Mark's Square in Venice. I was there for three days. I was jet-lagged, and it was the middle of the night. I went to take a walk and the pension door locked behind me. The streets of Venice were empty, except for the occasional vendor pushing a cart of food down the cobblestone pathways. One narrow corridor was lit in red and hung with scaffolding. The moon and the street lamps shone obliquely against the canals. The echoes of birds were enormous, and every so often there was the shattering of the bells. I went to the square. I sat in front of the Byzantine church. The golden horses charged forward. Everywhere I looked was a lion holding an erect sword. The pigeons scattered and then they regrouped. I walked past the tied up gondoliers along the bank of the Grand Canal. I walked past rows of columns. I had never been to Italy before. I wanted to believe in it, but I had other concerns, drifts of thoughts, and longings, and all I really wanted was to get some rest. Across the Grand Canal was St. Giorgio Maggorie, which Samuel emphatically recommended I visit. It was designed by Andrea Palladio. Samuel knew all about him, and about how he was neo-Platonic, and about how he interpreted the architecture of antiquity through the reality of his place in time. From the distance in the darkness it looked white and circular. I tried to breathe it and everything else into me with admiration, but I remained clogged and anxious. As the sun crept up and started to light up all the gondoliers and the stones and the people now making their way to stores, I headed back through the winding roads to the pension.

****

Dennis and I met at a pub called White Horse across from the circular side of the Sheldonian Theater. The Baroque details were hidden behind sheets of rain. Dennis was wearing a leather jacket, his hair was longer, and his face was scruffier. He came towards me confidently and we gave each other a hug. I thought he looked very sophisticated. We sat down on a bench alongside the window. "What's the deal with this Victoria?" "You didn't seem too excited so I told her not to come." "I thought it was a little strange, you offering me a girl like that. Felt like some weird erotic transference." "I thought I was doing you a favor." "Sending me a woman?" "Yeah. She's a beautiful woman. I don't know why you wouldn't want her." "Maybe I'm unavailable." "You never told me. I thought you said Dolly ditched you." "No, I'm having an affair with this older man. I wrote you about him, Dr. Samuel Horkheim." Dennis guffawed and his mouth dropped, "The art historian?" "Technically he is an architectural theorist, and yes." "I'm shocked... He is brilliant though." "Yeah..." "Have you?" "Yeah, just before I left." "And?" "It was nice." Dennis kept shaking his head. "And you get off?" "No, I don't get hard. But it's still very nice." "Okay, so you're not gay then?" "I don't know, I wouldn't put it like that." Dennis got animated, "I mean you don't get hard, call me old-fashioned but I think that's a pretty clear sign." "I feel my sensations elsewhere. What does Judith Butler say, non-genital erogenous zones." "You read Judith Butler now? Did Dr. Horkheim suggest this to you?" "No, I think it was some whining girl, what the fuck is wrong with you?" "I'm jealous, that's all." "What about this Victoria?" "You'll meet her tonight, we're going to a dinner party at a friend's house, she'll be there, you can decide." "What're you doing sending me pictures of women? Why don't you want her?" "She's a bit too crazy for me, I think you'll like her, she's a lot sexier than Dolly." "No one's sexier than Dolly." Dennis rolled his eyes.

Victoria Everheart was sitting on the couch in front of the table of food when I arrived. She was fidgeting nervously, picking at the runs in her leggings, and she smiled at me, and those enormous blue eyes ran up and down my skin. I was feeling drunk after the long bus ride through the English countryside. She had thick curly hair that came down to her shoulders. Her face was jarring. She had such healthy cheeks and she kept smiling at me. Her chin was over-defined, like that of a witch. She was full-figured, her cleavage was staring at me, and she kept on wiggling, and she did not stop looking at me. "What? What? What're you looking at?" "It's strange to see someone in real life. I saw your pictures and I heard so much about you." Dennis came in and sat down next to Victoria and put his hand on her thigh. She shrank back a little. He whispered something into her ear. "He's very cute," she said. "Victoria here out drinks all of us. She has to tuck me into bed every night." I walked into the other room.

Everyone at the party was commenting on the shirt I was wearing. I bought it at the Peggy Guggenheim museum, it depicted what is known as the Angel Guardian of Venice: a metal sculpture of a fully aroused, rotund boy straddling a horse. The actual sculpture is in the back patio of the museum facing the canal. One of the Indian aristocrats stopped me for ten minutes to discuss Venice. I was only thinking about Victoria and how much I hated Dennis.

I went back in, Dennis shoved Victoria's hand in my face and said, "Can you believe the way she bites her nails?" "Oh, it is terrible, my mother begs me to stop every time she sees me." "You pull it off, it's part of your charm," Dennis said, and then, "Let's get some more to drink."

I sat down next to Victoria the moment Dennis got up. She snuggled her thighs against mine, and we stared at each other until we both started laughing. "I can see why Dennis is friends with you?" "What does that mean?" "You're very different from him, but I see what he sees in you." "Yeah, well, to be honest, I don't know what I see in Dennis." Victoria laughed. Her black dress was cut very low, and I could not help staring. "Do you believe in fantasy?" "Believe in it?" "Or do you like it?" "Yes, I guess." "I want to live in the fantasy world. Where everything is good or evil. Where I am a princess. I hate everything being so gray." "What kind of fantasies do you want?" "Why?" "Because I've been known to make fantasies come true, it's a power I have." "Oooo, sounds cheeky." She stared at me so intensely. We kept laughing.

"Tell me a secret." "I have a very good secret" "Ooo, tell me, I'm so excited." "Come on." I grabbed her hand and we went and sat at the bottom of the staircase facing the front door of the home. "Let's be brother and sister," she said. I shrugged, "You want to hear my secret, sister?" "Yes please." "So, I just recently got buggered by a man for the first time." "Oh, that is a good secret." She turned her knees inwards and leaned her body towards me. "Was it good? Did it hurt? I've never done that?" "It felt strange. I liked it. It was about control. It was about breathing, letting the trauma of it all spread through my body." "Who was the man?" "Oh, he is this Professor of architecture. He is very sweet and very smart. He knows everything, and he does all these funny imitations." "He sounds very special. I love professors. Does he have a beard?" "A goatee." "Mmmmmmmmmmmmmm. I love facial hair. I have this obsession with priests and even more with rabbis." "You know I teach at a Yeshiva?" "Yes, I know. I love the Jews. They are so hot."

I really could not help myself. I leaned over and put my mouth on Victoria's, she pulled away embarrassed and surprised, "But we are brother and sister, we can't do that." "I thought it would be even more appropriate that we do it, because of that." "I don't even know you." "I know myself well enough to know we are getting along, anyways, I'm sorry, I was probably too forward." "Are all Americans like this?" "I don't think it has to do with me being American." "Maybe it's because you're Jewish, can you grow a beard, you should grow a beard." "Last time I grew a beard I had my hair very long and I looked like Jesus." "Ooooooo, mmmmmm... you have to do it, Jesus is so fucking hot. I used to have these fantasies about him when I was younger. Dennis thinks I'm crazy. It is very sexual. You see this naked man in front of you, and you bow before him." "I get it." "Dennis is a cheeky one, you know. When I first met him I thought he was a total sleaze, he was like 'Hi Dahling.' It was gross. But then I see he is so brilliant." "Yeah..."

We walked home together that night. Victoria and Dennis walked ahead with their arms around each other. We passed monuments and imposing facades. The smell of the rain from earlier was still in the air. Victoria was very loud and easily excitable, she swayed her hips violently. Dennis turned back towards me and made a face which was supposed to impress me with the position of his hand as it crawled along Victoria's shoulder.

Dennis lived across from Christ Church. It had big spires and domes. It had a giant archway with Gothic folds in the vaults. Victoria pointed to her favorite angel in one of the building's recesses. They had stolen a large bottle of Bell's whisky and were drinking it recklessly. I did some cartwheels to get out all my energy. Dennis's room looked just like his room in ChinaTown, he had all the same pictures and icons posted on the walls: Dylan, Caravaggio, Shakespeare, and Rembrandt, the only addition was a quote by Derrida. We had to pack and then catch a bus to London, "So you're gonna come to Morocco with us, right?" I asked Victoria. "I thought you didn't want me to come?" "That was before I met you. Now I want you to come." "Ooooooo, I don't know. I think you're both drunk and are going to change your minds in the morning." "I don't get drunk. Dennis?" "I always wanted her to come." "So?" "Write me from Morocco saying that you want me to come, and I'll come."

We walked out together, all three of us. Victoria and I were staring in each other's eyes again. She shook out of it. "What?" I asked. "I just can't believe this is real. I can't believe this is real." "Fine, just come to Morocco," I said, not wanting to push her. She rode off on her bicycle, and Dennis and I ran through the small city to catch the bus.

****

Djemaa el Fna is the busiest public square in the world. It is in the center of Marrakech, surrounded on three sides by souks. The other end opens up to a park with Palms and further down the road is the Koutoubia Mosque, a slender tower of subdued elegance. Dennis and I were hassled by everyone as we walked. He was wearing his leather jacket, bomber shades, and tight jeans. I had on an Indiana Jones hat and a Cashmere red sweater. Within seconds two snakes were thrown around my neck. The place smelt like donkey shit, and everywhere people rode around in trucks, in motorcycles, and in carts pulled by donkeys. The men looked like snakes or donkeys. We did not meet a single Moroccan who did not eventually try and sell us something. The first man to come up to me was wearing a worn out Shaquille O'Neal jersey, his eyes caught mine too fast for me to prevent his advance. "Snake, very good snake." And then the snakes were around my neck and Dennis was encouraged to take a picture. Nearby were men on a carpet drunkenly humming on hand-crafted recorders. In front of them lay two lazy cobras. They were immune to the music.

The man held both snakes around my neck. I made a real sour face for Dennis when he finally got his camera off his wrist. On all the edges of the market were reddish, sandy buildings which offered food for tourists. Orange juice vendors screamed at us from far in the distance, and young boys came up with plastic snakes and waved them around, saying, "Snake, snake, you want snake?" Off the plaza the souks were full of grains, colored carpets, and jalabia vendors. Everyone looked at us and waved us over to buy something. Some men came up and tried to offer directions. Dennis knew French so we got suckered into following a few of these guides. One of them took us to the tannery, and he gave us mint to put in front of our mouths because the smell was so bad. The place had rawhide lying over these cesspools of chemicals and donkeys. Dennis nearly fell into one of the pools. He was really shaken up, and we had to go back to our hotel, which was in the religious part of town, so there was no place nearby to purchase alcohol. An Arabic star was tiled into the floor of the lobby, and an identically shaped fountain was inscribed within it. The outdoor hallways to the bedrooms reached four stories high. A computer offering Internet services was in a gated space on the second floor:

Dec. 11th
Hello Jonathan and Dennis...

So if I were to come, with your permission (!), I would arrive in Marrakech at 7.45pm on 14th....

Yes? No? Only if I stop biting my nails? Let me know.

If I don't see you... be safe, explore blah blah etc and possibly see you on
18th...

Vxx

Dec. 12th

So yes you do have our permission. Note: this has been declared under the soberest of conditions. Were it to benefit the possibility of
your arrival to make all sorts of declarations and flatteries I would do
so... Currently the men of Marrakech are pray-moaning to Allah in all
sorts of odd harmonies—the voices are broadcast through loudspeak-
ers on the tops of the mosques; there are snake charmers and donkeys
aplenty here—so if it is fantasy you are seeking, this place, which we
have yet to fully discover, is more than ripe for the imagination. And it
is fine if you bite your nails. Be in touch with your plans

J and D

"Listen Jonathan, if you're gonna make moves on
Victoria don't be sloppy about it. I'm not gonna change anything, so don't get all pissy if she is more interested in me."

"Do you want her?"

We were lying in bed together, our backs turned.

"No, though sometimes when she gets close, it's hard
for me to not touch her, she's very sexy."

"Yeah, I know... I tried to kiss her you know?"

"And?"

"She rejected it."

"You're a real bonehead."

"What is it about women, Jonathan?"

"What do you mean?"

"What is wrong with them?"

"Samuel says that they identify with their degradation,
it is not that there is something specific and universal about
them. It is a role they are playing, and they are scared to stop
playing it. And it is the same for men who play into their
games."

"What about their tears? You think that is part of the
spectacle too?"

"Of course, that's their best act."

"That's where my critical eye falters. I have too much of a soul. The only way I can assess someone's pain is to imagine what it would take for me to feel like that. I never cry, it takes so much to make me cry. I have to give women the benefit of the doubt and believe that they suffer more than I do."

"That's idiotic Dennis. They just have a different threshold. You can't make a hierarchy of pain. Why do you fetishize suffering so much, treat it like something so valuable?"

"That's very interesting what you're saying, Jonathan. In truth, if I fetishized suffering then I would no longer treat it as seriously. I just can't imagine that these women are crying purely as an act."

Dec. 13th
In the soberest of conditions I have booked my ticket....
Will be arriving on 15th (Thursday).
London Gatwick to Marrakech - flight 5305 arriving at 19:45, with easyjet.
Leaving morning of 19th.

Want to meet me at the airport?

I am very excited.... the fantasy is going to be a real treat, an excellent antidote to any cheekiness... :)

See you in a few days...x

p.s is it cold?

-V

Dec. 13th

Hey Samuel, I arrived in Marrakech yesterday. As always occurs when I travel—I discover myself to be disturbingly too similar to the person I was before having left. This may simply be nerves and lack of sleep. I guess I have much to tell you—but I want to gesticulate awhile more. I have been thinking of you—fondly of course, and I wonder what shall come of this 'relationship.' I must say that my

most recent debacle with romance has—perhaps wrongly—taught me not to burden others with emotional confession. I have a hunch this is not the case with you, but still I am teetering. I bought some Venetian ghost stories and am reading Levinas' No Escape. This may give you sufficient cause to think me cast in a gloomy light. But really I am just tired. Dennis, or as we should call him, Lawrence of Arabia, has been an utter bore. The Moroccan keyboard is very confused, so I am going to sign off. I have been missing you.

J

Dennis came and looked over my shoulder. "Writing love letters to your sugar daddy?" "Something like that." "What does he think about you not getting hard?" "I think it makes him a little uncomfortable, but he knows that I like him a lot." Dennis guffawed.

We drove up into the Atlas Mountains. We got out and looked around at all the trees. The clouds were contoured richly and left large shadows on the far peaks. Shepherds lived up where we were, and two of their daughters, wrapped in cloths of all colors, ran towards our car. They were smiling and so happy to see us, they ran all the way up a hill, and then when they saw what we were, they froze up and walked away... We drove down during the sunset and waited at the airport for Victoria to arrive.

I forgot how it felt to look upon Victoria's face. I was looking for her features, but then when I saw them, I felt something so very different than a recognition that it was Victoria...

In the morning Victoria woke both of us up. She opened our door and jumped in between us. Her hair was wild, and she wore a thick, red sweater which hid her voluptuous, marmoreal features. "Come on you sleepy boys, let's go." We got out as quick as we could and made our way to the bus station. We had to return the car from the day before, and it took a lot of concentration for me to steer through all the donkeys and the rather careless drivers. Dennis was speaking to Victoria the whole time, I could not tell if it was about mutual friendships or paintings, but I felt bad for Victoria every time he made her laugh.

It was a relief to board the bus, and I managed to procure a seat next to Victoria. Dennis sat across the aisle wearing a blue and white poncho he had bought at the market. He was reading Aldous Huxley. Soon enough he fell asleep and Victoria and I started staring into each other's eyes. "What was Marrakech like?" "It has all these alleys and turns, sort of like Venice. If Venice is heaven, Marrakech is hell." Victoria had taken off her red sweater and was wearing a white tank top from which her breasts squeezed out towards me mercilessly. She opened her eyes to me, and I gesticulated madly as I explained myself to her as best I could. She was very interested in Dennis and all the women that he had conquered back in New York City, and I had no choice but to indulge her. I told her mostly about how cruel he was, and I made a point of emphasizing his impotency problems. She was surprised. She said that everyone at Oxford was terrified of him and that all the girls were trying to get into his pants. "You're in love with him, aren't you?" She asked. "No." "He thinks you are." "Seriously?" "Yeah, he says that you have this father complex. Because your dad is so rich... It's okay, I have a father complex too." "I am not in love with Dennis." "Sure you

109

are." We stopped talking to each other. She climbed over the seat and lay back in the empty row behind me. The bus was speeding by sparse desert landscapes. A handful of dilapidated homes painted pink and light blue rose up every so often. I peaked back at Victoria, she had taken my digital camera and was posing for it. The sun coming through all the windows lit up Victoria's blue eyes as she pouted her lips.

We stopped halfway to Essaouira at a busy restaurant in the middle of the desert. I bought a fried crepe with cheese and a water bottle for Victoria. When I came back to the bus, she was way up above me staring out the window. She looked like a vision. Like a Greek statue. Like a Leonardo. She waved happily at me.

We got the penthouse room at the Majestic Hotel inside the walls of Essaouira. We went out onto the roof and found a ladder that led to an even higher rooftop. We climbed up the ladder and took our shirts off. The Atlantic Ocean was crashing in on the rocks all around us. Whitewashed homes with small patios and satellite dishes stretched out to the Sea. A few minarets rose up above the homes. It was dilapidated and beautiful. Dennis and I had bought weed from one of the guides in Marrakech so we rolled a joint up there and got real stoned. Victoria had her bra on, and its latticed satin revealed the dark skin of her nipples. She kept taking pictures of us. I sat at the ledge and looked out at everything and sighed. "You're like Pan," she declared.

"Me?"

"Yes."

"Who is Pan, like a faun?"

"He is the king of the fauns, the satyrs actually, it is Greek."

"Victoria is a Classicist, she loves her Zeus and her Apollo. Has she told you yet about how she goes to confession to get herself aroused?"

"Yes, she told me. I think it is very cute."

"Cute?" Dennis coughed, "Strange is a better word, Jonathan."

"You think I'm strange?" Victoria found this very funny, "I told my friend that I was going on a trip with the two strangest boys I had ever met."

"You should feel lucky," I said.

Dennis added, "Yeah, what must these Moroccans think of a young white girl strolling down the street with two handsome men?"

"Yes, but you only like me now, because I am young and healthy, when I am older you two will not have any time for me at all. It is a horrible thought, but very true."

"Don't be so morose," I said.

"I think Victoria has a point. Women only have a small window of time when they are in bloom. They have to do their best to capture you before they wilt."

"Ooooo, it is all so gross," Victoria added.

I drifted away from the conversation. I climbed down the ladder. I looked out over the street where all the vendors and shops were below. I tugged at a clothesline which still had some pins on it. Victoria and Dennis had moved to the edge of the roof, watching me. "I'm gonna take a walk," I yelled up to them. "You want us to come?" Dennis yelled down. I shook my head.

I walked lackadaisically through the shops. I bought some toothpaste and a toothbrush for Victoria, who had left hers on the plane. On my way back I stopped at an Internet Café. Samuel had written me:

Dec 15th
Jonathan, I too have been thinking fondly of you, and about fondling you, etc. etc. Have fun on your North African adventure, with Lawrence of Arabia. Perhaps more revelations will occur in the warm sands

of the Northern Sahara.... To strike a more serious note, I can't wait til your return: and don't worry about emotional confession, I am a good listener (or so I have been told) and you can tell me anything you like. Also just take the 'relationship' or whatever it is—I think we should call it something like the Ongoing Romp—as unselfconsciously as possible. But then again that's nothing short of impossible for people like us. I think about you often, and can't wait to see you. Not surprising that Mr. Lawrence of Arabia should still be a bit, well, boring. Great ingredients, not well cooked, that one.

When do you get back?

-Samuel

The three of us took a long walk through Essaouira. The air of the Ocean made all the vendors more lethargic than they were in Marrakech; instead of running up to us, they sat in front of their stores and screamed for us to come over. Many of the stores sold scarves, jalabias, drum sets, rugs, electronics, chess sets, and hand-carved bowls. The parti-colored goods hung on wires, racks, and shelves. The contrast between the white homes and the festive wares was hard to appreciate: the moment we looked into the stores, we were accosted: "Hey, nice sunglasses," "Hey, my friend, my friend, what, you don't like me my friend?" We learned to look straight ahead, darting our eyes strategically. Even out by the beach men sold space cakes and baklava. And even further out they sold rides on camels, which we bargained down to 200 dirhams a person. Victoria and I mounted one camel. She held onto me from behind, we tied our shirts around our heads so we looked like sheiks. A small, dark boy pulled the leash from the front. Dennis was alone on his own camel, wearing a scarf around his neck and a thick black sweater despite the beach and the warm sunlight. As we pulled further away from the town, Victoria and I started to playact. We sang songs we both knew from *Aladdin*. I pretended that I was her master, that she had served me well, but that once we came around the bend at the edge of the dunes, I was going to give her to another tribe as a peace offering. I told her that she must make sure to be as loving and generous to her new master as she was to me, otherwise an eternal war would rage in the desert. She promised that she would do everything that she had done for me. "Even that thing you do?" "Even that." Oddly enough, when we reached the dunes, a man appeared riding a large, black horse, and the horsed reared up, lifting its front legs to the sky, and this was an auspice which completed our game.

We drank a lot and bought a whiskey bottle outside of the town's walls. We had to walk through a crowded market. Goat and camel meat hung in front of butcher shops. We ended up back on the high rooftop just in time to hear the final shoutings from the mosque. There were always a couple men whose howls were like the groans from *The Tell-Tale Heart*. The sun was down, the moon and stars lit up the homes and the minarets. Across the street a red-cloaked figure with no apparent face clawed at the window on the fourth storey. He did so with intense deliberation. He raised his head up at the three of us. Victoria and Dennis got spooked and backed away. I clawed back at the man, and when he seemed to respond, by clawing viciously at the window, I backed away too. We went inside to our room and got ready for bed. Dennis put on his sunglasses and started speaking in a French accent. Victoria wrapped a blanket around her body and imitated the poor women on the road. She cradled part of the blanket to make it look like she was holding a baby, and she put out her hand begging us for money with tearful eyes.

I came out of the shower with a towel wrapped around me, and Dennis got all excited and said that Victoria and I should reenact the Pietá. I lay out splayed and smiling uncontrollably on Victoria's lap, and Dennis told me where to move and how to position my arms. When I was where he wanted me to be, he took a photograph.

I rolled off of Victoria. My towel fell down, and I scurried over to my bag and threw on the gray jalabia I had bought from the market. I moved to the corner of the room and crossed my legs. Dennis lay down in one of the beds and Victoria lay down in the other. The walls were tiled to keep it cool in the summer time but it was freezing now that it was winter. I was angry that they were going to sleep. I began to laugh silently to myself. My laughter grew louder and louder until I was cackling demonically. The two of them asked what was the matter with me, and I kept laughing louder and louder. I thought that I could stop but when they said I was possessed, this made it even funnier. I imagined I was the red-cloaked figure from across the way. I let the laughter continue on longer than I thought possible. When I finally stopped, Dennis invited me into bed with him. I got inside and put my arms around him. He was still using his French accent, "No, no no, zoo cannot touch zee Anus. It iz very bad. No, no, no. Zee anuz iz very sacred. Zoo cannot touch it, Jonathan. Zis iz very wrong." I was still giggling uncontrollably, and Dennis did not let up. Finally we both calmed down, and I felt a slight warmth from him as he buried his back into my caress. We fell asleep.

When we were on the beach the next day, Dennis drew a picture of a cock and a heart, so it said, "Jonathan loves Cock."

"Basically, Jonathan has found a way to transgress the norm while simultaneously eliminating the risk of heartbreak and obsession." Dennis told Victoria back in our room a couple nights later. "It is ingenious really. In a way the best thing has happened to you. You have been courageous enough to discover whether or not you're gay, and have proved that you're not. Every heterosexual male wishes to prove this to himself."

"I don't think you can say I'm not gay. I enjoy giving head to a man."

"But you don't get hard!"

"Well, you don't get hard with women. What does that make you?"

Dennis came at me with his fist, but I ducked. Victoria came between us and broke it up before anything happened.

On the bus ride back to Marrakech, Victoria and I sat next to each other. The setting sun pinkened the sky as we headed East. We stared into each other's eyes the whole time. I kept encouraging myself to have the resolve not to shy away. Victoria made many confessions about herself. When she was younger, she used her female charms to get the attention she wanted. She wore low cut outfits and acted all precious to get every male to laud her with compliments. Now she hated compliments. She said that if she heard people compare her to a Botticelli one more time, she was going to puke. "It is called treasure map burning. I'm trying to get over it. My friend Catherine and I came up with it. See, if you burn the map there is no treasure at the end." "So you burn the map to draw attention to yourself, but by then you have destroyed the very thing needed to preserve yourself?" "We never thought it out that far. It just makes sense, doesn't it?" "I think I might be someone who encourages women to burn their maps, like I hand them the match." We made a deal that we were both going to stop.

That night we had our final dinner in Morocco. After the belly dancer finished throwing flowers at us, Dennis told Victoria how everyone in their program fantasized about tying her up in an open plain and raping her. "That's terrible, why would you tell me that?" "I thought you would be interested to know." "I don't want to hear those things. Did Erica say this too?" "Everyone." Dennis looked at me and found me scowling. "What, what, what do you think you see?" "...I think you're misguided, both of you. It's a giant web of misguidedness." "Don't think you can sit there all quiet and judge us without us knowing what you're doing." I got up and went to the bathroom.

Victoria and I found a dark alley around the corner from our hotel and I pushed her up against the wall and started kissing her. I melted into her rich body. She ran her hand down my pants, trying to be discreet, but bumped directly into my cock. "Oh, sorry, I wanted to see if you were gay or not." "I'm not, okay." "I really thought you were at the beginning of the trip, now I think it is Dennis who is gay. I think Dennis is in love with you." I redoubled my efforts, kissing her, squeezing my hands against her breasts, pushing my hand inside her blouse and twisting my fingers against her nipples. "Oh no, I can't do this, I'm sorry." She tried to push away, but I pulled her back towards me. "It's very nice," she cooed. "You're so beautiful, honey." She stared at me unhappily, "No, I'm sorry, I can't hear that. I can't do this." "Why not?" "What about Dennis, I feel bad about Dennis." "Nobody cares about Dennis. Dennis doesn't even care about Dennis." I tried to kiss her, but she ran away from me before I could do anything.

I leaned against the wall, too drunk to want anything but Victoria...

Dennis was on the roof terrace of our hotel, staring down at me with a cigarette in his mouth. He started laughing when I looked up and caught his eyes...

A few moments later Victoria appeared alongside him and took a few drags of his cigarette...

I ran up four flights of stairs to the terrace. Upon seeing me Victoria turned towards Dennis, begging "Oooo, get him away from me." "What is your fucking problem?" I asked, angry. "Just go away, go away." "It looked like you were trying to rape her down there, buddy," Dennis added.

116

"She's like some French parlor maid. It's outrageous." "Have a cigarette, we ain't ever gonna get to the bottom of the female psyche." In the middle of our cigarette Victoria took my arm and led me to the other end of the terrace and started kissing me. "This is very bad." "Why?" "I don't do things like this, you don't know me. I ruin things that are beautiful... I wanted to touch you so badly on the bus, that was very cheeky." I kissed her again, but this time she stopped me for good and ran downstairs to our room.

The room was tiny, Dennis was in one bed reading Aldous Huxley and Victoria was in the other. I shouted, "I'm getting in bed with you, Victoria." She curled up into a big ball and said, "No, no, please, I just want to go to sleep." She did not move. "I don't fucking care, this is ridiculous." "Why don't you calm down, Jonathan." I ignored Dennis and got into bed with Victoria. I tried to put my arms around her but she curled up tighter. I was forced to turn over and stare at the ceiling... Everything was quiet. My head was drunk. Dennis said, "Why don't you both come in bed with me?" Victoria jumped at the opportunity and I followed her. I immediately had her whole body wrapped under mine. Her mouth was on mine, and my hands were under her shirt and squeezing at her breasts. Dennis lay right alongside us, and since I felt bad for him, I took one of my hands out of Victoria's shirt and caressed it along his stubbly cheek. "You're incorrigible," Dennis said, "I don't know how you can think you're gay."

I didn't care and I kept kissing Victoria, but she was wasted, and she passed out on me. Dennis passed out too. I was wide-awake, lying atop the two of them while they snored. There was no room for me on the small bed so I went to the other one. All the blankets were wrapped around Dennis and Victoria, and I lay there freezing, listening to the two of them continue to snore. Around six in the morning I crawled back into bed with them convinced that I was going to get sick if I stayed there shivering any longer. I snuck into the small space between the wall and Victoria. She woke up, and she wrapped her arms around me. I pulled her into me tightly, holding her head against my chest, my hand palming her thick hair. Her face smelt of whiskey. She kissed me once, then put her head back on my chest. I held her like that, alert and praising god, until the alarm went off at 7:30. Victoria had to catch an earlier plane than the two of us, and I offered to walk her to get a taxi. We started kissing immediately, once we left the building. We kissed in the narrow streets of the souks, and we kissed on the edge of Djemaa el Fna, and we kissed at a small table outside a café while we waited for our espressos. "I'm gonna write you a nice letter, the moment I get home." "Don't you think we should just forget about each other?" "I won't be able to, I'm gonna write you, I promise." "Oooooo, this is so bad, why do things have to happen like this?" "It'll be okay, just promise me that if I write you, you will at least respond and say you received it." "I promise, of course I will." I kissed her... her blue eyes and her thick cheeks, and her round breasts... I wanted to devour her. The harder I squeezed and the closer I pulled her towards me, the more excited she got.

We had to walk down to the taxis. We clung to each other. One of the Moroccans yelled out, "Respect! Respect!" and he came up to us and shook his finger menacingly. We smiled. The taxi pulled up. "Goodbye." We kissed more, our tongues trying to taste something permanent. She got into the cab, she was so darling, and then the cab drove away. I walked back through the Moroccans with my head cast skywards.

****

Back in Oxford...

Dec. 20th

"Doubtless the tragedy out of which life was created occurred along the avenues of the garden. There were two of them and they were beautiful and they wanted to be something else; love waited for them far off in the tedious future and the nostalgia for what would be arrived as the child of the love they had never felt. Thus, beneath the moonlight in the nearby woods, for the light trickled through the trees, they would walk hand in hand, feeling no desires or hopes, across the desert of abandoned avenues. They were just like children, precisely because they weren't. From avenue to avenue, silhouetted like paper cut-outs amongst the trees, they strolled that no-man's land of a stage. And so, ever closer and more apart, they disappeared beyond the fountains, and the noise of the gentle rain-almost stopping now-is the noise of the fountains they moved towards. I am the love that was their love and that's why I can hear them in this sleepless night and why I'm capable of living unhappily." –Fernando Pessoa

That was all, Dolly didn't write a thing. I decided not to write her back, though I did entertain calling her once I returned to New York. I wrote to Samuel and told him I would be home soon and that I hoped we could meet up over the weekend. Dennis got a phone call and he started to act very surprised; I looked up from what I was doing. "Victoria is here. She's on her way over, she just took a bus from London." "Why is she here?" "She said to see some Ruskin exhibit." "I'm gonna stay at her place tonight." "Well, why don't you wait to see if she wants you there." "Fuck you Dennis, she wants me there. We consummated in the morning." "She seemed pretty annoyed with you the night before." "I'm gonna wait downstairs for her, alone."

I packed up all my bags, I was so excited to get away from Dennis and his insipid room. My heart was beating so fast. "You're really pathetic you know. You have this Christian sense of love and romance." "I feel things, I'm excited, you don't get anxious before you see a girl?" "I'm too aware of what's going on, maybe when I was in high school I felt like that." We hugged each other goodbye.

I stood out front of the gate to his dorm staring at Christ Church. Victoria came bounding up the road in tights and a long, sleuth-like dress coat. We kissed, her eyes were frozen blue. "I'm gonna stay at your place tonight, okay?" "Yes please. But..." "Don't worry, I just want to see you naked and be affectionate with you." She crumbled after I said that, and we walked clumsily hip to hip through the freezing mist. We stopped and kissed. Everything was indecipherable in the fog. We kept walking and watching our breath and giggling and then we would kiss. When we made it home we stripped naked immediately. Her body was more delicious than I could ever describe. It was so full and rich and I dug myself into every corner of it. Her pussy hair was not shaved, and her pussy itself was perfectly warm and wet for me when I began to touch it. I found her clit, I made her cum, and she was so happy. She looked like a little puppy dog. I slapped her face a couple of times, and she stared at me in awe. I wrestled her down, I dug my teeth into her breasts, cupped them at the edge of her nipples. She was screaming, and she made this face of complete terror, over and over, and yet whenever I asked her if it was too much, she ordered me to continue. She asked if we should have sex, I said no, that I just wanted to please her. I buried my face in her thick thighs. My hands on her skin, on her breasts. She stuck her tongue straight out and panted as I played with her.

In the morning the sky was gray and everything was frosted. Victoria lived in the wealthier part of the neighborhood. It had giant Sycamores and Elms and three story brick houses with towers and bay windows. The air was fresh and we were bundled up and still staring at each other. The hedges were all hung with spider webs which glistened with tiny crystals of ice. There were over a hundred of them.

We kissed at the café.
We kissed in front of the bus stop.
…And then I flew home.

****

I stood by the cube at Astor place on Friday night waiting for Samuel to arrive. I was dressed up in a navy Ermenegildo Zegna suit my father had bought me when I was younger—Samuel was taking me to see Daniel Barenboim perform a series of Bach fugues at Carnegie Hall. I had not eaten all day. The trip had taken most of my money, and the Rabbi was still holding out on a few of my paychecks. The cars all rushed by, and the glass and spires of far off buildings capped the horizon. The streetlights and the flood beams emphasized the fog drifting through the city. I was nervous for Samuel to arrive because I knew he would smile happily at me and then he would grasp my body and push it into his. Then he would push his mouth into mine and we would start kissing. If I could make it past that moment everything would be fine. He took awhile to come, and I imagined a scenario where, when he came, I was already talking to Dolly, who serendipitously ran into me on the street. Samuel would initially react as if I had betrayed him, so I would have to explain that I had bumped into her unintentionally…

After this was all cleared up, the two started discussing what they knew about each other, and I interjected, "Well, it is good you know so much about yourselves, because I don't know either of you at all." And then the scene reversed, and they started talking about me and about how I had these claws and these strange powers of persuasion, to which I interjected, "Well, I'm happy you two know so much about me, because I don't know myself at all..." I laughed out loud, trying to raise

121

my spirits; next to me, a couple skateboarders were pushing the cube around and around.

Samuel came up to me wearing a stocking cap, it was on a bit cockeyed, covering one of his eyebrows. He was smiling and he pulled me into him and he kissed me. I took a deep breath and let him enjoy me, I tried to forget everything. He noticed the facial hair I was growing and said, "You know I love facial hair. I mean don't get me wrong, you were very cute before, but now," He made a growling sound, "And this tan you have. I told my friends all about you, they don't believe that a smart sexy straight boy exists who fools around with men and gives amazing blowjobs. I said they would just have to see for themselves. Your letters were very nice by the way, I received them at just the right time. The dean at New School is this little Japanese aristocrat and she say, 'That no good Samuel, mustn't do that, you fired next time you talk about women like that'..." We were walking down the street, I had all these stories in me, but Samuel never stopped talking, "I thought a lot about you. I was thinking that this experience has been as new for me as it must be for you. In a way the student has become the teacher. Now, of course I still take the position of the teacher if you know what I mean." He stopped me on the sidewalk, took my mouth in his, and placed his hand on my ass. I stopped the kiss short and interjected my whole story.

He kept making conclusions about it before I got to any of the climactic parts. "You know what Dennis needs, now this may sound too easy, but he needs a cock in his ass, and I think we all know he wants that cock to be yours, Jonathan, and I cannot blame him, you do have a beautiful cock." "How would you know? It hasn't even been hard around you." "That's not true, it has been hard, three-quarters hard." "In the morning when we woke up, yes." "Listen if you wanna deny that you've gotten hard with me that is just fine, but I know what I've seen. You're very open-minded Jonathan but you

122

have a limitation here, you cannot believe that a man could arouse you." "Let me go on with my story, please." "Yes, sorry…"

Samuel decided that though Victoria seemed very insecure, she sounded much more suitable for me than Dolly, and he said that he was happy to share me with a woman as long as she was out of town. "I mean you're really what the Romans would call a full man, taking it up the bum, giving it to the ladies, this is outrageous…"

Sitting at Carnegie Hall on the highest balcony, watching Samuel push his head attentively towards the music, the piano and pianist tiny figures in the giant hall… I imagined Victoria emerging from the drapes of the skybox directly overlooking the stage. She had on a black dress and she was holding herself with that vibrating sensuality she has, staring her blue eyes at me with such blind curiosity. I let her stay there and watch me.

Samuel mentioned my inattentiveness later that evening and told me how he used to lie underneath the piano while his mother played. He would start crying whenever she missed a note. We were naked, and I was lying on top of his large, hairy stomach. My legs felt extra skinny. I wanted him to put himself inside me. I wouldn't have to be as close to him then. He fumbled with the condom, and he hurried to stuff his cock inside me. The dinner we ate after the concert was still in my belly and my asshole felt clogged up, so when he pushed up against it, nothing budged. He tried to force it in, and his cock kept sliding up my backside. "One more time." He pushed very hard and managed to stuff himself inside. The condom was dry, it scratched against the skin inside my asshole, and I leapt away. I didn't want him to feel uncomfortable so I took the condom off and put his cock in my mouth and made him cum. He held me in his arms, and I turned away. "Your generosity is very unusual. I know that you must enjoy doing it, but I still feel bad that I can't do anything for you. It is almost too perfect of a fantasy. A young sexy straight boy who likes to give." "It's okay, you're the nicest person I've ever met. I like giving to you." "I'm surprised you would say that. Many people think I'm a bit bossy. Thank you." "No, I think you are very nice. The day after I first slept with you, I cried when I got home. It wasn't the sex, I don't mean I didn't like the sex. I just had never had someone treat me so kindly. I thought about Dolly and Dennis, and how until I met you I thought the way they treated me was normal. You freed me from them."

"This is one of the nicest things anyone has ever said to me." I stayed quiet, bracing myself as he pulled me into his belly. He chattered nonsensically for a while, I tried to keep up with him until he began to snore. I was not feeling too affectionate, my ass was still a bit sore, so I left the room and went to sleep on the couch in my living room.

****

When Samuel left in the morning, I went straight to my computer. Victoria had sent me a very funny email about her being rubbish at writing emails but still wanting very badly to stay in touch with me. I assured her that she was far more articulate than she believed. She was back in her hometown Salisbury living with her father and her mother in her Victorian Mansion. It was Christmas and she was going to Church. At Midnight Mass, while the priest lectured about abstinence, the open windows let in the clamor of revelers across the street.

Jan 3rd
If a girl felt for a guy like I felt for you, she might tell him that there
honestly is a root of intimacy, and this is perhaps the reason why he
touched her like no one else

It is the issue of location which walls me in, its rationalizing force
weighing me so incredibly down. I won't be seeing you for months, our
only common ground being the one week we knew each other. Just
like you, I am worried about the 'point' of honesty because of our
situation. I don't want to lose contact, I wish I could see you, or talk to
you but we can't….should we really be honest with each other? And if
so what is the true honesty when our only reference is the past. I miss
you. I think about you more than often—far too much, I love your
words, I miss your affection, I miss you.

Just this morning I was looking at Titian's Bacchus and Ariadne, laughing to myself at how Bacchus' leap reminded me of you when you were
proving your manliness...!
But maybe we shouldn't talk of Ariadne, after all she died of a broken
heart, at least she was forever immortalized in the stars, surely watching
those who wander through her spider webs...

But today has been fun, I am wearing a Christmas hat, eating a mince
pie and playing with my friends, boring them with Moroccan tales - the
space cakes, the camels, and Pan :)
Vx

Jan 4th
Sometimes I have the silliest dreams. They concern notes I wish to
hit, through the use of words, which will silence
all doubts—all bugaboos of the soul.
These notes will be seamless in their clarity; topics previously discussed
(Bacchus flying in robes, Christmas festivities, and all the hidden winks
scattered in the well crafted prose) will be received, enjoyed, and then
forgotten—so no formalism of exchange limits the interlocutor from
expressing what is current in his vision; and, such is the case, he
must admit to having no concern whatsoever with spider webs nor
with Titian paintings and certainly none whatsoever with mince pies.
What does concern him is communion—one which could hardly be

accused of stinging, which lights no flames, sets no sails, and demands no treasure. Still he wants it to move. For it must trail along the thread of time if it is to be revealed—this dialogue. He sees now that evoking the thing he wants, whether it be stated with words like love or statements like, "Oh, to feel you again against my skin..." would immediately deny and then perturb the location of—let us call her 'his muse', if it suits her fancy. And now he grows shy and his face is red, for all he wanted was to wave his hand through the Ocean so she knew that when she speaks he listens. Does he reveal too much? Why is it he cannot say exactly what it is he wants to say? Victoria... you have stirred something silent and enchanted within me...and the wish would be that I never abuse such fortune. Oddly enough, doesn't it feel like we are growing closer through these emails, though we continually speak of having parted?
john

Jan 7th
You popped up in my dream two nights ago in a very sexual way, woke up quite wet and tried to force myself back to sleep again to re enter the same dream. I remember you telling me that you like that I got wet, and in my strange state of wake/asleep I thought if I re entered my dream I could show you how wet I was…hummmm!
Vx

Jan 8th
I feel like I am living two lives. One in the real world, where I do my work…play with my friends…watch Planet Earth..And then the other life is conducted through sneaking off to check my emails, the beat of my heart as I open 'TransAtlantic Companions…" to see what words my secret non-physical cyberspace lover has to kiss me with.
Vx

Jan 9th
Last Year I went a little insane. I thought I was dying. I was Positive that my soul was leaving my body. I went to the Doctor and told him that my soul was leaving…he was rubbish, prescribing me pills and sending me off to see people when all I kept on saying in complete

seriousness was 'I don't need anti-depressants, I know what is wrong with me—I am dying because my soul is leaving, tell me how I can stop it from leaving me?" It was a strange feeling, like I had no emotion; I was not happy or sad…just nothing. Everyday felt a little bit more like nothing-like my soul was seeping out of my skin. I thought I was going to turn into a vegetable, that all I would do was Function and nothing else. The Funniest thing was that any type of repetitive noise increased this rubbish sensation…the shower was the Worst. Quite Comedy really. In the end, I locked myself away and wept for two days solid, this led to a realization that there was emotion in me. How could I cry if there was nothing?? Thus my soul had not left me…If I could cry, I could (technically at least) be happy, giddy, dizzy, uncontrollably euphoric.

…am feeling a little taste of the soul leaving. I know NOW that my soul is not actually leaving, but it is still the best way to explain my state of being.
Magical X
V x

Jan 10th
#1 "How can I posses with my body, when I don't even possess my body?

How can I possess with my soul, when I don't possess my soul? How can I understand with my mind, when I don't understand my mind?

There is no body or truth we possess, nor even any illusion. We are phantoms made of lies, shadows of illusions, and our life is hollow on both the outside and inside.

Does anyone know the borders of his soul, that he can say 'I am I?"

Is there anything that we possess? If we don't know who we are, how can we know what we possess?"

#2 "I feel like screaming inside my head. I want to stop, to break, to smash this impossible phonograph record that keeps playing inside me, where it doesn't belong, an intangible torturer. I want my soul,

a vehicle taken over by others, to let me off and go without me. I'm going crazy from having to hear. And in the end it is I—in my odiously impressionable brain, in my thin skin, in my hypersensitive nerves—who am the keys played in scales, O horrible and personal piano of our memory."
-Fernando Pessoa

I'll write you my own words soon…

J

****

Dennis had been in the U.S. visiting Isabella. They were on tenterhooks, as they had been for the past three and a half years. He came to my place the night before he headed back to Oxford. He got very drunk and read me a passage he had written in his journal about Essaouira. The basic point was that I lacked profundity of spirit because I denied the mask I wore. This mask he informed me was my Romanticism. It was an over-compensation for my inability to seduce most women; when I did find one who suited me—I latched on to them with all my poetic might. The journal ended with Dennis congratulating himself for being brave enough to confess that communal existence required perpetual manipulation. He then picked up my guitar and sang me a song he had written. It mentioned Samuel and it mentioned my tone deafness, it listed my infidelity to his heroes, Bob Dylan and Lawrence Durrell, all of whom I had professed to love under his guidance—and its chorus sang, "Idol Envy, It's a Precious Thing." Dennis could barely get the song out he was so drunk, and as I sat patiently aside him watching his timid, hateful expressions devolve into burps, he continually apologized, saying, "This is a really mean song, I'm sorry." Only to continue until the end,

"Idol Envy, it's a Precious Thing. Don't Worry, I've Felt the Same."

****

Samuel invited me to a party with a handful of fellow professors. The party was uptown, near Harlem, at the apartment of Euphori Manishevitz, an aging Phenomenologist with no tenure and no hair on his head, save two giant white wing dings above each of his ears, which accentuated his ruffled suit and his professorial persona. It was Euhpori's birthday that day. Samuel warned me about Euphori. He compared him to Dennis, saying, in Euphori's German/French/Israeli accent, "'You know that I know that I know more than you know.' He is more a megalomaniac than I am," added Samuel, "But he is a sweet guy. What you don't know about Euphori is that he committed himself to an Asylum a month after moving to New York City. I asked him how he could have been crazy if he knew enough to commit himself. He said, 'Well, it was not me, it was what my friends told me about my disposition. You see, I was so happy, everything in the world fit into place, so I thought I was the Messiah, and I walked around naked and crapped all over myself.' So basically you became a phenomenologist for your sanity? 'Yes, yes you could say this but you American thinkers are always too explicit.'"

Euphori answered the door to his 13th floor apartment without looking me in the eye or shaking my hand. To Samuel he said, "You're late and you don't bring wine. The things you do for love." I stared at Euhpori waiting for him to greet me, but he just pointed to the coat rack and walked away. I knew I was going to be terribly bored, but I did not realize it was going to be such a small affair, and I had no other option but to take my seat around the glass table where most of the cheese and bread had already been eaten. I was introduced to everyone. On the couch sat a Portuguese woman who studied architecture, a frumpy Austrian Architect with glasses and a sour face, and a beautiful shy Jewish/Italian violinist named Eva. Across from me at the other end of the table was a Vietnamese colleague of Samuel's named Phuong. He wore a colored bow tie and black thick-rimmed glasses. Samuel pulled up a chair next to me and started making a joke with the last bit of cheese, holding it up to look like a nose, calling it, "Spinose-a." On our left sat two women wearing party dresses. Euphori was around the corner preparing our dinner.

Samuel immediately took center stage. He knew French and Italian and he started talking about Turin, Prague and Lyon—the triangular hub of Black Magic practices. I had managed to grab a piece of bread and a crust of cheese and was picking at them slowly. Samuel turned to me and asked, "Do you want me to explain what we're talking about?" "Not really," I said rather smugly. Samuel laughed. He went back to charming everyone, pausing briefly to inform me that I was very funny. He turned back to the guests and said, "Now you may all think that I am some terrible lecher who runs after innocent young men, but you can ask Jonathan himself, he ran after me. I mean my god, I was just an innocent lamb, and this ferocious child swooped into my path and before I knew it..." Samuel bobbed his head to feign shyness and embarrassment, "Well, we don't have to say much more." Euphori came around the corner and said, "Between the two of you, you make one reasonable person."

The food came, it was a notch above pasta and butter. I devoured it. Samuel whispered to me, "I don't know what this is Euphori is serving us. I've tasted his food before, it is much better than this." I could not respond. Samuel blurted, "You know my boyfriend teaches at a Yeshiva." Everyone looked at me. I said, "It's true." Someone asked how it was,

"It's difficult but fulfilling." They stopped talking. They pointed to a small statue of Mao Zedong on the kitchen counter and got into a heated argument about fascism and the possibility of evaluating dictators. Samuel was the most adamant about anti-totalitarianism, probably because he was American—though he would never concede to this type of 'biographical psychologizing.' He did not stop asserting his stance until Euphori took the statue down and put it in the cupboard. They all got a big laugh out of that. I could not look at anyone. My wild eyes took over, and I felt that where I was was a vacuum which would immolate all the smiles and feigned candor of the party if any pressure were to be applied to it. Samuel whispered, "We'll go soon, you look like you're gonna kill someone."

Walking along the sidewalk towards an intersection at Broadway, I explained to Samuel how patronizing he had been. He understood, "I must seem very naive. My mother used to treat me like that, no wonder you're angry." "It wasn't just that, I can forgive you. I mean, you're you. I get it." "You make me sound like a disease which you have learned to live with." "It's not exactly like that. Anyways, I just can't handle sitting still for so long. I get very antsy." "You can move all you want now that we're alone." Samuel tried to take me in his arms. I pushed him away. I moved to the edge of the sidewalk. We walked underneath a large parking structure whose lights on the dark street confused everything into an eerie existentiality. Samuel kept talking, I answered him with blunt aspersions. It disgusted me to think that if I did the simplest thing, like smile, tell a joke, or look into his eyes, he would immediately try and kiss me. I remained firm. We were in the neighborhood of his apartment, he asked if I wanted to stay over. "Yeah, but can I sleep on the couch?" "It would be fine with me, but my landlord won't have it, she says, 'Samuel, that couch is an antique. I know you need to have your fun, but please do it in private, not on this valuable

131

furniture.'" Samuel contorted his body upwards to mock a pompous, big-breasted old woman. It was how he imitated all women.

We went into his kitchen and made tea. I thought that I needed something clean inside me. I turned my face down to the wood chipping away on the kitchen floor. "I've never seen this side of you. It is very interesting. You have a very cruel side, but you direct most of it internally. I don't have a side of me like that exactly. I get angry, but not in the same way. No, there is something masochistic about the way you're behaving. Euhpori and I concluded that masochism is a way of filling up a hole, it is a form of diversion." "It's a little different, I'm just acting like this so you don't kiss me." "You think I'm that out of control," He bobbed his head to feign shyness and embarrassment, "Well, I mean you know what Nietzsche says?" I shook my head. "Physiognomy is destiny. You must think I have the appetite of a Pasha," he said the last words like a little baby. "My friends say I'm the id, do you think I'm the id?" My jawbone weighed a thousand tons, and it was painful to say, without breathing too much fire, "I don't know."

I endured Samuel's snores for the last time that night. In the morning the weather dropped, and Samuel lent me a black sweater. It came down long over my hips and my hands, and I felt snug inside it. I was really sad that things were going to end with Samuel. He knew not to kiss me when he let me out the door.

****

Jan 15th

My term has got off to a flying start…whiskey in Dennis's room…! I am not sure who corrupts who. It was nice to see him, he seems somewhat Warmer—He was not trying to dig into me. He did play me

132

the song he wrote for you. Cheeky indeed. I told Dennis I could never handle such a song, and he said that you were strong…! It focused on your 'figurephile' nature very strongly. How you obsess over your muses. I have not finished analyzing its significance. Ummmmmmm. I have made a decision to try not to talk about you with him…he has a great capacity to tell me things I am not sure I want to hear, things I am sure are true but seem somewhat negative. I suppose in a way this helps in putting my feelings for you in perspective but sometimes there are bits of magic even if fake or constructed I do not want destroyed. It is a bit like watching 'the making of…' your favourite fantasy, beautiful, magical movie and the reality of what makes it work hits hard.

I hope…well..i know you won't mention these things to Dennis—I do not want to sound like I am being negative about him, because I really do appreciate his friendship here, but I guess you two have such a close relationship, and I have only just scratched the surface of trying to understand it—and I do not know what is real or not, what is an illusion, what is manipulative or pillow talk.
Vx

Jan 16th
Are we in some 19th century romance play, or even some lost Shakespearean tragedy? My gosh! I see it all playing out now. Dennis as Hamlet. I as a sort of Romeo crossed with Prospero. And you as Ophelia, Juliet and Cordelia all wrapped up in one. I am the tragic hero, my flaw that I love. Will Hamlet seduce you with his existentialism? Or will you just go insane? That sounds fitting… As I, now I am Odysseus, am mid-flight across the Ocean—at last to return to my Penelope—from all my travels and adventures (in GayLand and ChassidTown) Hamlet plays a song to you in which he confesses that though he never believed in love your eyes convince him of its certainty—and his unexpected passion drives you to suicide—just as I knock upon the door. And so the showdown begins. I am the victor, naturally, but oh, at such a cost!

Oh, Victoria, pillow talk, magic, truth, negativity, lies, manipulations, honesty, doubt, distance, fantasy—I think we both know without Dennis's help that such is our relationship. Fact is—saying word's like

manipulation and then seeing how vacant and insignificant they are makes it all the more real, not less, despite what Dennis might believe. And in the end...I like you and enjoy thinking about you.
john

Jan 17th
For my own peace of mind I would just like to probe deeper into our Shakespearean tragedy. I want to make clear that I do not think it is Dennis's intention to take aim at your sincerity, I really do think (or perhaps just hope) that his words are not designed to attack, but what happens is they remind me of what I already know about you....
I will try and explain...It is nice to feel special, and it has been nice that you make me feel so, especially as it seems to have occurred without me having to burn my map for your affection. I knew already – as we discussed – that you are a 'figurephile', and that perhaps sometimes you enjoy making others feel enchanted (as you told me, you help the burning of the map).

I think it is best that I just do not talk about
you with Dennis... I came to this conclusion when Dennis and I were looking at the Morocco pictures, I kept on making little noises when you came on the screen, and Dennis made me feel like an idiot!

As far as the Dennis planned seduction goes, he is not a suitor. I honestly do not think he sees me in such a light. But in the game of tragedy, if I was to be the victim of Eros' sport, I would certainly choose insanity over love or suicide.

With concerns to the revealing of the juicy relationship you two boys have...while I am drawn to try and explore its caves - it is probably best not to let me in. I spoke to a close friend about the three of us. He thinks I am being naive, and there is some form of power struggle between you and Dennis and I am quite
insignificantly in the middle of a vast amount of other things
that you guys play with as part of your relationship. He tells me to be wary of both of you!!

Any truth in this? Damn the games people
play... 'All the world's a stage...' huh?

****

"Hey Samuel, I wanted to call to apologize for the other night."

"It doesn't bother me. I was just surprised to see you act like that."

"I was surprised myself. I didn't want you to think I was angry."

"I hate to tell you this, but you acted just like these girls in your life, who you always accuse of receding into themselves."

"Yeah, maybe I should send out my forgiveness, now that I know what it feels like."

"You mean to be ravaged by an uncontrollable sexual force?"

"You never quit do you?"

"Why would I?"

"I guess you have no reason to."

"I'm surprised you called so soon, happily surprised. This whole relationship—I hate that word—has been a welcome surprise. I mean who would have thought it would have lasted this long. Four months. Five... And even more importantly, I think we're becoming friends."

"I feel that way too. I really don't want any sexual incongruities to get in the way of that."

"There's no need to worry. You must think I can't control myself at all. What you don't know is that it is very common in the gay community," he made fun of this phrase as he said it, "To make friends with our ex's."

"That sounds nice. I've never heard of such a thing. Straight people are too cruel."

"You can't generalize like that—there is always the exception. You are living proof of that."

"You don't understand what I'm saying. I know it's possible, it's just rare."

"Well of course it's rare, that's what makes it the exception. I don't think you disagree with me at all. If anything I would say that women identify with their degradation. It doesn't have to be like this, it's just how it happens to be today."

"Yes, you tell me this all the time."

"You think I'm some old fuddy-duddy Professor who repeats the same rhetoric over and over without realizing it."

"Yep."

"Meow."

"Cow as a Puppy."

"Look what I've done to you. Could you imagine what Dennis would think if he heard you speak like this?" Samuel lowered his voice, "'Ummm... you realize cow as a puppy does not make any sense, Jonathan.'"

"Listen, I already have too much of Dennis in me, let's talk about something else."

"Can you say Darling or Dahling?"

"I think I'll talk to you later Samuel."

"But wait, wait. You have to hear this. Even daddies need daddies, right? Even daddies need daddies?"

"Goodbye Samuel."

****

Jan 21st
I just don't know anymore. Snakes whispering, minds contemplating....Whatever you feel for me, real or not I will take it with happiness until it ends. HA. I am going to say that to Dennis. He said yesterday that he didn't want me to ruin your relationship with each other. Damn him. Then he would not explain when I (very bravely) questioned him

136

on what he meant. I know why he says such things...it is to stop me from typing his words, it is to stop me from spreading his words. Well it works, his sentences are safe with me. But what I hate is that after all the crap he talks to me about (concerning Jonathan Direx and his relationships) he tells me to not bother wasting time over it—to not bother thinking about it. How>>>>>? Jesus.

Vx

Jan 23rd

Dennis,

I am very confused. Do you want me as a friend or as an enemy? If it is the latter then I guess I am not so confused, if the former...please help me understand why you make me mistrust you. I am very tentative about writing to you. I fear that by doing so I am being lured into some odd trap. I know all too well how your brain works. I would hope that my words hide from its duplicity and touch you beneath your breast. Please advise me how I should perceive the nasty journal entry, the songs...I am aware too that you have been a bit bold in private with Victoria. What the fuck? Are you just a bad person? Please help me understand. I am not in competition with you. If I was once...I have not been for months. You are making it hard for me to want you in my life. Is this what you want? I will leave...honestly, if you cannot muster the courage to win my forgiveness. I am utterly confused. I am almost fearful that you will find some way to condescend to me in response. I urge you not to—it will reveal too much. Just come out and say what's on your mind.

J

Jan 24th

Jonathan-

I never think of you as anything less than the most important friend in my life. The journal entry and the song...both were a bit 'nasty', but the latter was the inevitable result of art conforming with its ideal purpose—i.e. the expression of an 'unformed notion'...As for the journal entry—blowing off steam, the natural invective that one inflicts on a challenging (not necessarily competitive, or at least not in an unhealthy way) comrade around which one has spent perhaps a tad too much uninterrupted time. I felt incredibly happy to see you when I returned from out west, and I felt it my duty to declare all the 'nasty' things that had been swirling around in my head—my duty, that is, as

Your friend,
D

P.S. Regarding Victoria...I have a very 'sweet' relationship with her, which I think can be maintained without compromising the one she shares with you. I did play her the song, which maybe you think was some devious maneuver intended to cast you in a negative light, but I am sure she can affirm from my interactions with her, that I have never sought to portray you as anything but my most loved and admired accomplice, and if anything, I wanted her to have a greater knowledge of the complexities of the relationship we share. Moreover, this issue should benefit from the advantage that I have no desire to sleep with her, and so the toils of sexual jealousy which, however petty, often arise in these sorts of triangulate situations, should not haunt us here.

Jan 25th
If such is the case, as concerns your feelings for me, then I will ask you a favor. Do not talk about me with Victoria. She does not like being pulled into our world, and I do not blame her one bit.
john

Jan 26th
If it will make you feel better, I'd be perfectly happy not speaking to Victoria at all. In fact, I would probably rather uphold some anxiety-stricken call to responsibility such as that, thus affirming my loyalty to you, than attempt to carry on with a person I have been asked to censor myself around. Effectively I am asking that you not be threatened by things so benign—by doing so I think it is you who jeopardize this friendship, by giving it too little credit, and by revealing your purported generosity of affection and love as impecunious, a sad sort of jewery. I'll await your advice.

...If I have wounded her confidence in you, it should probably be taken as a compliment. The less embraced we are by the listless partakers of the pseudo-reality of the world, the better—and this pertains particularly to the vixens…

D

Feb 1st
I just wanted to apologize for whatever I said in last nights email. I was running on a sleepless night and stupid amounts of whisky, if I could remember what I wrote my apology would be more specific but I can only imagine that I embarrassed myself immensely.
Vx

Feb 2nd
That was so strange, as I sent my last email you were sending me one back! I just kissed my screen x…

Feb 3rd
Re-read what I wrote, I am sorry to explode on you like that, I just feel Dennis can be so intense and I spend the evening trying to hold myself together while he stabs me (and us) with his prong, then I get home and just want to cry. God I sound pathetic. Sometimes I think it is just because he does not like me at all…he really hates part of me at least. But as he confessed—all he cares about is sex and power, which—I think—is very cheeky,

It is so frustrating because things I don't actually care about—like you loving everyone you meet, or you thinking that Dolly has prettier fingernails than I, he manages to get me with, and then I feel bad telling you because he is concerned I am going to destroy your friendship. And why does he have naked pictures of you and Dolly on his computer? Gross! What a pickle. He is such a smart man, I guess it is easy for him to pick me apart, and if he enjoys it—well, why shouldn't he?

ARRRRRRRRRRRRRRRRRRRRRRRRRRRR

Frustration
Vx

****

No matter how recent the last time I opened my computer, the proliferation of possibilities always seemed to multiply. So many breasts soaked in lotion and cocks, women with phone numbers, and live dens I could visit if I was a good enough boy. Late one night in February, I visited I OWN YOUR COCK and found, to my delight, that a few new operators were working for Alessandra. I clicked on Hannah, immediately turned off by the opening sentence of her manifesto, "I am your salvation." There was a link to a voice recording but the file was corrupt. I cycled back to the icon-list of mistresses—must have been over thirty phone sluts working for Alessandra. I found Sandra. She was pictured as a smiling strawberry-blond. Inside was a different picture of a 30ish year old woman in a silk garter with a look of feigned shyness on her round, honeyish-hued face:

I am already becoming your addiction. It feeds off of my coquettish laughs. Sensuality, my slave, is serious. It would take sheer courage to bow down before me.

I am not interested in the toys and the sissy boys. I am interested in a man who knows he is one, and this is why he kneels down and lets my cunt juice drip past his eyes. It would please me to make you cry. It would be proof that you cared. When we begin, which we already have, sweetie, I would ask that you be honest with me, that way I can better fulfill your fantasies—soon, they will be mine, and you will want whatever I demand.

I have desires too. I want to be challenged by a man who pushes his limits and knows how to handle his cock. Don't bother me otherwise... XXX

140

I searched for more on Sandra, for a review or a voice recording. I couldn't find anything. I looked to see if she was taking calls. Her face popped up *available*. I yanked my phone out of my pocket. I had to listen to an obnoxious song for a few minutes. I turned off the lights, got naked, and snuck into bed. When the operator came on, one of the I OWN YOUR COCK ladies, she told me Sandra was on another call but if I wanted I could arrange a call back. "Okay…"

I was lying in bed with my hand on my cock wondering how long I would have to wait like that. I decided I should be loyal to this excitement and not move. I gave Sandra a head start on me by teasing myself. I pictured her fairly large breasts and that serious facial expression, emphasized by her serious prose, and I got dizzy off of these notions, moaning in bed as I traced two fingers up and down my shaft. Time passed. I said aloud, "I can't wait here like this." But something inside me said I could, and I was patient again. I started to leak, and I gently rubbed the stuff all over, and there was an exaggerated satisfaction from the feel of my pre-cum. I wanted the sensation to stay… I fought against its ebbings by speeding up or tightening my grip. This brought me too close to the edge, so I slowed down again…

I let my phone ring a couple times. My window was open and I caught a whiff of the garbage heap outside. I waited for the operator to connect me. "Hey, this is Sandra." Her voice was firm and nurturing. I pictured the fleshy part of her cheeks as they became her pursed pink lips. "You are my first caller… So what can I do for you this afternoon?" "I saw your post on I OWN YOUR COCK." "By the way, I wrote that myself." "I assumed you did." "My boss wanted to know where I copied it from—like phone sex operators are supposed to be stupid." "Yes… I was very impressed. I think most of all with how you asked to be challenged. If I read it right, you're saying that you're vulnerable too." "Did you ever think you were reading too much into my words, and that was exactly how I wrote them, to get you caught in your own projections... Is your cock hard right now, sweetie?" "Yes, it is." "I've got you by the balls, don't I?" "Yes," I laughed. "I'm assuming you like dominant women like myself to make you feel helpless and totally desperate? Did you see my pics?" "Yes." "You're not touching are you?" "No." "Oooooooo, someone has been trained very well. I like that. Bark for me puppy." I barked for her. "Oh, you're such a well-trained, mind-fucked puppy dog."

I leant the phone against my pillow and took a deep breath, I forced myself into Sandra's voice. "I am on my knees. Completely naked. Grab your cock and stroke it for me. My nipples are over your eyes, now they're in your mouth. Suck them puppy. I lean back. I have a tight little body. I'm only 5'2". I'm very fast. I kneel back and stuff your cock all the way down my throat. I gag on it. Now we are outside. We are near a pond. I pull you in. It's dark out. You're floating. I inject myself into you. Pump your cock harder slut, faster. I have my long wet hair between your legs, brushing against you. Your skin heating up where I have snuck in all over you. My head bobbing harder and harder, my hand squeezing tightly against your balls. Now cum for me, CUM for me, say 'I worship you Sandra.' Say 'I worship you Sandra' while you cum for me."

I hadn't had that good of a cum, my cock had felt the urge to pee the whole time, and this made my focus fade in and out. I was disappointed, and I knew when I said I would call her soon that I meant it, because I felt like I had missed out on something special.

I went back to my computer. Victoria had sent me a series of four pictures of herself drinking at what appeared to be a costume party. Her eyes and her blatant cleavage were the center of every picture no matter how many of her friends she posed with. She wore a white toga—dressed like the Venus she hated being compared to. Her eyes were so fucking blue contrasted against the white sheet and the two thick lines of kohl... In one picture she was lying full length and coy along a chaise lounge, eyeing the camera seductively with a drink in her hand... She and Dennis posed together in the final picture. He had painted his face white. He made a face of anguish while Victoria laughingly splashed into his arms. The text said that I had to come and visit. Everything was finally okay with Dennis, and they both really wanted to see me soon. I closed the computer.

I called Sandra two hours after saying goodbye to her. I could not concentrate on anything but Dennis and Victoria. "I didn't expect you to call back. You were very quiet when you said goodbye." "I get shy after I cum, and in all honesty, it was not a very good cum—because I had to pee, and I should have done it before I called you." Sandra laughed, "You should've told me, we could have done something interesting with that urge." "I need to feel like my cock is completely empty, but I guess you're right, it's a kind of prejudice." "You should do what makes you comfortable. Do you have to pee now?" "Yeah, when you put it like that I do." "Good, I wanna make you feel like you need to relieve yourself whenever you talk to me." "Should I go and then call you back?" "Are you on a cell phone?" "Yes." "I want to hear you pee. Go!"

I opened the door to my bedroom and crept through the hallway to my bathroom. The paint on the ceiling was clumped up and pealing near the overhead light from all the humidity that accumulated when I lay on the bathroom tiles listening to the shower. I picked up the toilet seat. I was cold. It took a lot of concentration for me to pee because I had a hard on. I asked Sandra to be quiet. She giggled when the first tinkles hit the bowl. "That's a good boy, your shaft is ready now?" "Yes." "One more thing." "Ok?" "I have heard horror stories of women taking men for all they're worth. That's not what I'm interested in. I am very nurturing. Alessandra does not know how to advertise me because, though I am dominant, I am still a caring human being. So please tell me you're not hurting yourself financially by calling me. You can afford this right?" "Yeah, I can. It's my mother's credit card I'm using." "She doesn't care?" "I don't use it for anything else. Technically I am not supposed to use it, but she doesn't have much power over me. It's a strange situation. I'm an underpaid schoolteacher—but I have access to some of my parent's money—but since I use it for my perversions, I can't use it for food. I can only use so much before they would cancel it on me. Anyways, I wouldn't jeopardize myself, I'm not interested in that fetish." "Can I ask you something?" "Yeah." "Why aren't you a rich asshole? You could have fooled me?" "I don't understand what you're asking." "Why do you live as an underpaid school teacher instead of working for your father or a bank? You wouldn't have to struggle like you say you do." "So you're my fantasy and my conscience?" "Quit it puppy, you don't get to be witty when I'm asking you questions. Tell me!" "I don't know. I hate all these words. If you know what I mean you know there is no right and good way to put it. Around the age of nineteen my eyelids pealed back. You know it happened to Prince Guatama. It's not that strange." "It's just very hard for me to hear because I would do anything to have what you have." "Why don't you seduce it all out of me?" "You wouldn't let me." "Don't let me decide." "How old are you?" "Twenty-Five." "You're a baby." "I thought I'm a puppy." "You want me to use your prick for my pleasure now?" "Yes." "Bark for me puppy." I barked for her. "How big is it?" "It's eight inches hard." "Girth?" "Average." "Are you happy with it?" "For the most part." Sandra quit chitchatting and I went silent.

My cock had been hard the whole time we were talking, it felt so good to put my cold hands on it. Sandra had me

144

do a number of different strokes for her. She made me use my palms on the side of my cock as if I was starting a fire. She had me put my finger in my asshole and say, "I like getting fucked in the ass!" She had me stand up and fuck the air without using my hands. Then she told me to pour lotion onto my pillow and fuck it until I came. While I was fucking it, she had me picture her large wet pussy rocking violently against my hips. "You must be tired now." "I am, exhausted." "…It was nice talking to you. I'll be hearing from you soon." Click.

Feb 10th
So this is john... the teacher/Prince Guatama...

Sorry about the first somewhat aborted phone call. Definitely interested in
you... like the thought of you on all fours, all cat-like and
purring... Okay... Hopefully we shall talk soon... I only really meet
sexy people in the airwaves.
john

Feb 12th
Yes, I remember you clearly. I'm so glad to see you sent a note. I felt strange guilt after speaking with you. I am rather cat like in motion but not mentality. A cat will hold a mouse by the tail, let it go, then catch it again...let it go, grab it, catch it again. Let it go...grab it....you know what's coming...I should say something here like "I guess I am cat like" - but really only my "purr" is.

I like how you enjoyed being with sensation. I probably have never wanted a webcam so much in my life!

With regard to sexy people on the airwaves, though. So much of what we experience is disembodied as it is, even when it's right in front of your face. Strangely enough, our anonymity allows for something curiously authentic, and I think we should explore that. Yes I do.

145

Thank you for your sweet murmurs,
SandraSandra

Feb 12th
... I do have one misgiving SandraSandra (is this really doubled, or is
this me hallucinating?), it concerns the money factor. What I mean to
say is that the fact that I am the one investing and you the one collecting creates a certain lopsidedness in the ambition of our sexual interests
which makes me doubt authenticity. Then again, I like the idea of being taken for my money. But, you must admit, somewhere in the desire
to connect with others the commoditization of it all weakens the con-
nection. I do not know if this is too much to the point of the matter--
your thoughts are welcome, as you seem to have many. As for me, I
piss and I cum and I write... Yeah!

J

Feb 13th
I recently re-read through most of JP Satre's "Nausea". I remember
the description of his hand, where it seems as though it is independent
of him - that he is somehow amazed at his incarnation in flesh and
bone, pissing and cumming...and overcome with seasickness at the
unconsciousness around. These sort of things strike me. Shake me...
leave me wondering what it really is that we do. But then, my gawd, to
look at just a hand for the first time - recognize its fragility, its miracle.

To just suck fingers can then be a joy all its own.

Perspective being everything, I respect this response. This excites me
also (the sexy talk), but I'm more happy to see you question than anything else. I thought you would. Maybe I'm naive, but I have this be-
lief about being able to divine a zen experience from anywhere - within
any environment.

The level of illusion here is what's up for discussion, and although it is
my job to cast a line and bait a hook and reel that line in, I am more
concerned with being a human being - and being good at that. In my

146

personal set of definitions, a "good human being" is described by an integrity that's present in any environment - even the theatre of the mind. Hard to manage? You betcha - it demands humility, mostly.

Under any other circumstances, you and I would not have the op to roll the dice in this way and come across each other. I would not read-ily cast out my home phone number.

In "real" life, I'm told I talk too much, and I write way too much. I'm seen as cute. A good kisser. But intimidating in ways that don't allow for the vulnerability of me to be as visible. I am here to take up the task of bringing in an income that supports my art (photography) but is not devoid of the human touch - fascination with what's base and ever-evolving.

Yes, what you do in calling supports me, but it supports me in ways the greenback, the boss, and the system at large would not suspect or even understand. The commodities exchanged are more rare than cash but the cash is ever necessary to allow me to be here at all.

(we've spoken once; all that is the world we're in compels me to heed warnings too - so it is double vision for now - meaning, SandraSandra)

Feb 14th
Interesting you bring up Sartre and his existentialism, only because it is in a sense antithetical to the ideas I am posing about cash crops—if the pussy were to be harvested. Meaning: one can never simply suck a finger—that finger has symbols, mythologies and values which will never allow us to simply suck the finger, and, twould be a nasty lie for us to believe that in sucking a finger we were at last sucking the finger as it should be sucked... I did not mean to stir up so much with this question; now I see it is essential in a way; and I would say to you, in terms of being authentic, I would prefer you to be bluntly persuasive in getting me to cough up the dough—otherwise we would be ignoring our hands, if you will. Realize that since you are in the position of pro-fessional there is a certain respect and subordination immediately im-posed on me; once the cash is transferred, it is you who subordinates yourself to me—for you have to give me my money's worth. I agree

147

that an opportunity appears in this situation which should be appreciated, indulged, explored—but let us not forget its parameters…

I guess web cam, another call, are next of order, Sandra…Sandra…

J

Feb 14th
I wish to hear you read that first statement up to "nasty lie" while I do in fact listen and suck your fingers, and could you be a bit feisty about it? I can tell you have the ability to speak with passion. I can listen as well as I suck. Sometimes doing both at once.

Which is rarely the case, anywhere - ever. We listen as if it is all a familiar tune; listen to catch the beat we recognize, rarely daring to think a note might come that is newly evolved- just right this minute. Not likely. What is the sound of my tune hummed into the soft space at the back of your scrotum?

What is a moment for you? Do you believe we have one -ever- that is fresh or, Dear, is it all an amalgam of past tense? And what is internal mythology - to you. Granted, so much - these words for instance, are not discovered; we are regurgitating what we know. A processed block of experience spam. The mystery meat of being. How dare we be so arrogant that we think we'll stumble on some fleshy organ of yearning that is a private secret of a few who are brave enough to push their boundaries of ego, embarrassment, and making of sense.

We have our reversal of roles, of course. If you are not starving, but I am - then you're accurate that the obligation falls to me as the needful thing. But you do look a bit hungry to me. It appears we can flip flop on occasion? Or is "Daddy has the cash" - a function of your laziness - an expression of the only time in your life you are really, truly elementary?

Is my sight clear, as I blink at the light that is John - happily?

And yes, a fat wallet - the smell of money - is a scent I like. You should consider it the strongest of aphrodisiacs in general - will serve you well, as can I.

But Don't forget, this whole exchange excites me.

A call yes...and oh, to see you touch on webcam...to have the visual of your edges and cliffs.
Sandra

Feb 20th
You haven't let go yet Jonathan; I realize this. It's a tad disappointing, but I suspect we'll find your lungs. The want is there, and I think the ability.
.
Fork to mouth. You chew; I chew. I feel your saliva, the movement of your jaw. Know that I am pleased by chocolate, chai, black tea, Indian food (spicy, not mild), hummus, a doughy pretzel with mustard, water, wine, fruit. And each time you please me in taste, I will rub my cheek against your testicles and hum in pleasure.

Expect it to begin as an itch. The itch in your back will be too hard to reach as I instruct it to present itself. Or a tingle in your scalp as I move my lips along the underside of your every follicle. This is how you'll know I've arrived.
You might walk with utter confidence in one minute and then find yourself huddled in the grass, fetal and without will - frantically jerking your pretty penis in the open air. As the police carry you away, I would send breath through your lungs in a fit of inappropriate, mad laughter - much to the dismay of onlookers, even friends.

I so enjoy silky panties, and wish us to buy a pair. Some shade of rouge. And a ring for your cock. I want to feel our scrotum hugged tight.

I want to see through your eyes. Go to the Flower District, take pictures for me. Let me feel how you see.

From you, I want all that there is to experience. In a word, everything.
Sandra

149

I received this email from Sandra at a time when I was waiting impatiently for Victoria to respond to the flight information I had proposed. My window, which rarely let in light, was oddly generous that morning. I felt rested, I put on a fresh pair of jeans and a warm, black fleece. The air in my room had a sweetness to it, as if I had recently tidied up and done my laundry. I grabbed a brown winter cap and my digital camera. I walked anxiously out my door. It was Saturday. I had the whole day to myself. I scurried down past the scuffed enamel on the walls and staircases of my apartment building, opening the black gate to a gust of cool wind and a slash of sunlight palliated by the cumulus clouds hurrying through the line of brownstones towards the East River. I walked quickly along the sidewalk. My balls humming.

At the café it turned me on just to order Chai Tea. I sat at a wooden table and stared shyly at everyone. They were still hidden behind their laptop computers. The taste was sharp, herbal, it flooded through me—and my cock got hard and I wanted to run into the bathroom and stroke myself vigorously. My clothing felt fresh. I sipped more of the tea. My balls started humming. I wondered what would happen if I stopped focusing on Sandra's commands, would they still hum, had she reached that far inside me?

I finished my drink, then I took the long subway ride into Manhattan. I got off at Broadway & Lafayette. Everyone looked very sexy. I felt myself in the wind, brushing up against satin coats and other delicacies like cheekbones and lips. The colors radiated solidly in what was now a precise white light. Some of the buildings had large fenestrations, tinted blue. Monstrous women bathed in grease and seductive postures loomed far on down Houston.

Inside Victoria's Secret everything was pink and yellow. All the women had bronzed cheeks. I was proud of my embarrassment, my cheeks were the color of all these undergarments, and I had an itching premonition of how satisfying it would be to place the silk on my hard cock. A cheerful black lady with rouge on her face came up to ask if I needed assistance. "Yes, I'm looking for pink, silk panties." "Do you know what size you're looking for?" "I think a medium." "Do you know what size your girlfriend usually wears?" "A medium." She fingered through a stack of panties. "Nothing with ruffles, those plain ones are fine." There were fluorescent yellows, oranges, greens and pinks. I walked out with a pink bag and a pink box with a bow. Right outside I found a vendor selling pretzels. The mustard made me cringe as I watched the Polish man squeeze it all over. I did not like mustard much, but that somehow got my balls to hum even stronger—and I again pictured myself dashing off madly and stroking myself without conscience.

I had never been to the Flower District before. I felt silly about the idea, but once I let myself go, I got a little lost in the tiny block. The owners of the stores encouraged me to take photographs—seeing as my objects of affection were so undeniably photogenic. I mostly aimed my sight on small, enigmatic flowers, ones which were worn like autumn leaves. I was getting horny—I took a walk through a forest of orchids and through full-sized plants with giant leaves—and I could not resist, behind the view of the convex mirror, shoving my hand onto my cock, and it felt like each pore was an individual thought, and my nipples shuddered as my mind subsided. I took fifteen photos in all, and I was still completely eroticized as I walked back to the subway to go home.

****

Feb 22nd

Dearest Pan,

I wrote a letter as to why you coming = bad idea but fuck it - just come. Will send the email tomorrow explaining why it is a bad idea then we can have a discussion and a vote. After all we live in the free world, democracy please.

But the truth is thinking of you coming gives me shivers, disgusting. I don't think I like feeling out of control. Remember the rubbish rotting out of me?

How is Samuel? How is Dolly?

better get back to the party; I can hear the piper blowing up her pipes again. How sad am I that I sneaked away to write you an email, like a little squirrel gathering nuts for the winter. That is such a cute image! One day let's gather nuts together.

VEX

Feb 23rd
About all those people in my life...more to come, but to summarize: Dolly completely gone, Samuel (he is away in Italy. I fear that our slumber parties are over, though I have a good feeling we are going to remain close friends). My oft dreamed of bedmate is across the ocean, as you know. Thankfully, she often flirts words my way. Ok, again, you are very very cute, Victoria, and funny, looking forward to our plebiscite tomorrow. Hope our citizens are looking towards the future and do not stay enmired in reactionary politics.
J

Feb 23rd
More Confession. Ever since your email--with all that imagery, and your presence, the way it has crawled into me—and I know I cannot turn my head to ward it off, for it is within. I have already stormed into my room and cradled my cock-buried under the covers, knowing that I have your nipples to excite, pinch, stretch and swell—and my watering jaw is your tongue. Already this has caused me a bit of para-noia, the intensity—the delusion or non delusion aspect of the situa-tion. Also, I feel that I am disobeying this other woman in my life... Can I ask of you favors, or do you grow of your own accord? Were I

to get a favor from you it would be to temper yourself until March 13th—oh this pure paranoia, but I would hate to have to explain to this girl that I have been seeded by you. Where does one begin to explain such a thing? It is that I am caught between what is a healthy sexual drive and the ethics of relationships. Maybe you can teach me new ethics. Like that my hard cock has priority. Oh, it is very dangerous all this. Surprisingly, I must say.

J

Feb 24th
My dearest vex,
On waiting

"In this extreme point of waiting where for a long time what is awaited has served only to maintain the waiting..." Maurice Blanchot

Am feeling a little uneasy after everything with Dennis, can you send me something sweet?

Over and Out
J
Feb 25th
So you want sweetness you say.... tonight, in all the glam, dresses, suits and fine wines, I kept on WISHING you would be there to hold my hand, giving it the odd squeeze when we got trapped into some stupid small talk with an insufferably boring banker. You would have eaten the half of my cake I couldn't finish, and played with the tassel on my long black dress, wanting to find a quiet corner where we could just kiss. That was my fantasy of the eve.
And I think it is pretty disgustingly sweet.

Maybe we are like 'unreal' close friends because it feels like we are just talking to ourselves? I hope it is more than that though.

MY PAN

Naked

Victoria

153

I waited for SandraSandra to accept me as a friend. Once she did, I pressed the video camera icon and my face came up on the screen. I messed up my curls and forced my expression away.

SandraSandra 1:31AM: i see you

sevendirex 1:32 AM: i feel strange

SandraSandra 1:32 AM: i see you

sevendirex 1:32 AM: i feel your eyes all over me

SandraSandra 1:33 AM: Look at ME!

I looked into the lens of the camera. I was shy. It had been easier to focus on my image at the corner of the screen. I felt like I had more control over myself that way.

SandraSandra 1:33 AM: you have very intense eyes. I'm getting shivers.

sevendirex 1:33 AM: Do I look like some smug, pretentious asshole?

SandraSandra 1:34 AM: no, you seem to have done your best to avoid looking like that

sevendirex 1:34 AM: Do you like how I look?

SandraSandra 1:34 AM: show me more.
SandraSandra 1:34 AM: get hard for me
SandraSandra 1:34 AM: get hard now
SandraSandra 1:35 AM: feel your balls humming

SandraSandra 1:35 AM: take your hard cock out
SandraSandra 1:35 AM: Show me your cock

I got giddy to find my cock so hard so quickly. I lowered the webcam and made sure my cock was in the center of the picture.

SandraSandra 1:36 AM: let me see you stroke it …squeeze it tight.

All my veins were bulging on the camera.

SandraSandra 1:38 AM: callmecallme, call me this minute I'll tell Alessandra to block all the other callers.

I went to get my phone.

SandraSandra 1:38 AM: Don't leave me…let me watch you call me.

I readjusted the webcam.

SandraSandra 1:39 AM: lie back down
SandraSandra 1:39 AM: want to see your face and your cock.

I stripped naked and lay against my wall. At the corner of the screen I saw myself. I had to listen to that obnoxious song before I connected to Sandra. I kept staring at myself, it was the only way to feel comfortable knowing she was watching me. She had me show her all the goodies I had bought. She wanted the cock ring on her cock. My cock's veins looked like they were going to explode with the added tension of the cock ring. Sandra loved the veins and she had me trace them with my fingertips. She told me to lube up my palm and stroke the shaft without touching the head. I had to take giant breaths of air to maintain my composure. She had me jerk fast—on a whim, and then to stop me from cumming, she had me squeeze it as tightly as possible. "Tighter!" She had me get a shoelace and knot it around my balls and the base of my shaft. She told me to make it hurt. My cock was bulging so much that when I took it into my hand it felt like a monolith grown over with vines. I gulped and I grew voracious. And that's when she had me pose for her in the panties. The feel of them on my cock was relieving, I dug the silk into my cock. My nipples were getting hard and I was feeling very pretty. She had me rub the spot under my head as if it were my clitoris. She had me pant like I was a little girl. I think she lost her cool then—because I could have lasted much longer. She had me rip off all the accoutrements and ordered me to cum. She had me go for it without hesitation. It took longer to buildup than I was used to. I was already orgasming a minute before any of the cum came out. When it did, it popped straight up, it hit the wall above my head. I could see my exhaustion on the screen. "That was so beautiful," Sandra said, "You have no idea how sexy you are." I looked at myself on the screen—"No, I just try to enjoy myself." "That's what's so sexy." "I want to clean up." "No, lie in your cum, you look so vulnerable." I lay there. "We should show you off to our other customers. You could be the success story. Jonathan and his indefatigable cock. Okay, I don't want to

156

charge you more, let's hang up, but stay, talk to me online."
"Okay." I hung up.

SandraSandra 2:45 AM: dont clean up yet.

sevendirex 2:45 AM: fine, but im gonna mess up my
        sheets.

SandraSandra 2:45 AM: did you take pictures of the
        Flowers?

sevendirex 2:45 AM: I did...was sort of embarrassing

SandraSandra 2:46 AM: good, you need to get over
        yourself.
SandraSandra 2:46 AM: i need to see through you. I'm a
        photographer.
SandraSandra 2:47 AM: images tell me so much. More
        than words.

sevendirex 2:47 AM: Are you really going to be able to do
        this?

SandraSandra 2:47 AM: Take you?

sevendirex 2:47 AM: yes, take me. take me away from my
        self.

SandraSandra 2:48 AM: brb
SandraSandra 2:51 AM: Do you want to know about me?

sevendirex 2:51 AM: the picture isn't real is it?

SandraSandra 2:51 AM: NO, I do have that color hair
        though.
SandraSandra 2:52 AM: and the smile on the small picture.

i chose it because it looks just like mine.

sevendirex 2:53 AM: where're you From?

SandraSandra 2:55 AM: I was born in Cali and I live in a small town outside Firebird, NV. I live with my grandmother. My grandpa just passed away and I've been taking care of her.

sevendirex 2:56 AM: i had a sense you were from the desert. I imagine you coming out from a crack in the dry sand…with your piercing green eyes right?

SandraSandra 2:56 AM: how did you know?

sevendirex 2:56 AM: obvious

SandraSandra 2:56 AM: i have an intense stare, like you. you would stutter if I looked at you

sevendirex 2:57 AM: I want to see them!!!!!!!!!!!!!!!!!!!!!!

SandraSandra 2:58 AM: I can't show you yet. There are things about who I am that would scare you. They scare most of the men in my life away. I would want to know you could handle this information before I revealed more of myself to you.

sevendirex 2:58 AM: i get it. i won't pry.

SandraSandra 2:59 AM: can you get hard again?

sevendirex 2:59 AM: Yes!

SandraSandra 2:59 AM: lean back…follow my instructions…

****

Feb 28th
Hello sweetness,

Glad to hear you emailed Dennis (nicely)… methinks he is looking forward to your visit, even though he calls you a bastard – which I think this time you might deserve! Should be fine us three hanging out right? Remember he was not trying to be cheeky about us, just told me things I already knew… Enough of that, everything is going to be fine and beautiful.

So on the 7th Christ Church is having a Christ Church only Heaven and Hell party, but because I am an honorary member (cough), we can go!! It is black tie, so you might want to bring something vaguely smart or borrow from Dennis. It should be fun, lots of free booze and girls in pretty dresses for you to look at.

VEX!! Hehe

****

I flew to Las Vegas the next weekend for my father's 60th Birthday. He had been trying for a while to get me to come on one of his fully paid-for shindigs and I finally acquiesced. My sisters were supposed to come as well but they bailed at the last minute. My father had flown all his friends out to Las Vegas, and he had rented out an entire wing of the Bellagio. I got a suite on the 5th floor all to myself. I opened the shades the moment I got inside. The fountains of the Bellagio were spouting above my window. Behind them were the strip, the Eiffel Tower, and a small line of people hurrying to the casinos. The imposing Rocky Mountains loomed flat as a billboard on the horizon. I opened the bar and took out a bottle of Champagne and started drinking it. In my giddiness I reread the text messages Victoria had been sending me the past few weeks.

Feb 16th 4:44 PM
In pub. Thinking about u…very naughty.

Feb 18th 2:55 PM
Oh Jonathan. If I could cycle as fast as the speed of light. I would be with u now. Tis been a lonely day without pan…even went & blew a kiss to the golden faun

Feb 21st 1:19 PM
Why do libraries make me feel so very naughty? Just imagined u appearing under the desk&pleasuring me here, heaving 2contain myself in this busy quiet place..?

Mar 1st 4:45 PM
Stop it. That is very naughty…. But it does work…touch me all over please

Mar 2nd 6:24 PM
So when does phone sexuality begin?

I had received the last text message waiting in line for a taxi at the Las Vegas airport. I had done my best to contain my relationship with Victoria to emails, but it was already crossing over to the phone, and I really could not help myself.

I had bought a calling card in the lobby of the Bellagio, and I was dialing away.

Victoria answered, "Mmmmmmmmmmmmmm…" She had the sexiest voice. "Is that you Pan?" "Yes, bunny." "Mmmmmmm, I am home in my bed." "Are you naked?" "Yes, I'm touching myself, I was thinking about taking control of you and telling you just how to touch me. You made me so wet." "Stop touching your pussy." "Okay…" "Just listen to me, I'll tell you what to do. Are your nipples hard?" "No?" "Are you okay?" "I don't know if I can do this." "Just don't think about it, do what I say." "Okay. Go on. You have a very sexy voice." "Touch your nipples, bunny. Squeeze them tight. Get them hard for me." Victoria lay in her bed. I longed to touch her body. I had been repressing this desire so as to not drive myself crazy. She was touching her breasts. "Okay, they are hard." "Pinch them honey, make them hurt a little." "Mmmmmmmm…. I want you so badly. I wish you were here." "Just listen to what I say, ignore my absence. Let me be there with you. Put one hand on your neck and hold it tight, then put one finger into your pussy. Is it still wet?" "Very." "Get your lips wet, rub your wetness up towards your clit… Rub your clit with the same finger, push against it." Victoria was touching herself beneath her flat, fleshy stomach. Her thighs were thick, and she was growing her pussy hair out at my request. I kept my eye on it. "I want to kiss you, bunny. I want to give you thousands of kisses and feel you smiling while I kiss you." "Yes please." "I miss you so much. It has been so hard these past few days." "Keep touching me." "Rub it harder honey, rub your clit harder." "Are you touching yourself?" "No, do you want me to?" "Yes, take off your pants. I want you to cum with me." "Put your fingers inside of you." "Imagine my mouth going down on you." I pictured her blue eyes looking up at me, her hair tied back behind her face. "Mmmmmmmm, I'm going to cum, are you getting close?" "Yeah, I can cum, tell me when."

161

"Mmmmm, you really are Pan, nobody makes me feel like this." "Cum for me baby. I'm inside of you. I'm fucking your pussy. Cum for me." "Ok, I'm cumming…" Her breathing started to expand, and I started to orgasm myself.

She was petting herself lightly, telling me she wanted more. "You shouldn't have had me cum then." "I wanted you to… Wait, hold on…" She fumbled with the phone and I could hear the ruffles of her bed. "Oh shit! Oh shit!" "What?" "Dennis and his friend Sofia want to come over and lie in bed with me, they just sent me a text message." "What?" "The two of them are so cheeky together. They play this game where we are all from The Story of the Eye. Dennis is Lord Auch, Sofia is Simone, and I am the virgin Marcelle." "That is disgusting." "I know, they wouldn't even know what to do with me if I gave them the chance. Not like my Pan." "Could you please just not talk about Dennis to me, he is so fucking annoying." "You're an asshole too you know." "I am not!" "You're an asshole to Dennis." "I don't like Dennis, of course I come off as an asshole to him." "Well, even though he is slightly cheeky, he is my friend, and I want you two to be friends with each other. Dennis is always telling me how much fun you two had together back in New York." "It was not fun. It was oppressive." "Maybe you need to get over your issues and be nice to him." "I can't have this fucking conversation, Victoria." "Sometimes I wish I never met either of you." "Look, it's you who triangulates things. I don't want anything to do with him, and I want to be with you. So…" "Ooo, oh no, they're here. I'm sorry petal, I'll call you soon." The phone clicked off.

I went into the giant bathroom and took a long shower. I took the Champagne bottle in with me and finished it off. My hotel phone rang, and I went to answer it, dripping water all over the plushy carpet in the bedroom. "Hello?" "Johnny?" "Yeah, hey Dad. How's it going?" "It's going fine. You like you're suite?" "Yeah, I have the view of the fountain and everything." "Mother and I want you to come upstairs in an hour. We need to have a conversation." "What about?" "It's not a big deal, just come up in an hour." "Okay, see you soon."

My parents had a penthouse suite on the 31st floor. They had to come down and meet me in the lobby because you had to have a key to press the elevator button to their room. My mother has thick brown hair, a rainfall of curls, and is very sweet and very elegant. She was dressed in pink terry cloth and looked like she had come from the Spa. My father is a short, handsome man, with big eyes and a Russian severity in his face. He is for the most part bald. He was dressed in sweat pants and a designer mesh shirt, and he was wearing a Chicago Cubs hat backwards. I always felt drunk when around my parents. They were always very happy to see me. My mother asked me about my diet, noticing that I was much skinnier than she remembered, and she also mentioned how she did not like my beard. "Well, I am growing it out for Victoria. She has this strange obsession with facial hair." "And she probably likes that you smell too?" "Actually…"

We all laughed as we walked down the carpet past a series of polished stone tables, and then we entered the penthouse suite. The windows looked out at the same view I had, it was just a lot higher, and instead of being dwarfed by the buildings and the mountains, I was now way above them. I could not see the people anymore down on the sidewalk. The fountains were no longer spouting. The room had an entertainment setup with couches and a desk area where my father had put his enormous laptop computer. There was also a circular table at which my father and mother had already seated themselves. "Sit down," my father commanded. I sat down. I smiled at my mother, she smiled back at me. She always smiled very warmly at me. "You look great," she said. I jokingly fidgeted with the color of my purple-striped shirt. "Is this about money, Dad?" "Yes, it's about money." "How did you guess?" My mother exclaimed, seriously surprised. "Listen, I'll stop using the credit card." "You're not gonna have a choice, we just canceled it an hour ago." "Alright, is that all?" "Well, we thought this might get you to change your lifestyle a little bit. Don't you think it's time you work for an employer who pays you on time. How much does the rabbi owe you?" "10,000 dollars." My father's face hardened, "It's not funny. How can you let him take advantage of you like that?" "Listen, I don't wanna talk about it. I pay very little rent, and I don't eat much. If you cancel my card fine, but it's not gonna make me be a different person." "It's going to have to." "How're you going to pay for phone sex?" My mother asked. "You guys aren't going to give me a monthly allowance for that?" My parents didn't flinch.

My father started giving a long lecture about investment and the possibility of giving me some money under the stipulation that he got to watch over it—if I started to use it recklessly, he would take it away from me. "Is that even possible to put money in my name and then have the ability to take it away from me?" "That is exactly the reason I am not about to go and give it to you." "Money is a pain in the ass, trust me. It is probably best you not give it to me, when I have money I indulge myself too much." My mother contorted her face in a giant smile, looking at her husband, "Fine, if he does not want any." "You guys decide. I'll be fine." I was looking out the window. The sky was blue without any clouds. I could see the reflection of my face in the window. I took out my cell phone and snapped some pictures of myself so I could send Victoria an image of my beard, and I knew she would laugh about 'how comedy' the penthouse was. I made very stoical faces. They were not that hard for me to muster. My father finished talking, and he gave me a big hug. He called me kiddo. He told me I needed to hurry on downstairs and take a shower because the limo buses were going to be here in an hour to take all of us to dinner—and afterwards, we were going to Cirque du Soleil. "Why didn't any of my sisters come?" "They are not as good of a child as you are," my mother said, facetiously grabbing me by the waist.

When I got back from Cirque du Soleil I was drunk. I went to the craps table, figuring, what the hell. I lost 200 dollars in a minute. I went up to my bedroom. I couldn't call Victoria because it was in the middle of the night in England. I thought about Sandra, I was in her state, but I couldn't call her anymore. I turned on the bathtub and lay down naked in the middle of the cold tile, using a towel as a pillow.

I woke up to find a thin film of water creeping into my nose. The whole bathroom was flooded. The lights were on bright. I went to take a piss, the water had made it in there too. I took a few towels, put them down in the doorway to the bedroom and got into bed. The bed was extra cushiony, and I fell asleep right away. Around 5:00 AM the hotel phone woke me up. "I'm sorry to wake you sir, we have a report of water dripping down into the engineering room which is directly below yours. Did you have a leak earlier?" For a second I forgot about the flood, and I was annoyed that they woke me. "Oh yeah, I left the bath running." "We are going to need to come upstairs and check for damages." I sat up in bed and turned the lampshade on.

The room was designed so that the bed faced the opposing wall at an awkward angle. Everything felt far away. A knock came on my door a few seconds after I hung up the phone. I could hear a walkie-talkie buzzing. A big man came in wearing a service uniform and asked me to show him the bathroom. "I'm sorry, I fell asleep." "It's not a problem. Luckily, it didn't leak down into a guest's room." "Is there any damage in the room where it's leaking?" "So far none... We're going to have to take some pictures and then we're gonna get a water vac up here to haul all this away, just stay put." I had a big headache... I read while the service men kept coming in and out of my room. One man came in and snapped all these photographs from different angles, another took down all my information. Finally an older man wearing the housekeeping uniform came up and vacuumed all the water. It took him awhile. He had to call for some towels to be brought up so he could dry up the corners.

I flew back to New York City that night, came in over the steel lights of Manhattan.

****

"You've been an animal for me sweetie." Laughter. "It is sweet you make these sounds. You are like a baboon, so stupid and so horny. You sound so pathetic. I can make you do whatever I want when you're like this. Your two fingers are moving at my command. You want to stroke with your whole hand but you can't. You're my mindless animal robot. Oh, you're so fucked. I'm fucking up your mind. You love that I'm destroying you. You want to give me all your money and all your cummies. You're more in love with me sweetie than you've ever been with anyone. I'm going to ask you a question and it's going to be very very easy for you to answer, and when you speak you will only fall deeper. Do you want to stroke your cock?" "Yeehszz. Plehzzzeezz. Goddess." I sounded like a pig. "Ha, ha, you are so desperately in love with me. You're going to have to speak to me once a week. If you don't a terrible pain will shoot through your body. Do you still want to stroke your cock?"

"Yeehszz, Plehzzzeezz, Pleeze, Goddess." My whole body was shaking.

"Okay, when I hit 0 you can stroke it. You will be fifty times deeper and more horny, but you won't cum until I tell you to. 5, you are in love with me, 4, you want to devote

166

your life to Goddess Dearheart, 3, you have no brain, you are a stupid and horny pig boy, 2, you are falling, you have no body—only my words, 1, you are so horny horny horny, 0, stroke it for me."

I grabbed my cock. I visualized the clusters rising all over me—it happened super fast. I was screaming, still not cumming. "Oh, listen to you, You're so sweet honey. I bet you really can't wait to cum." "Yeehszz!!!" I shouted. "Maybe I should tease you more." "No! Plehzzzeezz, Pleeze Goddess Dearheart." "Ok, you sound so pathetic and that makes me have so much affection for you. On the count of 3... One...twothree. Cum, Ha, ha, cum for me."

****

SandraSandra 11:58 AM: my real name is Sandrina Rox. I'm 36

sevendirex 11:58 PM: that's not so scary.

SandraSandra 12:00 PM: Two years ago I was obese. I weighed over 300 lbs. I was on the verge of death. I had gastric bypass surgery, and lost almost 200 lbs. I AM a photographer, and I do live in Nevada. And I do like Chai Tea, and I do live in the basement of my grandma's house. I also am definitely a dominant woman. So there it is, that is the real flesh and blood me. Sandrina. Are you turned off?

sevendirex 12:01 PM: i think that is unfair of you to ask. of course I'm not.

SandraSandra 12:01 AM: i can't trust you yet.
SandraSandra 12:01 AM: youre not even real
SandraSandra 12:01 AM: it must be easy for you not to care how I look

sevendirex 12:02 AM: i can't say one way or the other, you know that. i like that you've been through things.

SandraSandra 12:02 AM: who would have thought a young Jewish boy could have made me feel so much

sevendirex 12:02 AM: are you being Anti-Semitic?

SandraSandra 12:02 AM: just think it's funny, youre more the devil than a Jew.

sevendirex 12:02 AM: maybe the devil in me makes me Jewish. Look at my horns.

I pulled back my hair so she could see where they would protrude.

SandraSandra 12:03 AM: i love the veins on your arms. Show them to me.

I turned my palms out and raised my arms up close to the camera.

SandraSandra 12:04 AM: mmmmmmmmmmmmmmm
SandraSandra 12:04 AM: you are intoxicating
SandraSandra 12:04 AM: fully and truly..to the depth of me

sevendirex 12:04 AM: i am so happy for this

SandraSandra 12:04 AM: sonnet worthy
SandraSandra 12:04 AM: being an idiot human being
                          makes sense in this context

sevendirex 12:06 AM: i know what you mean by making
                        love a verb
sevendirex 12:07 AM: something like in the act of loving
sevendirex 12:07 AM: and cyclical
sevendirex 12:07 AM: rechargeable
sevendirex 12:07 AM: beyond the pale affection of a
                        married couple
sevendirex 12:07 AM: and by beyond
sevendirex 12:07 AM: i mean in different oceans
sevendirex 12:07 AM: outside of the realm of sleep
sevendirex 12:08 AM: as i see it it means transparency
sevendirex 12:08 AM: like you said
sevendirex 12:08 AM: constant
sevendirex 12:08 AM: even in shades of grey moods

SandraSandra 12:08 AM: ACK

sevendirex 12:08 AM: flushing them out this way

SandraSandra 12:08 AM: sometimes you don't know what
                        you say
SandraSandra 12:08 AM: John...
SandraSandra 12:08 AM: fuck
SandraSandra 12:08 AM: in
SandraSandra 12:08 AM: jesus
SandraSandra 12:09 AM: christ almighty
SandraSandra 12:09 AM: you know what's weird?

sevendirex 12:09 AM: tell

SandraSandra 12:09 AM: in a grey scale....there is a range
SandraSandra 12:09 AM: a camera meter reads 18% grey
as middle grey..the barometer of
all else that is..for a right expo-
sure..one is looking to have that
shade...be that shade...to
expose properly
SandraSandra 12:10 AM: there are ways and means to
test
SandraSandra 12:10 AM: things you learn
SandraSandra 12:10 AM: for instance...concrete at times
and green grass are close to
middle grey
SandraSandra 12:10 AM: but the good photographers
learn how many shades their
own palm is FROM middle
grey
SandraSandra 12:12 AM: assuming you are always with
yourself...you are always
there to read from.
SandraSandra 12:12 AM: people use this in the extreme in
other venues..being self-
referential.
SandraSandra 12:12 AM: all roads lead to the self it
seems...
SandraSandra 12:12 AM: when you tell me we will fuck
well because we can "be
outside ourselves"...I wanna
pass out
SandraSandra 12:12 AM: or I want to be hit by lightening
SandraSandra 12:12 AM: really bad
SandraSandra 12:13 AM: because its words..simple
words..that once strung
together..tap a nerve...I have

thought others have tapped
into it (and been WRONG)...but
you do it...in spades..over
and over..like a waving of flags
from the universe itself saying,

SandraSandra 12:13 AM: "Sandrina, don't look away just
yet. Not now."

SandraSandra 2:57 AM: your eyes..looking up at me...
reminded me of my own...a
mirror image of my drive and my
want..only blue..deepest blue...

sevendirex 3:00 AM: sounds like we are in for a long
turbulent exquisite ecstatic haul

SandraSandra 3:00 AM: and if it were one fucking hour..I
swear to you..I promise you...on
all that is holy and right

sevendirex 3:00 AM: you paint such a tremendous picture

SandraSandra 3:00 AM: if you walked out on the street
and died by a bizarre piano from
heaven incident

SandraSandra 3:01 AM: your last thought would be my
honest, pure

SandraSandra 3:01 AM: passionate, crazy love

SandraSandra 3:02 AM: rooted, firmly with authority, in
understanding..not to
oppress...EVER...only to buttress
this shit of life

SandraSandra 3:02 AM: away

SandraSandra 3:02 AM: from your sacred back

SandraSandra 3:02 AM: the spine I long to trace with my
finger tips

SandraSandra 3:02 AM: and rest my head in

sevendirex 3:03 AM: when I am done pounding you
sevendirex 3:04 AM: caressing you
sevendirex 3:04 AM: pleasuring you
sevendirex 3:04 AM: when i cum all over your tits and your
face
sevendirex 3:04 AM: more than anything in the world
sevendirex 3:04 AM: do i long to lie in tired non-identity
sevendirex 3:04 AM: in your sweat and your flesh
sevendirex 3:04 AM: !!!!!

****

Victoria sent me a picture of herself walking in a winter coat through a snow-covered street. Her scarf trailed behind her.

Mar 4th
How exciting!! You should jump into the picture, grab my hand and force me to
play...alas...I am in the library - 'working'.

Mar 5th
You really have a finger on my pulse...witchy woman...I'll join you in Everheart lane, follow the scarf and the mist of snow kicking off your feet... get lost, get warm, get buried...

Then you can boil me in your kettle.

Mar 6th
Boil you in my kettle aye? I have an oven to put you in instead, I prefer my meat roasted. I think you would go very well with runner-beans and roast potatoes...with custard as dessert.

Just to clarify, so you don't get your hopes up...the bop is more

like a mini posh party than ball as it is only for the graduates in a couple of small rooms...but I like small and to be honest I don't really care
as more excited about seeing you. More admin: dietary requirements –
I know you aint Kosher...but there's pork and shell fish on the menu?
Or is that a no-no?

Mar 7th
No concerns about the particular, from my side of the pond... Boil me,
Bake me, Brew me, Rape me... as Jesus, Pan, Tumnus or John... at the
party, away from the party, in St. Edmunds behind Mercury's fountain,
in your bed, the bathroom... really, I think about one week ago...when
the snow all settled, I grew patient... Like the fantasies I have had and
had been having of you...all just withered into smoke... It will be like we
never said goodbye that day at the bus station, not even rushing to
embrace each other, because we have been embracing these past few
months, and then of course embracing still... we will both laugh while
it is happening because we knew that such a thing was bound to happen, even though we could never foresee a single touch or sensation...
But time's accordion will string us along... Besides... I think my mouth
will just start watering when I see you... Tomorrow!

****

At 4:00 AM, I got up to shower. In the mirror I could
see my worn eyes. I packed my toiletries and took a long
shower. The water did not wash away my discomfort. I accepted as much. I called for a cab. I waited outside on the
front stoop in the gray and cold. Nobody was out there. The
wind blew absent-mindedly against the naked branches. The
cab pulled up. We headed to Queens. At the Kosciusko
Bridge the city was absent, covered in fog. The gravestones
fluttered past as we drove on, tediously, through morning rush
hour.

I could not sleep on the airplane, the engine was too
loud—my legs cramped and my body dehydrated. I was

173

counting the hours I had been awake. I feared I would be sniveling when I finally met Victoria. The city and its lights came in through the six hours of fog. I wanted the energy to kiss Victoria, just once. I wanted to see her in her black dress. I wanted to stare back at her. We touched down. I had intentionally brought only carry-ons. I ran past a series of advertisements in the endless halls.

I made it to the bus stop and called Dennis from a payphone. "You're in Oxford?" "No, I'm still at Heathrow... I'll be in in an hour." "Jonathan?" Victoria's voice came anxiously through the phone. "Hey Victoria, one more hour." "I hope your flight wasn't too miserable." "It was awful, it doesn't matter. I'm excited to see you." "Oooo, me too." Dennis came back on, "Alright, alright. Go catch your bus Jonathan." The bus came ten minutes later. There was nighttime traffic on the British highways. I curled up on the seats trying to stop my heart from knocking on me. I couldn't stop it... Trees started to fill up the windows and I knew we were near.

We pulled in behind a plaza of food shops. No one was there so I went to a payphone booth. After putting a pound in the slot, Victoria and Dennis came out from a side alley, all dressed up and smiling. Dennis had on devil's ears and a tuxedo, and Victoria wore a low cut black dress and Brazilian earrings. Her eyes stayed on me, "I love your beard." She started crawling her hands through it. We did not kiss right away. Dennis barged in and said, "You look like shit." "I didn't sleep much." We walked around the corner and headed to Christ Church. Victoria had been worried that I would not find her beautiful anymore because she had dyed her hair black, but it only accentuated her eyes, and I told her as much as we walked down the cold streets looking nervously at each other and politely joking with Dennis. We had to open a heavy wood gate which led into a giant plaza. In the center was the fountain of Mercury.

Victoria took me into a changing room and locked the door behind her. I took out my suit, which was folded at the top of my backpack. We started to kiss. I had never seen such a happy expression on someone's face. I kept kissing her more and more, nibbling on her lips and on all the squishy parts of her cheeks. "I really like your beard, it's hot." I pulled away from her. I undressed to my boxers. Victoria, with the way she lusted after me, made me feel sexier than I had ever felt before. I was something strong, wild, and nimble. I put on my navy Ermenegildo Zegna suit and knotted a deep blue tie over a powder blue shirt. Victoria complimented me with a flurry of kisses, then she took me by the hand. "Everyone is waiting for you. Well, not everyone, but a lot of people are interested to meet you." "I don't want to meet anyone, I just want to be by you." "Come on silly." We went underneath some streamers and a sign that read 'Christ Church's Heaven and Hell Ball.' All the guys were wearing tuxedos, and the girls had sequins, pink lipstick, and high heel shoes. My hand was tossed around.

The dance floor was in a large, high-ceilinged lounge—and it seemed that Victoria and Dennis were hosting the party because they had special access to the drinks and the music. Victoria had already left my side. She was flirting with a classmate and then dancing with another. She was steadily getting drunker and drunker. Dennis was dancing too, with a skinny German boy who studied architecture. Victoria came up to me and we kissed against the nearest wall. "This is very bad. I feel very cheeky. I do this thing called planting seeds. Dennis knows all about it. He does it too… It's where I flirt with someone so I get all his attention, but I never really want to do anything. Oooo, oh no. I feel very naughty. There are three guys here whom I planted seeds with. They are all very jealous of you." "It's okay, I like watching you flirt, makes me feel like I have achieved the ultimate feat. The shy boy who has lured the social butterfly into his unrelenting clutches." "You're quite vain aren't you, Mr. Direx?" "No, it's just part of the act." She caught the eye of a friend she had not expected to see and ran away from me. I took my drink to the large oriel window where the rain was coming down. Victoria was kissing some other guy, it seemed, but then I wasn't sure. She flittered about so pretty-like. I was totally in love with her. Everywhere I stepped she remained my focus.

Victoria and I were lying on a pillow kissing madly underneath a staircase. The little nook was protected from the outside eye by a curtain. Taped to the front of the curtain was a paper sign designating the nook: 'Purgatory.' "You are so fucking hot, Victoria," I said as I grabbed her all over. She stopped suddenly, and she held my hands with each of hers, like she had a very serious matter to discuss. "Dennis makes me so mad, John. He is so brilliant. He says such mean things to me. Like the other day he made fun of me because I scuff my feet. I could kill him. But he is so smart." She tried to make fun of the final word but affirmed it instead. "You know I don't even like him." "Yes, and that really confuses me too. You're supposed to be his best friend. It's mean how you ignore him." "Listen, Victoria, smart people don't force people to recognize that their smart. Being smart is about ethics not knowledge, if it's about anything at all." Victoria lit up when I said this, "You always make me feel so much better. I wish I could believe in what you say when you're not around. I feel very strong when I'm with you." "So stay with me..." I went to kiss her, but she backed up. She was shaking her head, knitting her brow. "Come on..." I tried to pull her close again, "I don't get this at all, Victoria." "I can't, I know you'll leave me. Dennis told me you would." She ran off before I could catch up with her.

Victoria, Dennis, and I were all lying in 'Purgatory.' Two friends of theirs, Russell and Erica, were making out on the floor. The two of them fell in love right there in front of us, even though Victoria had rejected Russell that very night and Dennis had rejected Erica the night before. They were both blond and strong and beautiful and brilliant. Dennis was pale and whining about how drunk he was. He had himself laid out very dramatically. "You fucking people and your illusions. It's pathetic." "Dennis, are you well enough to walk home?" Victoria asked. "I'm fine, darling." "Okay, is it okay if Jonathan stays with you tonight?" "What?" I said, looking at her angrily, "What're you talking about?" "I just really want to sleep alone tonight." "I came all the way here to see you, not Dennis, Jesus Christ." "Ooooo, please don't make this hard, I can't make decisions right now." Dennis importuned, "You don't want to sleep with me tonight, darling beaver? We don't have to do it head to toe, if that's what you prefer."

I pulled Victoria into the hallway, "What the hell?" I kissed her so she could make no other decision. She kept changing her mind, kissing me, then backing away. Dennis came up with his shirt untucked and unbuttoned, he pulled Victoria away from me. When I got back to them in 'Purgatory' after collecting my bags, Dennis said, "She is going to let you stay, but you have to promise not to have sex with her." "I'm not a fucking retard, Victoria, just tell me what you want. All I really want is to hold you. Why the fuck do you have to make me out to be some—" Victoria started reddening, and Dennis turned her face towards his and mumbled what must have been consolations.

We all left back through the gates. We had to dodge under the vaultings and the façade ornaments to keep from getting soaked in the rain. When it died down, Victoria and I took a long clumsy walk past all the Colleges until we reached her room on a small side street. We fell asleep naked smelling of alcohol.

Victoria's giant window looked out on a backyard and a small, shingled home. In the morning, the light peering in lit up her walls and one side of her face. She had Picasso's, Degas', Zeus, Priests, Rabbis, Girls in Bikinis, Bearded ex-boyfriends, collages, and bowls filled with bracelets all about her room. We woke up at the same time and started kissing heavily, my cock was stiff. We smiled happily and dove for each other. I asked if I could fuck her and she said please. I didn't wait. I arched my back so I could aim straight, and when I hit the initial resistance, I slowly stretched it open, feeling all the sensations push into my stomach. Victoria cocked her eyes, she looked distressed, and this made me want even more to start pounding her as hard as I could possibly fuck. I was so fucking angry with her. I hated her for being such a coy cunt. And I squeezed her mouth and gritted my teeth and slapped her face as I gave her an ear-splitting orgasm which was punctuated by the opening of her enormous blue eyes—as if she hadn't seen the sun in months. I continued to pound furiously. I pulled her hair. I thought my teeth were going to break loose, I gritted them so hard. Her eyes were closed, and her mouth was expressing agony. And I just tried to increase it more and more until her eyes burst open again. She wanted and needed more still. I twisted my body so that she ended up on top of me. I had her push her hands against the wall. I rocked my hips incessantly, pumping like a fast precise motor; she came again, this time it was on my chest. And I squeezed her breasts so hard, I tugged them, I feared I was going to rip them off. I slapped her face. She panted her tongue. I told her to keep it open, to stick it out, to pant for me. I slapped my hand against her wagging tongue. "Good Girl." "Good girl." I fucked her until she had cum six times, then I lay back and enjoyed the bliss of her mouth on my cock—and I screamed as I poured it all into her. She was all giddy and cuddly and loving and we laughed about how nice things were.

It was warmer in England than it was back in New York. Many of the trees were already starting to bloom. Even

178

an anomalous blue sky hung over Oxfordshire. It had been a long time since I could go outside in only a sweater. I wore the black one Samuel had leant me. Victoria liked it very much, kissing me once she saw me in it. She put on a long forest green dress made of cotton. It was her grandmother's. Everything (her little hand bag, her amber ring) was once her grandmother's. Over the dress she wore a black zip-up sweat-shirt, it was open so that her cleavage protruded. I made a joke about her cleavage always staring at me. "It gives me vertigo." "Fine, I'll just hide them away." She zipped the shirt up to her neck.

Five minutes later, as we entered the Plaza of Christ Church to meet Dennis, Erica, and Russell for brunch, the zip-per had fallen down, and her breasts were staring at me again. "There's nothing I can do. They want to be seen. I think they must be very inviting because everyone is always trying to grab them. I don't get what all the fuss is about, they are just like everyone else's." "No, they're perfect, they're like no-body else's. And you're always presenting them. You don't fool me." "I do like that you like them. I don't want anyone else to see them at all. They are just for you." We were kiss-ing by the fountain when Dennis came up with Russell and Erica.

We walked to a stairwell made of thick slabs of stone. Dennis informed me that Queen Elizabeth had once graced these steps. He was also complaining about all the Japanese Tourists who came snapping photos while he and his class-mates were eating in the famous dining hall. "We have to wear caps and gowns to dinner. At first I thought that this was some godawful antiquated ritual, but there is a charm to this type of aristocratic formality."

Long, dark wooden tables carried all the way to the far end of the room, where the floor raised up a step—separating the faculty from the student body. All around the room were paintings of famous Christ Church alums: Philip Sydney, William Gladstone, Christopher Wren, John Ruskin, Albert Einstein, Lewis Carroll, WH Auden... and more. A buffet and a cash register had been set up alongside one of the long tables. I filled my plate with mushrooms, beans, bacon, sausage, and roasted tomatoes. Dennis advised me to use the delicious brown sauce. Victoria filled her plate with broccoli.

Dennis was defending himself while we walked to a table and continued to defend himself once we had sat down. He had made a mockery of a girl's advances the night before. Lauren, a classmate of theirs, had confessed how badly she wanted to kiss Dennis, and he responded by opening his mouth extremely wide and then sucking on her cheek. "I don't care what other people think about me. If they can't handle me, they can get out of my way. It's not my fault everyone refuses to see the spectacle. The least I can do is call attention to it. This is my ethical standard." Victoria had her eyes on Dennis—listening to him patiently, without disgust. I concentrated on my English Breakfast—I thought it was delicious.

We took a walk around the meadows. Four trees were clustered in the center of a large patch of grass. The area was fenced off, only cows of the elite alums were allowed to graze in it. Victoria spoke of the maenads and satyrs and their Dionysian celebrations. On the other side was an ornate building with ivy crawling all over it. Through a high fence could be seen the Alice Tree, a many-tiered, many-branched sycamore. It was there that the big smile of the Cheshire Cat was first imagined. All of Oxford had the air of an intellectual fantasyland. There was the lamppost and faun of C.S. Lewis' Narnia and somewhere the shire of J.R.R. Tolkien. Victoria loved all these details.

The path around the meadows led along a small pond where the athletic Oxonians went punting. A fluorescent moss covered the trunks of the largest trees. Dennis walked ahead of the two couples: we were both relaxed and embracing. Victoria and I joked about how Dennis was more jealous of her than he was of me. "I never told you this. It was very clever of me. When we were all being cheeky in Morocco, I grabbed for Dennis's cock, it was not hard at all. That's how I know he is gay." "Samuel thinks that all his problems will be solved if I fuck him up the ass." "Would you want to?" "No!"

Victoria and I lay on a couch with all the light from the high windows covering us as we kissed and giggled. The others were picking up the mess from the party the night before. "The two of you are like a pair of children," Dennis said, disgusted. We kept kissing. My heart, all of a sudden, as Victoria put herself on top of me and buried her loving looks all over my skin, started to palpitate—it skipped beats. I remembered how little I had slept. I tried to breathe patiently, but I barely had time to—with Victoria so giddy and energized, begging for me to return her affection. For a moment I thought that all this pleasure was going to kill me. "Are you okay, petal?" It made me melt when she called me that; but then my heart started palpitating even worse. "I'm exhausted. Lie still." I took her head and embraced it against my chest. It sunk up and down as I tried to expel the imminent blackout I felt coming over me.

She decided to take me to Dennis's, whose key she had, and she tucked me in, and I fell asleep in a frantic state of over-exhaustion.

When she woke me I was rejuvenated. Her body wiggled up alongside the bed. I could not help myself. We were naked again. It all repeated itself. I kept asking, "Am I being a good boy?" And she would say, "Mommy is very pleased with you... that's a good boy." And she would stroke me, imagining I was the faun she loved to dream about.

The next morning Victoria let me sleep. She went and made me porridge which she served me in bed. I didn't want any. "I want to touch you perfectly. Tell me exactly what you want. Hypnotize me. Don't let me cum until you are fully satiated." …Kiss my neck. Pull my hair. Good Boy! That's a good boy. Put your fingers in my pussy. Play with my nipples. Fuck me, sweet faun. Fuck me. Start slow, hold my face gently. Kiss my face. Kiss my forehead. Put your tongue in my ear. Turn me over and fuck me from behind as hard as you can. Harder. Don't Stop. Don't Stop. Good boy. Let me get on top of you… I grabbed her breasts, tugged at them, breathing heavy. I felt sick. I kept pounding away. I felt nothing. She was cumming over and over. I showed her how agonized she looked when she got close to cumming. She apologized. I said it was really sexy. I felt like I was fucking demons out of her. She wanted more. I got on top of her. I held my stomach in so I could arch my cock directly into her g-spot. I was fucking her organs. All her cums were different. The bed sheets were soaked with her cum… She did not want to touch my cock. She said she wanted to cum six more times before I could cum. She jumped out of bed, stepped her foot directly in the bowl of porridge, and it splattered all about the room. "Oooo, I knew I was going to mess it all up. My mum told me I would." I hugged her and said I loved her and I thought she was beautiful—she shouldn't be embarrassed…

I lay still looking out the window while she went to wash off. I joined her in the shower after a few relaxing minutes. She teased my cock with soap. She said I had the most perfect cock in the world.

"So are you gonna tell me what's going on or are you gonna brood over it for the rest of your time here?"

I was sitting on the ledge of Dennis's window, he was sitting at the desk in front of his computer. I could not look him in his eyes. He held them out with such woeful insistence—these big green, sheepish things. He wanted the whole world to sink down into his stupor. "I'm tired of this Dennis—It doesn't interest me anymore."

"I have no idea what you're talking about."

For a second I believed him, that it was all my imagination—that he was just a good friend of mine.

"I'm tired of you saying shit about me to Victoria. I told you to stop talking about me, but it has not stopped. She keeps telling me how you've convinced her not to get too caught up in me because I'll drop her as soon as I find someone new to obsess over. She also told me that you showed her pictures of Dolly and I having sex, and that you told her that I thought Dolly was sexier than she was, and that you have written an entire song about how she is my new obsession, and you get drunk and ask, 'Who is this, who is this I'm singing about?'"

"Are you trying to make me believe you're going to marry Victoria, come on, you know I'm right. I shouldn't have shown her the pictures of Dolly, but I was drunk. It was harmless, and she begged me to let her see them."

"Please stop talking about me to her."

"I don't tell her anything I wouldn't say to your face."

"I don't fucking agree with what you think about me. I can handle your misperceptions. Victoria, on the other hand, thinks you're speaking the truth—and why would you lie when you're my 'best friend'"

"I never realized Victoria made such a big deal out of what I say. She should know I run my mouth."

"She cares. She comes straight to me. Man, the whole fucking past three months our emails have consisted of me defending myself against your words."

"I didn't realize Victoria was like this."

"What do you mean by that?"

"I told her things in confidence. And I always spoke of you as my most loyal companion."

Dennis stood up and started doing stretches. He shook his head, "I didn't realize what a liability Victoria was.

I feel stupid for trusting her. I don't know if I can be friends with her now that I know how she behaves."

"It's not like that Dennis—you don't get it. You have a way of preying on the weak. Victoria tells me how you make fun of her for scuffing her feet when she walks, for having holes in her runners, for believing in Jesus—she's always talking about you, and it's always about how insecure you make her feel."

"I cannot apologize for this, I have no time for other people's insecurities."

"How do you justify yourself?"

"I don't understand what you're driving at."

"You're the police man of self-possession, you must be aware that you impose this on others."

"You've been reading too much. I'm opinionated. I'm not going to hold back my opinions to please everyone. I'm happy everyone is so threatened by what I have to say. Come on Jonathan, they're all blind, they don't see the hypocrisy of everything they do—and you want me to be quiet about it. What about putting up a fight, fighting to end all this secular ideology? I thought you stood for these things."

"I don't, or not the way you say it. You're just a bully, you're not a hero. Samuel calls you an impotent bully."

He looked me in my eyes, "How do you think I feel, or felt, when you met this brilliant older man and used him to malign me. Let's just put it all out there, it's not like I don't have my own annoyances with you."

"I know what you're saying. But that's not the point."

"You're just replacing me with him—how am I supposed to feel about that?"

"That's not what it's like. You don't have to see it like that. I can be with both of you, but not if you keep acting like such an ass."

"You're still dating him?" Dennis nearly shouted this question.

"No, things ended. But we're still friends."

"Of course! You're not gay. I've seen you in action. I always knew it was doomed to failure…"

"Yeah, I wished it worked out. I think a hermitage is the next gamble."

"I don't entirely blame you."

"Hell is other people, right? That's what your good friend Sartre says to comfort you."

Dennis laughed… We talked things through for an hour more and everything calmed down. Dennis pulled me over to his side and gave me a hug. "I'm happy to see you're no longer glaring at me with the fire of a thousand suns," he joked.

I met Victoria by the Narnia Lamppost. Around the corner was a magnificent Magnolia tree in full bloom. Its pinks fore-grounded a spiraled pillar—leading into one of the thousand churches. Pan was there, the sky was layered with clouds. Above our heads were all these gargoyles: witches, screaming goblins, twin demons, thousands of frightening little guys, one after the other. Victoria immediately offered, "I'm sorry about talking about Dennis. I realized when you left this morning that I must put you in a tough situation. I'm not going to listen to him when he talks about you. I'm going to block it out from now on."

I felt bad for having made Victoria out to be so undependable. Before we headed to the meadows we stopped at the library. I sent a quick email to Dennis, and Victoria ran in to check out a book on Jesus & Apollo.

Mar 14th
Hey D,
Just wanted to note that the irrevocability of which we spoke of yesterday should somewhat be reconsidered. Because the moment I saw

Victoria today she apologized rather profusely for having said things which were irrational, and vowed not to speak of such things again. What I mean is, it seems she was rather aware of what we were working through last night—I think a good sign. Of course everything is your own prerogative, but, since I am warming up to her, I should say she does care for you greatly, and I myself would be rather disappointed if all of this confusion caused serious breakage. Oh, and I wanted to apologize or admit guilt for using Samuel as a lever to help me take a sort of vengeance on you. I felt I did not adequately fess up to this last night... Take care,

J

We passed underneath The Bridge of Sighs on our way to the meadows. We sat down on a polished slab of tree raised up on a couple stones. It looked out on an idyllic curve in the rowing pond. Willow leaves hung in front of the pond. A large sycamore with a large, gaping figure eight in its trunk stood beside us. All the green in the forest was tracing on down a winding path. Across the pond bushes of white flowers curved over to form a trellised pathway.

"When I was younger, like eleven, I had an affair with my brother's girlfriend. We wrote letters to each other every day. We would have to sneak off because my brother would have killed us both. It was very cheeky. One day my mother caught us. We had our breasts out and were kissing each other. She stood there, like the mother in The Story of the Eye, completely silent. Later she said she thought I was spending too much time with Susanna. It was my only real love affair."

"I was thirteen when I first had sex. I was in love with a Swedish girl my age. She had beautiful breasts. We had systematically rounded the bases and it was only logical that we carry on to home. We were both too embarrassed to buy a condom, but at the same time we were too terrified not to use protection. I went down to my cupboard and grabbed a plastic bag and a rubber band." Victoria gasped, "You're kid-

186

ding, right? That sounds so painful." "No, it's true. We were young. We didn't know what we were doing. In the end I just held the plastic bag with my hand and pushed in. Only the head really. She said it hurt and I took it out. She let me hold it in without a condom for a little. I pushed it halfway. I don't think I felt anything but nervous."

"You are Pan, I knew it."

"Maybe you're right. Maybe I am Pan."

"I think you confuse lust with love. That's another reason why you're Pan."

"I don't think this is true."

"Have you ever loved someone you didn't lust after?"

"I don't think that would solidify my Pan-ness."

"You've got the cock!" Victoria thrust her hand onto my lap and squeezed my hard-on through my jeans. She gritted her teeth, moaned, and I saw her breasts curving out of her shirt. My mouth was on hers, then on her cheeks, and then on her cold, sensitive neck. We saw someone coming in the distance so we looked back out at the pond. We waited silently for them to cross in front of us and carry on out of sight. It took over a minute.

"Nobody should be bothering us like that. It's rude," I said.

"Don't you wish this was our own little garden and nobody would ever bother us?"

"Maybe if we will everyone away."

"Maybe they'll smell our sex and move off... I can't believe we're here. I've never done anything like that, with the emails."

"Neither have I. It's strange how different things are, but then again this feels exactly like what we wanted."

"There should be a movie about our Romance. And some actor with a really sexy beard should play you. You must think I'm such a freak. Whole parties are spent making fun of Victoria's taste in men. They say I like the weird boys. But they don't know how much sexier the weird boys are."

She sidled up alongside me. She smiled without restraining herself. I was doing the same. I looked to see if the path was clear, and then I stuck my hand under her dress, pulling her tights back. I pushed a finger inside her already wet pussy. I turned all my attention to it. Victoria started to pant and to close her eyes. Her body jerked with each slow spasm. I pulled out and touched her clit lightly. "This is very bad, very bad, Ohhh..." She pulled down her dress and looked up at the sky. She pointed, "He sees us you know?" "He doesn't mind," I said, heading back, "He's on our side." I pushed my fingers inside, and she let herself indulge. Her pussy was even wetter. I was getting her to make small yelps. "Keep going, keep going." Over Victoria's shoulder I spotted a man dressed in a black shirt with a white collar hanging out from it. I didn't tell Victoria, he could not see us through the trees yet. "I'm gonna cum." I kept my pace steady. She stayed on the edge, pushing herself. The man came into my sight again. I pulled my hand out. Victoria looked at me despairingly, then she realized why I had stopped. She pulled her dress down very properly and turned towards the man...

She turned back to me and buried her head in my chest, repeating, "Oh no, oh no, oh no." She stayed there until she was sure the man passed. "Oh no, this is very naughty. I don't want this. This is beanshed."

"What're you talking about?"

"It's the most disgusting thing you can imagine. Think about it, a whole shed full of rotting soggy beans. Dennis is beanshed. It's gluttony."

"Did you make that up all yourself?"

"Yes, I made up the treasure map burning, beanshed, and there is also the rotting pigeon with the golden nugget."

"Is that like finding yourself?" Victoria still looked very distressed, "What's the matter?"

"It was a sign."

"What, the man?" I laughed, "It just so happened he came by us."

"It was a priest, Jonathan, that is a sign. Ohhhh… These things only happen to me."

"He wasn't a priest…"

"I saw him Jonathan."

"No, he was just wearing a white collar shirt and a black sweater."

Victoria looked perplexed, "It's still a sign, just to have thought it was a priest."

"That makes absolutely no sense."

"You don't understand, I was brought up Christian, it's a very cheeky thing guilt."

"You shouldn't feel guilty, you didn't even cum."

"It's not funny."

We were quiet. She wouldn't look at me in my eyes anymore. She turned her head to the side and looked out on the pond. "You have to go away. You have to stay at Dennis's tonight." "Are you serious?" "Yes, I'm sorry. I need to go." I watched her walk down the path and out of sight. I sat still for a moment or two, taking in the moist air and the wafts of Evergreen. I went over to the pond and put my hands in the water.

I was exhausted, and I lay down on Dennis's rug. He was talking to Isabella: "I don't have time for people like that… Yes, baby, I'm gonna come back to New York after this year… Are your folks all there with you…? I have too much work the next two weeks… I love you too." He hung up the phone and then swung his legs down to the floor, nearly clipping me in my ribs. "Don't look at me like that Jonathan." "You can't even see my face." "I can't leave her. It's too hard for me. She always draws me back in. I can't hurt her." I was too tired to care.

"I made a very twisted arrangement with her. You'll like this. I told her that I would be faithful only if she cheats on me. And then she has to give me a full report on her rendezvous." "And then you jerk off to it?" "Even when I'm with her I imagine she is fucking someone else." "I know, you love telling me this." "This latest arrangement is the perfect critique of monogamy. It can only be preserved by giving it up." "And Isabella is into this?" "No, it has taken a lot of convincing." "You're fucked up." "Oh, and you're not fucked up?" "Not like you." I got up and instinctively sat down in front of the computer, I swiveled around on the chair. Dennis went over to the closet to get dressed up.

"Hey Dennis, what is the deal with Victoria and Jesus?" "She believes in him Jonathan. I tried to press her one night, and she started crying. She said she knew what I was going to say and she didn't want to hear it." "What do you mean you pressed her?" "She believes in Jesus, I was laughing at her. How don't you know this? You're the one fucking her." "I don't think it's as serious as you make it out to be. She uses it to dramatize her inhibitions. She doesn't care about Jesus otherwise." "Man, the girl believes in Jesus. She has fantasies about being his wife." "This is all play. You take things far too seriously." "For people who believe in Jesus, he is very serious." "Maybe, but if you go imposing that thought on someone like Victoria, you make her take it more seriously than she would herself." "Unlike you, I believe in other's suffering, Jonathan." "Where're you going tonight?" "You don't want to talk about this." "No. Where're you going?" "You'll be happy, I'm probably not going to come home tonight." "I thought you're supposed to be faithful." "Yeah, but I met this smoking thirty year old blond chick who is really into me. She's really wild too, she might be perfect. But something about her is off. I can't get into the sex. She even asked me the other night why I didn't have a raging hard on. These Brits have the most unsexy way of expressing themselves. And they are all ugly. This one's pretty hot though." Dennis pulled on his leather jacket and tied his grey scarf snug around his neck. His pretty face was buried within all his winter clothing. "Clean up after yourself, darling beaver."

I went straight to the computer.

On the desktop I saw a folder entitled JONATHAN'S CASE. I clicked it open. There were only a couple lines: "Jonathan must delude himself, how could he tolerate Victoria's pathologies. He wants to believe that he has a natural voracity; he is too desperate to see how he disguises himself. In his ignorance, he believes in his potency. On the seabed shores of Essaouira, his greediness dismissed me, and I was banished to the shadows of existence. He could never know what this loneliness feels like—he is far too selfish to care. I know that one day... he will realize I taught him everything he knows." The file ended there. I next looked for the pictures of Dolly Dennis had shown Victoria. I had been stranded at his home in ChinaTown for a few days and couldn't wait to see them... I had loaded them onto his computer and put them in a folder I named PRIVATE. There she was... smiling at me. Twirling the small white flower. I took out my cock— but I couldn't get hard. Everything felt staged. I went to I OWN YOUR COCK and saw that Sandra's icon was available. Dennis did not have Yahoo Messenger so I downloaded it. Sandra texted me the moment I popped online.

SandraSandra 9:18 PM: hey you.

sevendirex 9:18 PM: hey Sandrina, its nice to see you online.

SandraSandra 9:19 PM: im surprised to see you…Nice to
see you too. I thought you got
scared away.

sevendirex 9:19 PM: been thinking of you.
sevendirex 9:19 PM: scared away? No, im out of town.
im in Oxford visiting my girlfriend, I
guess.

SandraSandra 9:19PM: been thinking of you too, you
never sent me the flowers.

sevendirex 9:20 PM: it's been strange out here…you're
right. I took some good pictures,
I think.

SandraSandra 9:20 PM: What's your girlfriend's name?

sevendirex 9:20 PM: Victoria.

SandraSandra 9:20 PM: Do you have a picture of her?

sevendirex 9:21 PM: yeah. should I send?

SandraSandra 9:21 PM: yes. Do it now.

I forwarded the pic. of Victoria walking down the snowy street

SandraSandra 9:25: she's beautiful.

sevendirex 9:25 PM: Yeah. you with anyone right now?

SandraSandra 9:26 PM: no, an art gallery owner from
Flagstaff has been making passes

192

SandraSandra 9:26 PM: but I think I got rid of him.

SandraSandra 9:26 PM: he told me I was too intense.

SandraSandra 9:27 PM: I asked him to stare back at me, and show me what he was really made of.

SandraSandra 9:27 PM: He got shy, and he left soon after that.

SandraSandra 9:28 PM: not for me.

SandraSandra 9:28 PM: I am missing out on an opportunity for my photography.

sevendirex 9:29 PM: if you asked me to stare into your eyes,

sevendirex 9:29 PM: i would stare right back at them.

sevendirex 9:29 PM: and you would fall down.

sevendirex 9:29 PM: you would lose all your powers of domination.

sevendirex 9:30 PM: your pussy would open up for me.

sevendirex 9:30 PM: I would have you writhing naked on the bed, begging for my touch.

SandraSandra 9:31 PM: And when you touched me, it would all reverse.

SandraSandra 9:31 PM: you would wonder if I had the power all along

SandraSandra 9:32 PM: I want to see your cock, show me your cock John.

sevendirex 9:32 PM: i feel it now.

sevendirex 9:32 PM: that opening of my pores

sevendirex 9:32 PM: you let me let everything go.

sevendirex 9:33 PM: i want to chew on you.

sevendirex 9:33 PM: i want to taste that thing, again and again

sevendirex 9:33 PM: so I really know what it tastes like

sevendirex 9:33 PM: please oh please, here, here is my cock.

I pulled down my pants and took out my cock. Dennis had a laptop with a built-in webcam, so it was no trouble sending her my image.

SandraSandra 9:35 PM: where are you?

sevendirex 9:35 PM: what? The charcoal drawings on the wall behind me?

SandraSandra 9:35 PM: are you at your girlfriends?

sevendirex 9:36 PM: at my friend Dennis's, no.
sevendirex 9:36 PM: he also goes to Oxford... its how i met Victoria.
sevendirex 9:36 PM: it's a long boring story

SandraSandra 9:36 PM: He's an artist?

sevendirex 9:36 PM: NO! he's an asshole.

SandraSandra 9:36 PM: I like you when you're angry. I can see your eyes tighten. I want to make you angry.

sevendirex 9:37 PM: I forgot how it feels to have your eyes on me.

SandraSandra 9:37 PM: I want to say things that annoy you. So you get that intense look in your eyes. I'll laugh at you.
SandraSandra 9:38 PM: don't look so confused.

sevendirex 9:38 PM: take me. take me away from myself!

SandraSandra 9:39 PM: touch yourself.

SandraSandra 9:39 PM: grab your cock.

SandraSandra 9:40 PM: get it hard for me.

SandraSandra 9:40 PM: stroke it for me baby. Stroke it for me hard.

sevendirex 9:40 PM: mmmmmmmmmm

SandraSandra 9:41 PM: im on my knees in front of you.

SandraSandra 9:41 PM: im crawling towards you.

SandraSandra 9:41 PM: my eyes are on you.

SandraSandra 9:41 PM: i stuff your cock down my throat.

SandraSandra 9:41 PM: i gag on your cock.

SandraSandra 9:42 PM: jerk off and cum down my throat, baby.

SandraSandra 9:43 PM: SHOW ME YOUR FACE

SandraSandra 9:44 PM: get it all over your clothes, all over your friends room.

SandraSandra 9:44 PM: CUM NOW!

SandraSandra 9:45 PM: that was beautiful. I wish you could see what I'm looking at.

sevendirex 9:46 PM: i can see it.

SandraSandra 9:46 PM: Yes, but you don't know how it makes me feel. You have brought so much to me Jonathan. I hope you aren't going to run off. I was really scared you had.

sevendirex 9:47 PM: do you want to cum now?

SandraSandra 9:47 PM: i don't have time...taking calls.

sevendirex 9:47 PM: alright.

SandraSandra 9:48 PM: You can go, I see that look.

you're bored.

sevendirex 9:48 PM: I'm worried about my friend coming
                    home.

SandraSandra 9:48 PM: Do one thing for me?

sevendirex 9:48 PM: I don't want to give you the wrong
                    idea.
sevendirex 9:48 PM: what

SandraSandra 9:49 PM: I want you to fuck Victoria harder
                     than youve ever fucked her
                     before.
SandraSandra 9:49 PM: I want to be there inside of you
                     while you fuck her.
SandraSandra 9:49 PM: She will never feel so good again,
                     for the rest of her life.

sevendirex 9:49 PM: I already fuck her good!

SandraSandra 9:50 PM: Fuck her better, you cocky brat.

sevendirex 9:50 PM: yes mommy.

SandraSandra 9:50 PM: You're beautiful, truly.

sevendirex 9:51 PM: so are you. i mean it... for so many
                    reasons.

SandraSandra 9:51 PM: bye for now.

sevendirex 9:51 PM: bye

"What time is your plane?" Victoria was dripping wet
and wiggling on the floor, reaching out her arm to check the

clock. "I don't care if I miss it. I promised you 10 orgasms."
"You think you can?" "Of course I can." I pulled up her silk
nighty, already wet with cum, and put my cock inside her.
Her pussy was getting more and more accustomed to my cock,
and my cock was more accustomed to finding the exact spot to
stroke, so whether or not she wanted to, I could bring her to
orgasm. Sometimes it was so sensitive what I was doing to
her that she would scream that it was too much, that I needed
to stop, and she would start pushing me, but then I would hold
down her arms, dig my elbows into her sides, and fuck her
even harder, forcing her over the edge she feared she could
never surmount. She started to hiss at me. Her blue eyes were
livid. She squeezed in her cheeks. All the skin around her
nose wrinkled. "You're scaring me." "It scares me that I
scare you." "Why?" "Because you scare me. I don't want to
know what I must be like to scare you." She hissed back at
me. And our bodies were in sweat, tearing at each other...

****

Mar. 20th
I figured it out...why I feel cheeky with you, Dolly etc...And it is simply because I don't like being involved in something I feel so very out
of control of. Because I am not 'special' to you, in that I mean I could
be replaced easily with Dolly or Sally or Mystery Woman No.1 if they
had been willing to reciprocate your emotions... I have never been in
this situation, tis mighty vulnerable. Of course 'what ifs?' are very
silly...but what if Dolly turned around all ready and good? Or Mystery
Woman No.1? How precarious our 'relationship' is if it is based on
simply reciprocation!....If I said fuck off you would. This brings me to
my next problem...that for me it has nothing to do with reciprocation,
it has always been and will always be about the individual...if you said
fuck off I wouldn't...therefore you are safe, but I am not. How nasty is
it to know that the person you are with still holds the same feelings for
another person as they do for you? I feel sick that

I am even telling you this.

You have had this before, and still could have this with others at this very moment, I have not and could not. I do not like this fact.

I hate you. You fall giddy too easily.

****

"Cow as a Puppy. Meow. Are you a little kitty cat?"

"No Samuel, I'm not."

"Do you think I'm a little kitty cat?" I thought about his question. "You think I'm insane!"

"No, I think you're a kitty cat."

"Meow… Can you say Darling or Dahling?"

"I say Darling honey baby."

"You never said that to me."

"You never deserved it. With your snoring and your hairy shoulders. I'm a young boy Samuel."

"You make me sound like some kind of monster. What you fail to remember is that you came charging after me. I was a little kitty. I didn't know I had to look out for young straight boys."

"I told Dennis that we broke up and he said that it had been doomed from the start."

"Dooooooom…"

"Dooooom and Gloom…"

"Can't he see anything in any other light?"

"No, it's his favorite shade."

"It's all very uninteresting. Goethe says, 'There is nothing more pitiful than a devil in despair.' I mean you really know how to pick them Jonathan. I must seem mild compared to all these other people in your life. You either have small waifish little fairy girls or father figures."

"What about Sandrina?"

"You're taking this too far. This person is not even real... Now let me tell you what happened to me."

The two of us were sitting alongside each other at a Sushi Bar in the Village. A giant octopus tentacle stared at me from within the glass case. I was scratching at the chips of wood underneath the counter.

"I was in STA Travel trying to get a refund for a flight to Italy I canceled. And behind one of the computers was this beautiful boy. We were staring at each other. He was just my type. Young, blonde hair, sweet face, tall and lanky. I mean he wasn't a curly-haired Jewish intellectual like yourself, but I can't just wait around you know... With my voracious appetite." Samuel threw back his head defiantly, "He was obviously checking me out. Now listen to this Jonathan. This is something out of your life. Four days ago I get an email from this boy, whose name is Todd, saying that he had gotten my address off the computer, he hoped he was not being inappropriate, but he really wanted to go on a date with me. I mean ever since I made it with a straight boy I have had to fend off thousands of boys looking to get their cherry popped."

"And you met him?"

"I met every part of him. And he was quite knowledgeable. He had very beautiful equipment, if you know what I'm saying."

"Did you?" I made a shape with my two hands.

"This is a little personal."

"Come on, tell me."

"Why're you taking so much interest in my sex life? If I didn't know any better, I'd say you were jealous."

" Are you gonna tell me?

"We didn't. Not yet, but everything was very nice."

"You just blew each other?"

"I mean my god. If you're so interested why don't you join us next time?"

199

"Maybe."

"Bimbatella."

"Mamallama."

"You are really crazy."

"I'm just imitating you."

"Who am I? Who am I?" Samuel stood up and arched his neck forward and started walking towards me, bobbing his head back and forth like he was a rock and roll star.

"Me, right?"

"Yeah, you're like." He kept bobbing his head and he pushed forward his lower jaw, "I don't have time for this. Don't bother me with this. Uh, get out of my way please. This is your Prince Hamlet side."

"I think I'm more like Romeo."

"No, Romeo is one-dimensional. You're like a transpeciatory erotic god."

"But I think Romeo becomes Hamlet if he doesn't commit suicide."

"I really don't know what you're talking about."

"Sorry professor."

"This is a very easy non-response."

"How about this for a non-response: You want to hear my story?"

"As long as there are no vaginas in it. I am just an innocent country girl named Heidi."

"There's none. You'll like it, it is more about the failure of heterosexuality."

"Go on..."

"And don't interrupt me. I know how hard it is to tell you stories. Just listen!"

"Yes daddy." Samuel held his face tightly, trying to control himself.

"So when I got back from Oxford everything started off very good with Victoria and I. We were emailing each other. Disgustingly sweet words. Sometimes we would be writing each other at the same time. Then it started up again. Dennis was angry that I was not writing him. Victoria included this in her emails to me, admonishing me about how I was hurting Dennis's feelings, and that I was undeniably an asshole in the matter. Apparently Dennis would spend whole afternoons forcing Victoria to show him the emails we were writing each other, looking for a sign of my affection. At the same time he was still mouthing off about me. He told Victoria that she was 'my latest muse.' Victoria wrote me a giant email about how she cannot trust me because she is not special to me. I fall 'in giddy'—this is how we rephrased 'in love'— she says I fall 'in giddy' too easily, and it does not matter who with—so there is nothing unique about her. She kept bringing up Dolly and how she knew if I ever saw Dolly again I would leave her immediately. Then she calls me up a couple days later, late at night. She is hiding in the bushes outside a pub, having run away from some bloke she had just kissed on the dance floor. She is all like, 'Oooooo, this is very cheeky. I feel gross.' And then she starts in on this Jesus act, how he is punishing her for the lust she feels for me. All of a sudden, while I'm on the phone, the bloke finds her and I hear them talking, and then the phone hangs up. She does not call back for 15 minutes. I am sitting there in my room, waiting.

"When she calls back, she is dodging behind houses, rushing me home because she wants to have phone sex. When we're done having phone sex, she lays into me for being an asshole to Dennis, who has been miserably sad ever since his girlfriend Isabella ended things with him. Then she passes out. Literally, I hear her snoring over the phone.

"Three days later she calls me up drunk and demands to know if I am 'Her Master.' 'What makes you say that?' 'Dennis says that you're My Master.' 'I don't know what the hell he means by that.' 'He says it's because you're better read than me.' 'That's ridiculous.' She goes into this whole thing about not knowing if she loves me anymore because she is not obsessed with waiting to see my emails like she once was. I tell her she is being drunk and dramatic and that I am not going to concern myself with what she is saying. 'Well then maybe we should end this. How do you think I feel if my feelings are never taken seriously?' To which I say, 'Maybe we should.' She starts screaming. She was on the toilet crapping, apparently, and the phone hangs up. I receive, ten minutes later, a text message that says, 'Fuck you! We are through. You're an asshole. Dennis was right about you.' She calls me in the morning sobbing, wanting to take everything back. When I don't let up, she says she doesn't even know whom she is talking to. She says that Dennis says that I am the most selfish person alive and that the reason I am breaking up with her is to get back at him. Then she tells me she woke up in the morning and when she went to the bathroom some bloody discharge came out of her. When she went to the Doctor, she found out she had had a miscarriage. She is now hysterical—she even says 'You make me feel like one of those hysterical women from the 1800s.' I break down crying myself, repeating, 'You ask too much of me. You ask too much of me. I can't give you what you want.'

"The very next day Dennis sends me a video of himself singing a love song to me. He has on a Brooklyn shirt, and his hair is all long, and he does not look into the camera once. The song goes 'Jonathan, let's look into each other's eyes, we know better than to make each other cry, but that's what I'm doing, lying here, in your cold revere, tonight.' Which he belts out, 'Tonigggggggggggggghhhhhhhhhhhhhht.' And the chorus goes, 'Darling, won't you be my friend?'"

"This is too sad. He loves you Jonathan."

"I know. But what do I want his love for? …I write back that I was very touched by his song but could not say yes to being his friend. It doesn't work like that."

"Of course not. You can't force friendship."

"Wait, wait.... so Victoria and Dennis are gone. I broke off with both of them."

"Do you mean that for real?"

"Yes, I can't talk to either of them. They pull me into this web. I need to be resolute. I know Victoria is totally broken up, but she doesn't realize the position she puts me in... So listen, meanwhile, Sandrina the cyber kitty and I have been speaking incessantly. She gave me her cell phone number. We send text messages, emails, and we spend all night chatting on the phone and watching each other on webcam. While she is taking calls from her phone sex clients, she types to me, telling me how I should touch myself. She will take me on drives down desert highways, or I will go to the supermarket with her. I lie in bed with my hand on my cock listening to her breathe. Whenever she says my name I get all these tingles. We have started saying that we love each other. We talk all night. She gives me the most intense orgasms. And I do the same for her. So..." I paused for dramatic effect.

"Yes?"

"I am going to visit her in Nevada next weekend."

"So cyber kitty becomes kitty kitty."

"Daddy kitty."

"You know what I think?"

"Yeah, I should just be gay and all my problems will go away?"

"No, they won't all go away. But, my god. I've never heard such things..."

When we got up after paying the check, Samuel took me in his arms and tried to kiss me. I pushed his cheek aside, and we laughed awkwardly, but it was not a big deal.

****

Mar 23rd
Dennis,
this all is very hard for me, and I think it best that I be brief. I want to
say that I do have fun with you, but it seems, and the reasons why
are too confusing to understand, that it hurts me too much for me to
continue being close with you. I also think it must not be so different
for you. I really hope you respect my request
to stay away from me, perhaps indefinitely. I also would prefer not to
delve into the whys and wherefores, as, in the end, they will not make
sense of the overriding ick and frustration that our relationship constantly fills me with. This is a sad turn of events, I know. Hopefully,
though, it will make things brighter for the both of us.

Mar 23rd
For you, John, maybe. What I wanted to say, but am not sure I managed, was I love you--I mean as a friend, not some deep hidden revelation. But maybe b/c of this fact, I will obey your request...I assume
this includes correspondences? Couldn't you at least have it out with
me one last time? I won't even respond. I just would like to know--as
I think it will help me reflect on this all--what it is, in your own words,
however tainted with sentiments noble or seditious, what it is about me
that is poison to you. Is this too much to ask?
-D

Mar. 23rd
Of course you may feel free to ignore my last request.

Mar 23rd
John, I hope that we can talk soon. I know that I made mistakes, but
you are not Mr. Perfect, you know… I hate feeling afraid of someone
who I once embraced so closely. You make yourself so inaccessible. I
really want to hear from you, but not if you are going to give me your
catty shit.

And… can we still have phone sex? (kidding, british humor)
Vx

I did not respond to either of them.

****

Mar. 17th

So...last night, S... I was exhausted as I said, but for an hour or more your presence was all around me—and I knew how powerful and warm and erotic you were, and it was immense...and I knew that you were definitely there to hold and wrap around me, that you could, if I just gave myself to you... I imagined this morning us holding a pose...like that Yoko/Lennon picture...and the sort of disappearance...STILLNESS... that this would create... Seeing you finally has burned an image onto what was once just an idea of your mind...and the body fits perfectly with everything that came before.... I know what I would be crawling into...gripping...clawing... pleasuring... we have been shedding our skin, revealing our masks before plunging... I love that you cum for me...and that you see me...laugh with me... I have the highest opinion of you and the way you have touched me...and I do not know you...but I must continue to draw you towards me...I must...and I hope this is to your liking...in fact, I would like you to be quite pleased by my reaching out for you...

Surrender!

SevenDirex

SandraSandra 2:00 AM: its resting
SandraSandra 2:50 AM: mmmmm
SandraSandra 2:50 AM: YOU

sevendirex 2:51 AM: you're unbelieveable
sevendirex 2:51 AM: really
sevendirex 2:51 AM: your directness
sevendirex 2:51 AM: mmmmmmmmmmmm

sevendirex 2:51 AM: love it

sevendirex 2:51 AM: right back at you

sevendirex 2:51 AM: staring, crawling, praying, begging, gnashing teeth, flailing

SandraSandra 2:52 AM: oh mY GAWD..you are the devil..THE DEVIL

sevendirex 2:52 AM: oh dear

sevendirex 2:52 AM: not this accusation again

SandraSandra 2:52 AM: say it..say it..LORDY LORDY

SandraSandra 2:52 AM: OH LORD

SandraSandra 2:52 AM: AHAHAHA

sevendirex 2:52 AM: cock stuffed in your pussy

sevendirex 2:52 AM: hard

sevendirex 2:52 AM: my dirty whore

sevendirex 2:52 AM: all mine

sevendirex 2:53 AM: k's

sevendirex 2:53 AM: wanted to say hi

sevendirex 2:53 AM: slap you around a bit

sevendirex 2:53 AM: i will be back

sevendirex 2:53 AM: always round the corner

sevendirex 2:54 AM: buzz if your pussy is in a state of emergency

SandraSandra 2:54 AM: **BUZZ!!!**

sevendirex 2:54 AM: it is shameless

sevendirex 2:54 AM: oh gosh

sevendirex 2:54 AM: this frightened me

sevendirex 2:54 AM: i was right i knew you would

sevendirex 2:54 AM: now i am drooling

sevendirex 2:54 AM: ok but no

sevendirex 2:54 AM: i need to go

sevendirex 2:55 AM: cause you are busy

sevendirex 2:55 AM: and i get frustrated
sevendirex 2:55 AM: i want to luxuriate inside of you you
know
sevendirex 2:55 AM: i will be back
sevendirex 2:55 AM: scouts honor
sevendirex 2:55 AM: devils honor, if you insist

SandraSandra 2:55 AM: don't go
SandraSandra 2:55 AM: I'm free to chat a
bit..love...hmmmm
SandraSandra 2:55 AM: mmmmmmmm
SandraSandra 2:55 AM: john
SandraSandra 2:55 AM: please.
SandraSandra 2:56 AM: please please please

sevendirex 2:56 AM: beg me
sevendirex 2:56 AM: more
sevendirex 2:56 AM: convince me to stay

Mar 19th
I want to be the invisible woman and jerk you off when you're out to dinner. Ugh, I'm angry at you just now for my swollen pussy.

Your ass was so pink and bright; I'm sure it stung. I was wet and swollen at the sound of the smacking, electrified by the proof. In many ways I want to judge my own reactions from a different vantage point, but that would leave behind our cave dug into the cliff where we let go. If anything, that is what I don't want to do. I want to explore you fresh, unreserved. There is a side of me waking, blinking at the light - digging in its heals to sweat you, bruise you, nurture your cock. I want your head. I want you to feel - sense at a higher pitch. The thought of your breathing makes me angry that I can't turn around, grab your hair, pin you and test you. Pinch you. Claw at you. Slap you. fuckfuckfuckfuckfuck. Yes, I liked it, but it certainly wasn't enough of anything. I can do more than I knew before last night, and that is heart-pounding pleasing.

wish to backhand you, with all my might - and then find solace in your prick across my cheek, furious

The hesitance you hear is me watching me some. I am coming at this sitting upright and attentive, aware of the opportunity for us to explore. If we can just put down what we know. And you feel cheapened? Get perspective. Handled with an abandoning of identity to get deeper, this can be priceless. Are you checking to see if I know this?

And this is meaningful. You know it too and somewhat hate/love me for it. What we're doing propels us both from the mundane and it highlights, quickly and with precision, what each of us brings to the table as strengths and weaknesses - it tests us both.

I am in a constant state of helper or challenge.Grandma.Money.Feeling Faint. The lower levels of Maslow's hierarchy. I challenge that pyramid, by the by, because I can envision that some types of awareness make You wait for the cheques. They come. Then what? *sound of crickets chirping*

Now I'm tired and irritable. I want the simplicity of fucking your mouth with my perfect clit until I cum and scream, and then I want you to truly slap the hell out of me. And yes, I'm disappointed because I don't know that you really could.

I want you to get a box of crayons and make a card. A sappy, child-like, card with hearts and flowers. You write with your opposite hand on this card. Big scrawling letters the following,

"Dear Mr. Man, touch me. I'm sure your hands are magic. Have a wonderful day, John."

And I want pictures of the card.

Sandrina

Oh john, u say thngs to me without effort that inspire even tempered quiet dillusional bliss. It takes effort to remain upright and yet strengthens me

Going for my walk

Hee

At german place for lunch. Thinking of u as I ponder brats and such

Ur a good man. Sigh

Please know I never intend to burst a bubble. I mean to be responsible when faced w love

I dnt mean to bring u dwn when I express fear or alternative scenarios

Its part of real love

It may be the only art left john

Want u to pin me and torture me with ur rigid insistemt prick

Wish to tend to ur every need

I picture u underground. Flashes of light. The people make less faces when alone. U make stares but mostly glances at the subtle writhe of task, journey, destination. If u read while riding no one knws ur crazy

I must make bacon and while I turn it I think of u trning me with violence and lightly teasing my mouth with a fingertip

Bring me back to consciousness with the extremities of the erotic. Bring me home for a worthy opponent

I cnt wait to feel u steadying ur cock in line with my cunt, breathing deep

Let me nourish u at my breast. My nipples need nibbles

My hand cnt be ur hand and so I dnt touch. Too teasing, comical, elementary

And I am jealous of the eyes tht make contact with ur gaze

When we get interrupted by my clients it has one advantage, the gentleman tht want humiliation GET humiliation

Such lightness in my step, kitten

U have tuned the instrument tht is commonly called 'cunt'. What harmonics we give voice to

All day, love! I attempt to quiet her, 'shhhhhh, punam. Someone will hear.' And she grows sad, mystified tht I ask joy to keep it down and nt disturb the sleep of the already unconscious

And u are more fulfilling thn sex. If I could never touch u, the fact tht u are here at all with such agility in love allows me to pray in earnest to whoever will take credit for ur being.

And I think they would line up to claim u-gods as well as demons

Blue eyes, baby's got blue eyes. Like deep blue sea—sea on a blue blue day…

And I u. dreams dreams these moments between us are. I slept so well after our play.

Thnk of me praying to u then between ur legs

The state of everything is more stimulating in light of u existing

Love u. want u. crave u. will fuck u.

Yes I know, want to fall and have you fall too and we climb on each other so as not to hit the ground

****

The night before I left for Firebird, Sandrina sent me four pictures of herself. Her webcam had been failing as of late, and all I could see, in the dark, were her green eyes. She showed me the room she was in: the parquet walls, and the cluttered mess with all her photographs. She showed me her pussy, but it was dark, and her hand was in front of it. Then she showed me, me. She turned the webcam around, and I saw myself, small, in a little box, staring back at her.

The pictures she sent me were grotesque, intentionally. She shot them in fluorescent light. They showed her tattoos, a rose on her thigh, a snake between her breasts, and they showed her big swollen fat pussy, that clit that I had told her again and again to tap with her finger. She had said in her email… 'This is me, let's quit the fantasy. I have seen how beautiful Victoria and Dolly are.'

I was relaxed this time. The plane touched down inside the Rockies. I walked slowly through the airport looking every which way. I tied my sweater around my waist. I was trying to let myself be washed away. I heard her whisper my name, "Jonathan," when I entered a large Rotunda. She was over on the side, leaning against a granite pillar. My heart dropped for a second. She wore Capri pants, and the whites of her ankles were showing. Her toenails were painted pink and each big toe had a flower drawn on it. She wore a black, loose-fitting shirt, and she had glasses on, hiding those green eyes I had dreamt about each night. Her face had broken out in pimples, from the sun, and it was hard for me to understand

211

what exactly I was looking at. When I came up she spoke to me gently, "Jonathan," and she took me in her arms. She wore a strong perfume, I liked it. Her chest and the way she enveloped me was all very pleasing. She had always said how softly she was going to kiss me, and her lips, small and pink, were very sweet as I put mine against them.

Sandrina took my hand and led me out of the airport. We were nervous, and Sandrina wanted to get out of the parking lot, off the highway, and into the hotel room. We said little more than, "I can't believe this." Sandrina kept telling me about all her friends and about how they were nervously awaiting her call. Most of them assured Sandrina, who was prone to rash decisions, that she would regret meeting me. Even she was wary, wondering if it was my youth—and nothing more—which had propelled me into this situation. I never knew what to say when she said this. Sandrina turned on the air conditioning in the car. It kept making me sneeze, but it was too hot outside to turn off. "This place reminds me of the last time I was in Arizona," I told her, "It was to see my Aunt, who was dying of Lung Cancer." "Is she okay?" "She died soon after I left. She was not married and she had no children. I think she was happy to go." "She told you this?" "A few years back she told me she would rather kill herself than grow old without a family, and only her job." "I felt like that for a while, when I used to work for Discover Card. It was a terrible job. And I have always wanted to work on my photography, and I thought I would never get to." "Why didn't you go to school for photography?" "I couldn't afford it. I got into SVA but my parents had no money. I went to UNLV instead." Sandrina was playing the Flaming Lips' Album *Transmissions From the Satellite Heart,* which I had sent her in the mail. It was nice to hear something familiar.

We turned off the highway and drove into a parking lot aside a Mexican Restaurant. I was starving. The Restaurant was insanely colorful, with murals of parrots, islands, cabanas and flowers draped all over the ceiling. We sat on the same side of the booth and put our arms around each other, "This is so nice, to be this close to you," she said. "Yeah, it is." I put my mouth against her neck and made her short of breath. She looked at me sternly, told me to decide what I was going to eat. "That's the tone I've been waiting for," I joked. "Just wait. Just you wait." We had a couple margaritas each and I ordered a chorizo enchilada. The wait staff were all wearing sombreros.

Walking back to the car the heat of the desert concentrated itself in thick gusts. Nobody was out walking. "I'm very nervous, I'm sorry." Sandrina apologized. "It's okay, I am too." We drove across town to the hotel. Firebird was a big cluster of shopping malls with an occasional apartment complex.

"I like it better where I live out of town. You can see more of the mountains, and there is a little more character. I used to live here though, when I worked for Discover Card." "What did you do for them?" "I was a phone receptionist." "Oh, I see!" She slowed down the car, "You're so beautiful John, I'm really happy you were brave enough to come." "It wasn't a big deal." "I'm not an easy woman to get along with, but you seem to get me. That's what's so amazing. I've never felt so vulnerable as I have with you the past few weeks... in my whole life. Sometimes I tell myself that I am being deluded, that you are just some prodigal son—but I don't think that is the case."

We pulled into the hotel. It was a funky little place— only a few stories high. In the back by the pool were giant yellow rubber duckies. Inside our room were metallic spirals, and the shade was a sliding piece of wood with a colorful painting on it.

We started kissing awkwardly on the bed. She got me naked and held my cock in her hand almost immediately. She had me jerk off for her, but I wasn't allowed to cum. She kept complimenting me. I felt bad that I wasn't eager to see her naked so I stopped jerking and took off all her clothes. She seemed reluctant. "I don't care, come on."

Before I touched her, she showed me everything she regretted about her body. She did not like the rose tattoo on her leg nor the snake between her breasts. She had cellulite and scars around her waist from the gastric bypass surgery, and as a necessary result of the skin removal procedure (performed after she lost all the weight), the skin below her navel was three shades darker than the skin above. She showed me the scars below her breasts from her boob job. "But I like the job they did, and my nipples are still very sensitive." She led my hand onto them, and I nestled my mouth on one, and pulled myself into her body. I thought it was very soft, and I was not displeased like she seemed to expect.

We played with each other tentatively, then I went down to her pussy to find the giant clitoris she always talked about. It was true. It was like a miniature penis. It was so easy to get her off with that giant, sensitive knob protruding from between her thick, large lips. I tapped it with my tongue... It was very moist. Tap. Tap... She orgasmed within minutes. She asked me to slap her face. I slapped it softly. "Slap it harder! Don't be a timid boy. Of all times to grow timid. Slap me harder." I slapped her hard. She slapped me back, and it hurt, and I got turned off and rolled over. "Awww... baby." I think she thought I was playing. She crawled down my body and put my cock in her mouth. She devoured it, and I was excited again. She wanted me to fuck her. I asked if she was clean. She said that she was. She did not ask about me.

I put my cock in, and it fell deep inside quicker than I expected. I held onto her breasts as I fucked her. From the corner of my eye I kept seeing the odd, artificial tan line on her belly. I started to get soft, I wasn't that turned on. Sandrina was getting close to cumming, moaning about my perfect cock and how I somehow had mastered hitting the G-spot every single stroke. But I wasn't even hard. It grossed me out that while I was going limp she was nearing ecstasy. I pulled out and acted tired. I looked down at my penis and there was blood all over it. "Are you having your period?" Sandrina put her hand down to her pussy and pulled her bloody fingers up to her face. "It's too thin to be menstrual blood. I think it's just been a long time since I had sex. Sometimes the hymen grows back." The bed sheets had blood over them too. "Come here, baby." But I didn't come there. I stayed on my knees at the edge of the bed. "Do you want me to finish you off?" She asked very seriously. "Yeah, fine." I hurried it up by not enjoying it at all. For the rest of the day we slept and showered, and spoke little to each other.

In the morning we did not kiss, but we were still sweet to each other. Sandrina took pictures of me lying on the beach chairs next to one of the rubber duckies. Then we went out to a sex shop. At the sex shop, with Sandrina's assistance, I bought an Aneros, an $80 state-of-the-art dildo that pushes up against the prostate and the perineum at the same time. We walked back to her car. Sandrina told me all about the horrors of obesity. She said it was even worse because of how erotic she was. She wanted so badly things she could never have. We met up with a couple she was friends with. They were both overweight. The guy was a computer programmer, the girl was a pretty, freckly, perky red-head in a red dress. I was quiet most of the time. I had nothing to share with them. I mentioned my teaching.

After lunch we hiked from the parking structure to a theater of concrete stairs. We had tickets for the *Bodies* exhibit. I had seen it already in New York, but Sandrina had planned for this before I booked my flight. They had redesigned some of the flayed bodies, and there were all these quotations on the walls by Kant, by Shakespeare, by Leonardo, and by Nietzsche. Sandrina and I were a bit horrified by some of the deadpan humor of the show. Like the bloody chickens and lambs put there for comedic relief. And a couple in love were placed on a heart-shaped mirror stand. "I feel like there is so much to learn," Sandrina said as we walked through the darkly lit hallways, "But I can't wrap my head around it." "I think that's all you can feel. They want you to think that by seeing the body in this way some truth is revealed, but what could that be?" "Maybe you're right." She grabbed for my arm. I backed away. "I'm tired of all this Christianity. The way they set this up even Nietzsche sounds like a Christian. I'm sorry, I just hate Christianity, more than anything in this world." "Is this because of Victoria?" "Her and everybody else. It's the way it manipulates everyone into kindness. There is nothing more unkind to me than Christian kindness." I quieted down, looking around at all the 30ish blond-haired men and women with their fanny packs and children. "You're home now, baby," Sandrina said.

Sandrina stayed clothed that night. She was upset, she said I was terrified of her pussy. I did not say much about it either way. She decided to focus solely on me. She put the Aneros in my butt after dabbing some Vaseline on its tip. She waited fifteen minutes because I was supposed to grow accustomed to it before I reaped its orgasmic benefits. She laid me down and proceeded to give me the most fucking shocking blowjob I have ever had in my life. She deep throated it so vigorously, and right before I ejaculated she squeezed the head with all her might—stopping me. Then she wiggled the Aneros, sending all sorts of sensations through my belly. She promised she was happy doing this, and she did it for an hour, at least. When she finally let me cum, it built up for minutes and I was screaming at the top of my lungs, and the Aneros shot out of my ass and dropped to the floor aside the bed. I started cackling madly. Sandrina wanted me to please her, but I rolled over, tired, and went to sleep.

My flight left late the next day. I had to get back for classes on Monday. The kids were having a test on Ancient Greece. Sandrina wanted to take me to Sedona where all the red rocks and Sequoias were. We spoke about how things were failing between us. We were out on the highway, crossing the border, winding through hills sparsely scattered with cacti. "I don't see it as a failure. Yeah, we're not in love like we might have thought, but we get along. I don't see a difference." "I guess I got my hopes up. I fear dying alone, especially seeing how depressed my grandmother has been since grandpa died... What is it? Why don't you love me?" "I can't answer that." "Don't give me that. You're not going to back out now. This is a question I need you to answer in all sincerity." "No, you don't get it Sandrina, I surrendered to the idea of loving you, it just didn't catch—there's no explanation." "Maybe you didn't surrender enough." "Maybe."

We drove all the way up to an old mining town called Jerome. We had some drinks at a bar with a lot of biker dudes. A band played folk and country music. Along the bar wall was a mural—I kept looking at the sad eyes of an ingénue in a black dress. The music played so loudly that Sandrina could not speak to me. She showed me a text message she wrote on her phone about a boy being there, but not being there at all.

We still had some time left so we went to Sedona. Once we entered the tall trees and sinuous roads, we pulled to the side and walked down to the creak. The rocks were ruddy, fleshy, red. The sunlight was golden far up against the evergreens. Sandrina ordered me to climb out to the long, red rock above a small, white rapid. When I got there, she assembled her camera and told me to strip naked. I felt a little cold. I tried to be comfortable in my body. I lay out on the mud running along the rock. She took a lot of pictures. The sun was setting. Sandrina gave me a thumb's up when I was in the right position.

We drove back to the airport in the night. Things were tense because we were cutting it close, and we didn't even say a proper goodbye because I had to run through the airport just to make the plane.

When I got home—all the pics were already in my mailbox. She had cut off my head to impersonalize them. In one, where my butt was sticking out as I climbed up a rock, she wrote between my legs the word: *homme*. There were lines cutting apart my body, making it look like I was climbing a ladder. The area around my body was black and white. The rocks and pond outside the lines of the ladder were colored vividly. I was really proud of the picture and I told her so. But Sandrina wanted more from me, and after a week of not contacting her, she wrote:

Apr. 1

What perception of you so glorifying do I have that believes you can do these things, honor these things well? Do you conceive of the mental energy I put into the last couple months, thinking we could take scrapes of misconception, focus in on what's real, and derive something at least erotically more free?

You are such a good salesman in the "sweet voice," sounding devoted and excited.

This whole escapade started from something simple. It didn't have to go this way.

Its stupid on my part to be here. I think too highly of you, based possibly on literacy alone.

And you know this. And you use it.

Go fuck yourself.

S

Blanchot, Maurice. Trans. John Gregg. <u>Awaiting Oblivion</u>.
  University of Nebraska Press: Lincoln, 1999.

Dostoyevsky, Fyodor. Trans. David McDuff. <u>The Idiot</u>.
  Penguin Books: London, 2004.

Kierkegaard, Soren. Trans. Alastair Hannay. <u>The Sickness unto Death</u>.
  Penguin Books: New York, 1989.

Nietzsche, Friedrich. Ed. Walter Kaufman. <u>Genealogy of Morals & Ecce Homo</u>.
  Vintage: New York, 1967.

Pessoa, Fernando. Ed. & Trans. Richard Zenith. <u>The Book of Disquiet</u>.
  Penguin Classics: New York, 2001.

Reich, Wilhelm. Trans. Vincent R. Carfagno. <u>The Function of the Orgasm</u>.
  Noonday: New York, 1973.

Sacher-Masoch, Leopold Von. Trans. Joachim Neugroschel. <u>Venus in Furs</u>.
  Penguin Books: New York, 2000.

Tzu, Lao. Trans. Sam Hamill. <u>Tao Te Ching</u>.
  Shambhala Publications: Boston, 2005.

If music be the food of love, play on,
Give me excess of it, that, surfeiting,
The appetite may sicken, and so die.
That strain again! It had a dying fall;
O, it came o'er my ear like the sweet sound
That breathes upon a bank of violets,
Stealing and giving odor. Enough, no more!
'Tis not so sweet now as it was before.
                    -William Shakespeare (Twelfth Night)